VOL. 1

EVEN A HERO NEEDS A VACATION EVERY NOW AND THEN

a novel by

AUGUST HEI

Cover Illustration by Elfe Carter

Interior Art Illustration by Kantuk Creative

www.august.art

Twitter: @augustdotart

CONTENTS

PRELUDE

Truly? *That's* the story you wish to hear?

You do know I was the one who defeated the Mad King Alberon, the Destroyer of Visseria?

I'm only saying... even my battle against the Demon Lord Izirath is a tale the bards will be singing for the next few centuries.

And then there are the countless stories that haven't made it into the taverns and history pages. Precious, delicious, vivacious stories that I haven't told a soul. Stories that would put fire in your heart, thunder in your belly, and lightning in your eyes. Stories far more enjoyable and far less embarrassing than what happened at the Tipsy Pelican Tavern.

Knowing all that, are you certain *this* is the one you want to get into?

All right, all right, I hear you. I was only checking on your behalf. Just don't blame me if the climaxes and twists are all out of place and your opinion of the *Hero of Our Time* takes a turn for the worse.

And remember, anytime you feel that churning in the pit of your stomach, that wince, that squirm—you wanted to hear the story of the Tipsy Pelican Tavern.

But where should a narrator begin when it comes to a tale as ungainly and confounding as this one? Do I start with when I first purchased the tavern? Or should I start with the moment I knew I wanted a tavern in the first place? Or do I begin even earlier? When I took my first sip of ale? My earliest childhood memories? The circumstances of my birth?

Hmm... I know. How about:

In the beginning, before humans walked the earth, before the dragons roamed the sky, before there was anything at all, there was only the Abyss and its endless emptiness—

Just kidding. The beginning of a story tends to be boring, anyway. Let's start with the night Elsa got into a fight.

CHAPTER 1: WELCOME TO THE TIPSY PELICAN TAVERN (ARC 1)

It was about to be a lively night at the Tipsy Pelican Tavern, and that was an unusual occurrence. A year had passed since we opened, and I could count the number of eventful evenings on a single hand. In fact, I could usually count the number of *daily guests* on a single hand.

But on this night, the city's Tournament of Heroes had just ended, and after leaving the arena, the people of Meritas were both in good spirits and the mood for a drink. The tournament was a major event, drawing the best fighters from across the duchy to compete in one-on-one matches in the city's grand arena. Thousands of citizens and visitors gathered to see the contestants fight.

Understandably, the tournament's results were the talk of the tavern, and at one particular table, an argument had broken out over which of the Rules of Ruin had ended the final match.

"It was Rule Forty-Six. Must have been," said Bran, who'd gained a foam mustache from the mug of ale in his hand.

"Rule Forty-Six is Bane's Blade, you fool!" Dalian said. He was the oldest of the three men at the table and a spirited talker, especially when it came to arguments. "Did you see a blade in Galston's hand when he delivered the final blow?"

"I don't remember all their names, but I'm sure of the rule's number."

"Bah," Dalian said, "I don't know about the number, but given the speed of his palm thrust, I say it was Hellish Hand."

"Both of you are wrong," Amberly said. He was the largest of the three builders and had arms the size of tree trunks and a beard that could put pirate lords to shame. "Galston used Rule Sixty-Six, Saffron Spear, the same spell the Stormblood killed the Demon Lord with."

I smiled to myself. They were all wrong. Galston had cast Rule Seventeen, Paralyzing Palm, in the final duel, and the Stormblood had not used any of Celeru's Seventy-Seven Rules of Ruin during his battle against the Demon Lord. Battle magic was uncommon to see in the city, and so it was no surprise the three builders had trouble distinguishing the spells.

"More Honeydew Lager, boys?" I said, approaching the table with a full pitcher.

"Ah, Master Arch, you have impeccable timing," Bran said, raising his large wooden mug that was emptied of the golden liquid, though his mustache still held at least a mouthful. He wasn't quite as immense as Amberly, but he, too, looked oversized on my wooden chairs.

Both Amberly and Dalian also opted for refills after quickly downing what was left in their mugs. "A full pour is the best pour," Dalian said as I filled his mug. He had a couple of decades on Bran and Amberly and often outdrank both.

"Best to keep them mugs empty, then," I said with my best tavern-keeper smile.

"Aye," Amberly said with a grin and clinked his mug with his two friends.

"Another empty over here," said a woman's voice.

I turned to find Elsa sitting slumped behind the bar, clearly already intoxicated, with one hand outstretched, gripping a mug. I walked over and filled it only halfway.

"Hey," she said, lifting her head from her arm to inspect at the contents of the mug. "That's not nearly full."

"You're supposed to be helping me with the customers," I said. "Not becoming one."

A feminine figure on the other end of the bar turned to me as I spoke. Her eyes were hidden by a white veil that fell to her nose. She wore the robes of the White Church, and at her side, a sheathed sword leaned against the bar. I had pegged her as a White Templar. This was her third time visiting the tavern this week.

I held the woman's gaze, or at least where her gaze would have been if I could see her eyes. She turned away and sipped on the glass of red wine she'd ordered earlier in the night.

"I need energy if I'm going to work." Elsa took a big gulp from her mug.

"So, eat something," I said.

"I already did." She lifted her mug at me again.

I glanced down and saw it was empty. "Good gods, woman, how do you drink so fast?"

She looked at me with a sudden seriousness that nearly made me take a step backward. Elsa had the type of beauty that could stop a weak heart permanently. And with her violet eyes trained on me, my heart was getting adequately tested.

"An ale addiction is a skill that one must train for many years to master," she said with mock sincerity. "Perhaps I will teach you one day."

"At least pour your own drinks." I placed the pitcher in front of her. "Maybe you'll get in the habit and start pouring for the customers too."

"As you command," she said, reaching for the pitcher while pulling up a strap of her dress that had slipped over her shoulder.

I had to tell my eyes twice to look away lest she notice that I was staring. I let out a small sigh, annoyed at myself, and rubbed my head. Despite my age, I still had the body of a nineteen-year-old boy. And since losing my powers, I was starting to feel the effects of my youth. *All the effects.* The problem was becoming both irksome and bewildering.

"If you don't mind, I'll buy her a drink," said a broad-shouldered young man. I hadn't seen him before. This was probably his first night at the tavern.

I immediately put on my tavern-keeper face and smiled politely. "Of course, sir. Elsa would be happy to take your order." I filled another pitcher from a keg at the bar and headed to the two new patrons who had just entered the tavern.

Despite Elsa's perfunctory skills as a barmaid, she attracted many patrons who were eager to spend money to impress her. Better yet, her liver seemed to be more robust than the Demon Lord's soul. So Elsa and I had come to a mutually beneficial arrangement: she got to drink what she wanted while earning a small wage, and I got a busier tavern.

As I passed by the builders to show the new patrons to a table, I overheard the men continuing their argument over Galston's match that had ended the Tournament of Heroes.

"Hellish Hand doesn't increase the caster's speed," Amberly was saying. "Therefore, it had to be Saffron Spear. He moved lightning fast."

"I still say it was Rule Forty-Six." Bran took a big pull from his mug. "I swear I heard him name the number as he incanted the rule. Perhaps Rule Forty-Six is Saffron Spear."

"No, it's sixty-six!" Amberly shot back. "It's the one the Storm-blood used against the Demon L—"

"If it had been Saffron Spear, the entire arena would have been destroyed," said a new voice—a woman's. It was the templar sitting at the bar. "And it is not known which spells Archibold Stormblood conjured in his clash against the Demon Lord, since there were none to witness it."

My ears perked up. This lady was sharp and knew her lore.

The builders at the table eyed her robes and sword and were undoubtedly wondering what a White Templar was doing in a tavern, as did I. Nonetheless, they did not say anything in reply. Everyone knew church templars were dangerous folk to be involved with, and my patrons wouldn't risk speaking to one—not yet, at least. The night was still young, and the ale had only just begun to flow.

Bran finished his second mug and began waving for a third. I quickly hopped over with the pitcher.

"Mmm…" Bran hummed as he finished a deep swig of his newly filled mug, leaving a fresh film of foam on his bushy mustache. "This must be the best honey beer I've had in the city. You must tell me how it's brewed, Master Arch."

"It's honey*dew* beer, Bran. And it's a trade secret, I'm afraid." I gave him a humble smile that hid the pride I felt. I'd spent months working on that beer. The latest iteration was my best batch yet.

"I'll have some of that," said a young man with his mug raised at a table beside the builders. I reached him swiftly and filled his mug. He put it to his lips and took a sip. "My, this is wonderfully cold. You must pay a mage a bright coin to chill this brew, Master Arch."

"Worth the cost, I'd say." This was a lie. I cooled my own brew.

The young man nodded, looking over at the table of burly men who had been discussing the tournament. He seemed a little eager, adjusting his fine linen tunic.

"Ahem." He coughed. "If you men would like to know which of Celeru's Rules of Ruin Galston used in the tournament, I'd be happy to ask him. The champion happens to be a friend of my father."

The builders said nothing. Bran drank his drink with a big smile on his face as if he hadn't heard the boy. Dalian murmured an unintelligible joke to Amberly, who burst out laughing.

The young man was a lordling called Herwin. He had come to the tavern on and off at first, but in the last month, he was in regular attendance for reasons only the gods knew. This was no place for nobles—namely because sensible commoners generally thought of nobles as stuck-up jerks during most interactions and thus avoided them whenever possible. In turn, nobles tended to be stuck-up jerks who avoided mixing with those of the lower social classes.

But Herwin seemed bent on becoming part of the tavern's slowly growing regular crew. I had no quibbles about it—a nobleman's coin was as good as anyone else's. If anything, their coins tended to come with better shines and larger sizes.

Just the other night, Herwin had bought the whole tavern a round of drinks with a silver shimmer. He'd gotten the same response from the men as he was getting now. Which is to say, no response.

"Ahem." Herwin coughed again, his mouth quivering as if battling his nerves. "I could even ask Galston to come by the tavern tomorrow night if anyone would be interested in meeting—"

"You're friends with Galston the Gallant?" Amberly said suddenly, looking at the boy.

"Er... yes. As I just mentioned—"

"Gods, why didn't you say so earlier!" Amberly said, standing and making his way to Herwin to clink his mug.

"Cheers!" Bran was also suddenly standing next to the boy. "I'm Bran, and you are...?"

"Herwin," the young man said, looking uncertain about the sudden attention.

"Herwin! Good name!" Amberly laughed and threw a tree-trunk arm around the boy. "So, you're bringing Galston tomorrow night, ay? It'll be a riot."

"Ah... well, I'll need to ask my father—"

"How about tomorrow at sundown?" Bran said with a big friendly grin.

"We're carpenters, you see," Dalian said. He'd joined the group too. "Got work on the city walls before then."

"Err... yes, of course, but I'm not sure—"

"Excellent!" Bran said. "Master Arch, get this man a shot of brandy. On my tab!"

I smiled and headed behind the bar, poured a finger into four glasses, and handed one each to the newly formed group. "On the house."

"There you go!" Amberly said. "You've got to come here more often, Herwin! Master Arch is never this kind to us."

Herwin smiled shakily, likely thinking that he'd come five nights out of seven for the past month.

"To Herwin and Master Arch!" Bran said, raising his glass. Amberly, Dalian, and Herwin held their glasses to Bran's, then they swallowed them in one swoop.

Herwin coughed violently, and Amberly rumbled a laugh, slapping the lordling on the back, which only made the young man cough more. Bran grabbed his beer and chugged it too. Dalian just grinned toothily as his cheeks turned pink.

I smiled. The night at the Tipsy Pelican Tavern had finally begun.

Not two rounds of drinks later, the front door banged open, and three figures entered, quieting the barroom. I recognized the three men instantly, and they spelled trouble.

The man at the front, and the leader of the little pack, was Mideon. He'd come by three nights prior and tried to take Elsa home with him. Forcibly.

She had declined his initial invitation. Then he had grabbed her arm and tried to drag her out of the tavern. Elsa did not like that one bit and split one of my tables with Mideon's back. And now he had returned with two pals.

Bran gave me a nod to let me know that if I gave the signal, he, Amberly, and Dalian would send Mideon and his cronies packing. But the real problem was that Mideon was the son of a *somebody*. A somebody who could cause a lot of trouble for a tavern keeper.

And that wasn't all. There was also the fact that Elsa refused to take help from anyone. The first week I'd hired her, some pervert had grabbed a handful. When I took him by the arm, Elsa pushed me off him and told me not to get involved. Then she broke the pervert's nose.

The next week, it happened again with a different pervert, and again, I tried to throw him out. She pushed me off him, threw him through the window, then quit on the spot since I had "interfered."

It took two more weeks for her to return and ask for her job back. She also demanded that I promise her I would *mind my own business*, which I found rather ironic since the tavern and everything within it were literally my business. But I had relented. Elsa's track record was that of an undefeated heavyweight brawler, and she had no trouble fending for herself.

However, I wasn't sure that would be true on this night. The two men whom Mideon had brought with him were almost Amberly's size. More problematically, one of them appeared to be emitting the thinnest wisps of halos.

"Sir Mideon!" I said, meeting the three men before they could get farther into the tavern. "Good to see you again. Unfortunately, we're entirely full. I believe the Grand Taphouse is open down the street if you are in need of a drink."

"Where is Elsa?" Mideon hissed as he scanned the room. There was heavy liquor on his breath.

His eyes stopped at the bar, and a grin that could be best described as rancid sprang across his face.

"Elsa is busy," I said in a monotone.

"Elsa!" Mideon screamed. "You're coming with me tonight!"

The last traces of conversation in the tavern died and was replaced with silent apprehension. I let out a small groan. Things were about to get ugly.

"You bastard," Elsa said from behind the bar, an opened bottle of brandy clutched in her fist. "How dare you show yourself here again!"

Wait... is she drinking that by herself? Directly from the bottle? I squinted. *Is that the good brandy? Who told her to open that?!*

"My gods, you look sensual tonight," Mideon said, running his rodent-like eyes up and down her figure.

"What's this about?" said the broad-shouldered young man she'd been speaking with. I sincerely hoped he had purchased the brandy for her.

Both he and Elsa stepped up to Mideon and his men, while the rest of the tavern separated from their path, pushing up against the barroom's walls. Even Bran and Amberly didn't make a move now that Mideon had made it clear he was there for Elsa. They'd been coming to the Tipsy Pelican Tavern long enough to know not to get involved with Elsa's "business."

Unfortunately, Herwin was passed out between them after failing to keep up with the builders. It would have been good to have the lordling as a witness if something happened. Mideon's father was the ward superintendent, but Herwin's father was a bona fide count—an actual land-ruling noble. Herwin's word would mean something if things really took a turn for the worse.

"You'd better walk out of here while you still have two working legs," Elsa said.

Her cheeks were a little red, which only made me more uneasy. I'd never seen Elsa vomit or collapse from drinking, no matter how much she consumed, but when her cheeks were red, it was a sign she could fall into a nasty and violent mood with sudden ease. Most people made the mistake of being blinded by the beauty and missed the building danger in her darkening eyes and drunken complexion. Mideon had done just that three nights before, and it looked as if he still hadn't learned his lesson.

"I'm not going anywhere without you, my dear," Mideon said. "I'm taking you home tonight, Elsa. We'll go together, all four of us, and have some fun. You'd—"

"How dare you insult this lady's honor!" The broad-shouldered young man threw out a protective arm between Mideon and Elsa, accidentally brushing her leg. "I challenge you to a—"

Elsa took his arm, draped it over her shoulder, and threw him through the table beside her. The wooden legs snapped under the force of the throw, splitting the table in two. I sighed heavily. It was one of my nicer tables with fine engravings in the wood.

Bran and Amberly, who in the past had each gone through a table themselves for the same protective action, shook their heads with empathy for the young man. Mideon and his two men looked at

Elsa with their mouths hanging open. However they'd expected the confrontation to begin, it certainly wasn't this.

"Sorry about that," Elsa said lightly to Mideon. "Now that the interference is gone, what were you saying?"

Mideon was still open-mouthed.

"Elsa..." I said with warning in my voice. "Please be more mindful of my furniture."

She shot me a glare like I was going to be next to go through a table.

"Why don't you all take this outside, where there are no tables?" I suggested. "This isn't the tavern's business, after all."

"Fine," Elsa spat. "That'll give us more room for a proper tussle."

CHAPTER 2: THE GREATEST HERO OF OUR TIME

The night was late, but summer had just begun, and a warm breeze swept through the street. Most of the customers and residents in the neighborhood of Kerrytown had gone home for the night. Those remaining were in the taverns and pubs that lined both sides of the cobblestone street. Muffled laughter and conversation could be heard from their half-opened windows.

If it had been earlier and the street busier, I doubted that Mideon would have agreed to such a public dispute with Elsa. He was the son of the ward's superintendent, which would let him get away with harassing the barmaid of a relatively new tavern, but only if he didn't make a villain out of himself in front of a street full of witnesses. At the moment, however, only the Tipsy Pelican Tavern's customers and Mideon's two men were standing on the street. The witnesses would have been the same had he confronted Elsa in the tavern, and other than Herwin and the templar, they mostly comprised builders, dockworkers, and day laborers—not the type of people who had much standing in the eyes of the nobility.

Someone had pulled up a seat for the broad-shouldered young man whom Elsa had split a table with and handed him a mug of Honeydew Lager for good measure. He was sipping it with a dazed look as he watched the confrontation. The White Templar stood at his side, her expression unreadable behind her veil.

"This is your last chance to come with me," Mideon said. "You assaulted me last time. It's the least you could do."

I wasn't sure how Mideon figured any of the others would allow him to take Elsa away if he did succeed in immobilizing her, but the guy clearly wasn't very bright. Then I noticed the aura I'd sensed earlier growing rapidly from one of his thugs. It was only barely visible without a Spell of Seeing, but I noticed a few small rings blossoming from the thug's torso. It meant the man was a caster, if not a full mage.

So maybe Mideon wasn't as dumb as I thought. Dumb as a brick but not dumb as a rock. Depending on his thug's ability, the mage could easily put down a tavern full of people. Well... assuming no one in the tavern knew magic. And there was at least one person who did—the templar, I mean.

"Enough of your dribble, you pointy-nosed bastard," Elsa snapped. "Are you going to fight, or are you going to keep whining like a little boy?"

That was the thing about Elsa. When she was angry, her tongue was sharper than a spear point.

It was clear from Mideon's expression that he was self-conscious about his strangely shaped nose.

"Y-You harlot!" he shouted. Embarrassment turned to anger all at once, and he leapt forward at the beauty.

But the balance of his body was all wrong—head and arms forward, fingers spread, torso and legs behind him. He rushed face-first right into Elsa's closed fist and landed on the ground with a thud. Everyone watching had expected that.

Upon seeing Mideon fall, his two men raced toward her. They seemed to fare slightly better.

The first man pulled his fist back for a punch, changing the plan to capture the woman to a fistfight. The second man, the mage, was right beside him with his hand raised. It was unclear what he was going to do until his hand began to glow with a red aura. He was casting a spell.

Things were looking bad until the unbelievable happened. The first man, with the balled fist, tripped on a raised cobblestone in the road. Or perhaps his knee buckled. It wasn't clear from the angle of the spectators, but his left leg twisted suddenly just as he began to launch his fist forward. The result was that he pivoted sideways on the leg that could no longer hold his weight. Instead of hitting Elsa, his fist smacked into the cheek of the unsuspecting mage, whose attention was all directed toward the beauty.

Elsa blinked as both of them toppled over a whole two paces away from her. The mage was knocked out cold, but the first guy stood again and hopped on one leg while clutching the other. Something indeed, had happened to his left knee.

But as he was groping his knee, Elsa slammed her fist into his jaw. The motion was smooth and swift and graceful as a royal dancer. He flew back, his jaw leading the flight, and landed neatly on the cobblestone road between his two sleeping friends.

There was a long silence. Then someone began to clap. Soon, everyone from the tavern was whooping and jumping up and down.

Elsa glanced at them with a radiant smile as she rubbed her shoulder. "Time to celebrate!" she said, raising her fist victoriously in the air to enthusiastic cheering.

Celebrate? I thought. *What are we celebrating?* Mideon and his idiots would undoubtedly return another night with even more men after being so badly embarrassed.

"First round's on the house!" Elsa exclaimed as she led the pack back into the tavern like a prophet among her loyal followers.

"On the house?" I exclaimed, but she didn't hear me.

There was nothing to be done about it now. Everyone was too caught up in the moment. The good news was that after a fight and a free round of drinks, there would undoubtedly be more purchases.

Which was exactly what happened. Which was why the rest of the night was a complete disaster.

Bran bought the second round and Herwin, who finally woke up, the third and fourth and fifth. Before I knew it, each person in the tavern was buying a round of drinks, and a dozen people meant a dozen rounds. I knew most of them couldn't afford such expenditures, so I only charged them half price. The price decrease was discovered as one of them settled his bill, which led to another furor of drink buying.

By the time the sun rose, Herwin was hunched over in a corner, puking into a bucket and Bran was dancing with the templar. She had drunk a second glass of wine, which was apparently enough to put her on an even footing with Bran, who by then was on his fifteenth ale.

And all of this was still manageable... right up until Elsa shoved into my hands the unfinished half of the good brandy she'd opened and drunk earlier in the night.

"What?" I said dumbly.

"You're not partaking," she said.

"Someone's got to be the adult."

"Not tonight. We're celebrating!" She hooked her arm into mine and took the first pull from the bottle. Then she handed it back to me. I sighed and took a gulp.

The whole tavern cheered. I guess they didn't get to see me drinking very often. One drink led to two, and that led to three. And before I knew it, I'd finished the second half of the brandy bottle.

I don't know how things ended. I woke up on some chairs that had been lined up against the wall, finding the tavern dark and empty of patrons.

Elsa was sprawled out on the bar, her feet resting on spilled mugs and bottles. For a moment, I thought she had finally died from overindulgence, but then I saw her chest moving up and down. I stared a second longer than necessary before I pulled my eyes away.

"Damn nineteen-year-old body," I muttered as I sat up.

"You're awake. I've been waiting for you."

I jumped as I saw the templar sitting a few chairs away. "Oh, it's you," I said. "Nearly scared me half to death."

She'd taken off the head mantle of her robes, and I could now see her face. She was younger than I had expected—perhaps twenty-one or twenty-two. Her hair was long and golden, and her eyes were bright blue and piercing. They were staring into me as if taking an account of my soul.

"I doubt that is possible, Master Archibold," the templar replied.

"Uh... it's Arch. Just Arch. Not short for anything." A cold sweat was forming on my back.

"I have come a long way to speak with you."

"With me?" I took a furtive glance at Elsa. She was still passed out on the bar.

"I am a templar of the Order of the White Church."

"That's quite the mouthful. Don't you folks just call it 'the Order' or 'the White Church'?"

"I have come to ask for your assistance in a grave matter."

"Assistance? From me?"

"Of course. You are Archibold Stormblood, the greatest hero of our time."

CHAPTER 3: DRAGONS AND SLAVES

I took another glance at Elsa. She was still sleeping—probably. I didn't want her overhearing this conversation.

"Sorry, I think you have the wrong guy," I said.

The templar shook her head. "I wasn't certain until tonight, when I saw you incapacitate that mage."

"Uh... why don't we talk somewhere more private." I motioned her to follow me into the cold storage room. I had to use the walls for support to keep myself from stumbling.

Damn Elsa for getting me drunk, I thought. I was going to suffer for the rest of the next day.

I closed the door behind me after the templar entered. "What's your name?"

"Cassia Hightower."

"Alright, Cassia. Listen closely. I'm not who you think I am. I'm just a tavern owner, not some hero of legend."

"I almost believed it," Cassia said. "But then I saw what you did to that man who attacked your staff."

"What are you talking about?"

"You disabled his leg, which caused him to disable his friend."

"No. He stumbled, and the mage just happened to be in the wrong spot. They'd been drinking before they showed up at the tavern."

"How did you know the second man was a mage?" Cassia asked.

"Uhhh…"

"You would only know that if you could sense his halos."

"Well… you said he was a mage earlier, and I assumed you knew what you were talking about."

"You shot a pebble from your hand into the back of the brawler's knee."

Damn, she got me.

"Fine," I said. "So, maybe I'm a little stronger than I look. Doesn't make me the Stormblood."

"The strength and precision required for such a feat are significant. Not only did you manage to hit his knee from thirty paces away with a small rock, but you did so without anyone noticing. Moreover, you hit the exact location at the exact angle to cause him to turn and incapacitate a moving target with his fist. Most people would be hard-pressed to deal a blow to another person moving at a fast speed. You made *someone else* do it with a pebble. This proves to me you are the legendary hero I've been searching for."

I opened my mouth to make a retort, but I had nothing to say.

"Archibold-don, I have come to you with great need," Cassia said, her voice turning earnest.

The *don* honorific was reserved for the highest honors that weren't nobility. I squirmed a little just hearing the word. It reminded me of war.

"The White Church recently discovered that an elder dragon has awakened in the northern lands of Visseria," Cassia continued. "As it begins to hunt and increase the territory of its hunting grounds, the dragon will inevitably attack the neighboring kingdom of Lareinti. Hundreds of thousands of people are—"

"Stop, stop. Just stop." I held up my hand.

Cassia looked at me, a small wrinkle forming above her brows.

"Sorry, but I'm not leaving on some quest. Not anytime soon, anyway."

"Then you admit you are Archibold Stormblood?"

Damn. She really got me.

"We can pretend for a moment that I am, and the answer is no."

"But you must help us. You are the hero—"

I held up my hand again. "I said, *no.*"

"But—"

"I don't care," I said.

"Y-You don't..." she repeated, unable to finish the sentence.

"I'm two hundred twenty-one years old, Miss Hightower. Do you know how many of those years I've spent training and fighting?"

"I do not..." she said with uncertainty.

"Just about all of them. I'm tired, and I'm... well, I'm on vacation," I said with a grin.

Cassia looked around. "Running a tavern, serving drunks?"

"Drunks are as human as the religious. They just attend a different type of house, little templar."

"Of course," Cassia said, going a little pink.

I suddenly noticed that she was, in fact, very pretty. She had a fair complexion and beautiful piercing eyes, and her lips were soft and...

Damn it! This is not the time for that! Good gods. It was as if my powers had been entirely replaced with adolescent lust. What an awful trade.

"But the people of Lareinti are in need of your aid," Cassia said, pushing forward. "They'll die if the elder dragon comes upon their kingdom. It has not awakened in two thousand years. When it discovers a city of people in its territory, it will destroy them."

"So, tell them to leave. Or find some young hero who has a name to prove. I don't know. It's not my problem."

Cassia looked at me as if she could not believe my words. She wasn't getting the hero she'd heard about in the stories.

"How did you find me, anyway?" I asked.

"High Lord Emdark informed me you had headed to Meritas to open a tavern."

"That traitorous long-eared elf bastard!" I spat. "I told him to keep his mouth shut."

Cassia looked like I had just damned Celeru himself. "He did not give me your location until I informed him of the impending threat of the—"

"Elder dragon, yeah, yeah, I heard you the first time. I'm sorry, Miss Hightower, but I'm going to have to pass on this one. I'm sure you'll be able to find some hotheaded fool to deal with it." I stood to leave the room.

"But you must."

"I must?" I said, turning back to her. "Why must I?"

"Because... the lives. People will die if you don't."

"And what about my life? Why is it that I'm always the one that must risk everything? The Mad King Alberon's armies are in the dust. The Demon Lord Izirath is no more. How much more do I have to give until it is enough?"

"Y-Yes, of course," Cassia stammered. "You have done many great services..."

"And what service have you given, Cassia? Why is it always my turn? What will you do for all those lives? What sacrifice will you make?"

"Me?" Cassia's eyes were growing brighter, and the color rose in her cheeks.

Her expression was filled with innocence and a desire to do the right thing. But that only incensed me further.

"You, Cassia," I said. "What is your sacrifice?"

"If I had the power, I would—"

"You have the power to sacrifice for me."

Cassia swallowed and shakily. "W-What will you have me do?"

"How about being my slave for the next two centuries? That's how long I've spent toiling for the people of Visseria."

"Y-your slave?" Her voice rose.

"You heard correctly. You'll have to do anything I ask. In return, I'll save the people of Lareinti. Hundreds of thousands of lives, did you say? A fair trade, don't you think?"

She took a step backward. "I couldn't... why should I?"

I shrugged. "That's fine. I guess all those people will just have to die, then." I gave her a smile not so different Mideon's, one that I'd seen time and again on the predators of humanity.

She shuddered. Templar or not, she was still too young and naive to face the realities of the world. My answer would send her packing, and next time, the White Church would think twice about sending some fresh-faced brat to sway me. I'd be damned to risk my neck for those righteous bastards again.

"Guess that's that, then." I turned to the door.

"I accept."

I paused in disbelief with my hand on the door handle. Then I thought better of it. She was calling my bluff.

I turned back around and found her stripping her clothes off. There were tears in her eyes. "This is what you want, is it?" she said, shaking. "Well, you can have me! I'll be your slave. I don't know if I'll live for two centuries, but by Celeru, I swear—"

"Stop, stop!" I exclaimed, catching her wrist before she could remove another garment. "Good Celeru, what is wrong with you?"

"I'm agreeing to your terms! If it means you'll save Lareinti, my freedom is a small price to pay for its safety!" Tears were flowing freely from her eyes, but there was also a hard-set determination in them.

We stared at each other for a long moment.

"Damn you," I muttered. "I can never win with your type."

I sighed and let her go and hopped onto one of the cold barrels of Honeydew Lager in the room. That put me a few heads taller, and I smiled down at her. If mock cruelty wasn't enough to send her away, the cold truth would have to suffice. Given her personality, it was no wonder she had not already noticed it. "Very well, Cassia Hightower, noble do-gooder of the White Church. Do you know the Spell of Seeing? I assume it's something a templar would know."

"Yes, of course," she said, rubbing away the tears.

"So, apply it."

"You do not mind if I...?"

"You have my full permission to crap on proprieties. Have at it."

She looked at me as if she was not sure what my intentions were, but she did as I asked, and her eyes began to glow with a thin blue aura. She ran her gaze across my face then down my body and stopped. The breath caught in her throat, and she stared at me as if examining my innards. Then she shot her widened eyes back to mine with an accusatory expression. Or a questioning one. Or both.

I was still smiling. "You see? Even if I wanted to help you, I'd have no chance against an elder dragon."

CHAPTER 4: WOULD NOT SPEAK ILL OF MY MASTER

"Your gates..." Cassia said, her voice quivering. "They're gone."

I nodded. Then I, too, cast the Spell of Seeing. I channeled my aura into my eyes, and I saw the energies emanating from Cassia. Each of the body's senses could interpret halos when properly attuned. The Spell of Seeing heightened the ability for spellcasters to discern halos via their eyes, and I saw several rings of light spinning around Cassia's heart. These rings were the primary source of one's magic. Cassia's rings appeared dimly thin, which was expected because she was not actively calling on them. Most people, even nonmages, had halos. And the best mages could often see a person's halos even without the Spell of Seeing. What was harder to see were the Gates of Awakening, and that was the primary purpose of the spell.

I raised my brows. "Impressive. You have two gates open. That would make you far stronger than me."

"I don't understand... this can't be possible. It was said you opened the Eighth Gate of Awakening."

I shrugged. I'd actually hit the Ninth Gate before I lost everything, but there was no reason to tell her that.

"But..." Her eyes ran up and down my body once more. "But none are open. All your gates are closed. I-I don't understand."

I looked down at my hands. "It's a strange thing to be aging again. I opened the Gate of Life when I was eighteen years old, and I stopped getting older." I rubbed my chin. "I can feel new whiskers coming in now. A few more years, and maybe people will stop calling me a baby face." I chuckled.

She didn't seem to find it funny. "How could this have happened?"

"And why would I tell you?"

She frowned and hesitated. "Can they be opened again?"

"Sure. Gates can always be opened."

"You mean..."

"Yup. The old-fashioned way. Last time, I got to the Seventh Gate in eighteen years. Then it took me about another century to figure out one more. I'm guessing it'll be about the same if I were to do it again. Not that I have any intention of doing so."

Cassia stumbled backward, her shocked gaze dropping to the floor. I could see goose bumps on her skin. Whether they had arisen from what I'd said or from the chilled room, I wasn't sure.

"You'll reach the Third Gate faster than me at this point," I said. "You've already opened Breath and Spirit. Most people spend their entire lives just to open Breath. You're a prodigy by most standards. I bet the church is very happy with you."

The Gate of Breath and the Gate of Spirit were the first two of the Twelve Gates of Awakening. Each gate could only be opened in the proper order. In other words, Cassia had to open the Gate of Breath before she could have opened the Gate of Spirit. The gates were also sometimes called the Twelve Gates of Ascension because anyone who reached the Twelfth Gate would become a god, though such an act had never been recorded except for Celeru and his disciples, if you believed in that sort of thing.

Opened gates increased the awakener's abilities enormously. The Gate of Breath made the awakener physically stronger, so much so that they seldom grew tired. The Gate of Spirit gave the awakener incredible mental dexterity and focus, which was often a prerequisite to casting higher-tiered spells. Of course, one had to call on that power to use it. Cassia certainly was not calling on it as she stared at the floor, looking lost and dumbstruck.

"My abilities cannot compare to yours," Cassia said. "I stand no chance against an elder dragon. But your gates are closed. All of them..." She was mumbling to herself. "Those people. What can I do? They'll be dead in five years."

"Wait. Five years?"

"Or seven. The historians are uncertain. It is said that awakened dragons go through a resting phase before extensive hunting begins. Even the most recent tellings are from a thousand years ago. It is hard to say how accurate they are."

"Good gods, girl. That's plenty of time. Just evacuate the city."

"The Lareintians are unwilling," Cassia said. "The king refuses to move his kingdom and give up his lands."

"Then he deserves to die by dragon fire."

Cassia frowned. "But what about his people? They are innocents, yet they must obey the will of their king."

"Maybe you should find someone to kill the king. Sounds easier."

Cassia looked up at me, shock returning to her features. Apparently, I was doing a lot of shocking in this conversation.

"That is murder," she said.

"Never claimed it wasn't. But so is killing a dragon that is committing no other crime besides following its nature. And from what you've described, I'm thinking I like the dragon more than the Lareintian king."

She shook her head. She seemed defeated and unsure of what to say.

"Hey, cheer up. The good news is you don't have to be anyone's slave. By the way, you should really put your clothes back on before—"

At that moment, the door opened, and Charm stepped in, carrying a crate of cleaned mugs from the night. Her youthful face turned to me then to the barely clothed templar. I had no idea how to explain the situation, though I had a feeling if I did explain it, it still wouldn't make me look too good.

"I see," Charm said simply, yet the expression in her half-lidded eyes was anything but simple. If I hadn't known her so well, I would have easily missed the slight arch of her left eyebrow. She turned around and let the door swing closed behind her before I could say a word.

I looked back at Cassia. "That was my, uh… cook."

She didn't seem to have noticed the impropriety of the situation. "What am I to do now?"

I shrugged. "Find another hero. I can't be the only option for the church."

"All elder dragons are of the Ninth Gate. What humans have gone that far? Even you only reached the eighth."

I scratched my nose. "Thought I did all right."

"Of course. I did not mean to suggest otherwise. You killed the Demon Lord Izirath of the Eleventh Gate. No one thought it possible, but you did it. Do you see why it must be you to help us?"

"Hmm… even if I wanted to, I doubt elder dragons are very vulnerable against pebble tossers. That's all I'm good for nowadays, I'm afraid."

Cassia looked numb, as if all her hopes had been dashed.

"It's late," I said. "You can use one of our vacant bedrooms upstairs."

"I couldn't trouble you…"

"Oh, really?" I gave her a look. "Asking me to risk my life to fight an elder dragon is perfectly acceptable, but taking one of my empty rooms is too much trouble?"

Cassia flushed. "I'm sorry, I didn't mean—"

"It's fine. Hurry up and put your clothes back on before someone else steps in and gets the wrong idea. I'm going to get an earful from Charm later."

Cassia got dressed quickly, and I led her out of the storage room and up the stairs to the second floor of the tavern.

"The place used to be an inn," I said. "There are plenty of rooms. Take your pick, other than the first three. Just watch out for Elsa. Sometimes she'll wander into a room randomly and pass out. Even if there's already someone in the bed. Unfortunately, the previous owner removed the locks when the property was sold and I've yet to get them replaced. The latrine is at the end of the hall, but if you want a hot bath, you'll need to wait until the morning. Charm already turned off the stoves."

"Thank you." Cassia gave me a short bow.

I watched her walk down the hall and enter one of the rooms. Then I entered my own, the first one from the stairs. I sat on the bed and let myself fall back against the mattress.

An elder dragon, I thought. *When will it ever end?* The entire world shouldn't depend solely on one person. Maybe once. Maybe even twice. Hell, maybe even thrice. But every damn time?

That was too much to take on. Too much to bear. Even a hero needed a vacation every now and then.

I felt the room spin as I closed my eyes. The brandy wasn't nearly finished with me. Drunkenness was still a strange sensation, even though I'd been experiencing it on and off for the better part of a year. When my gates had been open, poisons—including ales and spirits—had no effect on me. But now I had the tolerance of any other nineteen-year-old.

Not a moment after I pulled the blanket over my head, desperate for sleep to stop the room from spinning, a small knock sounded at my door. For a second, I thought Cassia was back to cajole me further. Then there was a split second of irrationality where I thought it might be Elsa entering the wrong room again. But Elsa wouldn't have knocked.

Charm stepped in. The young woman looked about Cassia's age—or perhaps closer to mine, as she was a bit shorter and scrawnier than the templar—but the light in her eyes was even older than my own. Her hair, which had once been fiery red, was now a shade closer to pink. It was drawn into two pigtails, one at each side. She wore a blank expression, just as she had for the past year. She was still in a sulk, and I was beginning to get irritated by it, but I supposed that was the point. Which made me more resolute to not show her that it was bothering me.

"Master," she said. "Charm has finished with the dishes and wiped down the tables. Is there anything else Master needs of Charm?"

Her slight foreign accent was, I'd been told, adorable to those who had not yet gotten used to it. I'd never met anyone else with a similar accent, despite my extensive travels.

"You didn't have to do that," I said. "I could have helped you with it in the morning."

She nodded then asked her question again. "Is there anything else Master needs of Charm?"

"Nope. Have a good night."

She nodded once more and turned to leave.

"Oh, wait. Uh... that girl, you know..."

Charm turned back to stare at me.

"It wasn't what it looked like..." I began.

"What does Master think it looked like?"

"Uh... well, I mean, uh..." I knew damn well whatever it looked like, it didn't look good.

"Like Master was coercing a young maiden of the church for his evil pleasures?" Charm said.

"Ah, it might have looked like that, but that's not—"

"Master does not need to explain himself to Charm. Charm is well aware of his... *personality*."

"Wait, was that an insult?"

"No, of course not, Master," Charm said without inflection. "Charm would not speak ill of her master. Perhaps Master's conscience is making its own interpretations."

I sat with my mouth hanging open, speechless. *Good gods, how does Charm jumble me up so easily?* Worse, I could tell that she was enjoying herself for once.

"What I'm trying to say is I was only trying to make a point to her, and she took it seriously, which is why she uh... got undressed."

"Is that so?" Charm said. "Charm was not aware that church templars become undressed when they take a point seriously."

"What? No... that's not what I meant." I was losing this bout of banter badly. The only way out was to be serious.

"She wanted me to kill an elder dragon."

Charm's half-lidded gaze suddenly intensified. "Will Master do it?"

"No, of course not. My gates are closed. Plus, I'm on vacation. We are on vacation. Taking a break. Someone else will deal with it."

Charm said nothing. Then, when I didn't continue, she asked, "Was there anything else, Master?"

"No," I said with a sigh. "Have a good night."

She nodded once more and closed the door.

I lay back down and closed my eyes, willing myself to sleep.

CHAPTER 5: BAD LUCK AND TROUBLE

That night, I dreamed of my father. I knew I would. I always did when my heart felt unsettled. We were sitting below the night sky on the water's surface in the middle of a far-reaching lake. It seemed entirely real as if it existed somewhere out there in the world, though I had never encountered such a place outside of my dreams.

"Hello, son," my father said with a kind smile.

"Are you ever going to tell me what this place is?" I asked, looking out upon the water's gleaming surface.

"What do you mean?"

My father couldn't answer questions like this. Any questions about why he was there or what place this was, he would not understand.

"It's nothing." I sighed. "The church wants me to kill a dragon."

"You'll do fine," he said with a proud smile. It hurt to see it.

"I'm not going this time."

"No?"

"I'm tired, and my powers are gone. It's been nice living quietly like a normal person. I'm not ready to go back yet."

My father smiled and looked out over the water and the night sky that reflected against its surface. "You must follow your heart. But sometimes, what you want isn't true to who you are."

"What the Abyss is that supposed to mean?"

He smiled again. "How's your love life? Have you found a nice woman yet?"

"What?" I said, taken aback.

"You're getting a bit old to be a bachelor, aren't you?"

"Do we have to have this conversation?"

He put his hands up, relenting. Then we sat together silently and watched the night stars until my eyes opened against the light of the morning sun entering through my bedroom window.

I found myself waking under the worst conditions possible. Firstly, Elsa had found her way into my bed. I had told myself several times to install locks on the doors of the rooms, but some part of me wanted to keep putting it off. I had a feeling it was the nineteen-year-old part.

That part was regretting his decision deeply this morning because in addition to Elsa, Charm was in my room. She looked like she'd just opened the door to wake me up, as she did every morning, but this time found Elsa in my bed with an arm draped around my neck—an arm that had somehow managed to fall out of the strap of the evening dress she'd been wearing the night before. Clearly, Elsa had drunkenly wandered into my room. At least, I hoped that was clear.

The expression on Charm's face told me it wasn't.

"Charm… th-this isn't what it looks like."

"Good morning, Master," Charm said with a voice devoid of emotion. It was always the worst when she spoke like that. Something dangerous was hidden in that voice. "Breakfast will be ready for Master downstairs when he is… *done*."

"Done? Done with what? Nothing is happening!"

She stepped out the door, ignoring me. But as Charm walked out, she bumped into Cassia, who was making her way down the hall, likely just having come out of her own room. Cassia apologized and inadvertently looked into the room that Charm was exiting—that is to say, my room, with the partially naked drunk in my bed. Cassia blushed then quickly looked away and hurried off.

"Wait!" I called after them like an innocent man before the executioner.

Charm didn't wait and closed the door behind her with a sharp snap.

"Why did you close the door?!"

"Ugh… no. Stop. Don't make me do it, Heru," Elsa mumbled into my neck in her drunken stupor. "I can't drink any more brandy."

"As if I'd ever make you drink!"

It was clear that my luck had suddenly taken a turn for the worse.

After slipping out from under Elsa's arm, I headed downstairs for breakfast. Charm and Cassia were eating silently in the dining hall as I came down the stairway. They sat away from each other at the table set with Charm's breakfast dishes and pitchers of freshly squeezed juices. Cassia looked at Charm, who avoided making eye contact with her.

"Don't mind her," I said to Cassia. "She's been a bit sulky lately."

"Oh. Um... how did you two meet?"

I stopped midstep as I was pouring myself a glass of orange juice. I glanced over at Charm. I'd been about to use our go-to story, but I could never tell what mood Charm was in. She had ruined the story while I was telling it in the past. I had a feeling it was going to be no different today.

"Charm is Master's obedient servant." Charm took a bite of her toast.

Cassia's eyes widened.

"She's joking," I said quickly. "I hired her. She helps around the tavern."

Cassia didn't look so certain about this. To make things worse, she was undoubtedly thinking back to my demands about her becoming my slave. *You're such a gentleman, Arch,* I thought to myself.

I shrank into my seat and began to help myself to the breakfast platter on the table while trying to come up with a plan to change the subject. "These are some perfectly cooked eggs, Charm."

"Charm obeys Master's every word," Charm replied. "Every. Word."

"Will you cut it out? You're causing misunderstandings!"

Charm nodded. "Charm will stop speaking about this topic now because Charm has been ordered to stop, and Charm cannot disobey her master."

I glared at her. Cassia looked worried. Charm, on the other hand, seemed pleased. A small smile curved at the corners of her lips. She took another bite of toast and munched it silently without looking at me, but I could tell she was feeling happy, which was a rarity.

"What is everyone chattering about?" Elsa came down the stairs, rubbing her head. "It's quite too early for a ruckus."

"It is two o'clock in the afternoon," I said.

"Like I said, *early*." Elsa grinned as she passed Charm and kissed her on the top of her head like a big sister would to a younger sibling.

In return, Charm gathered eggs, toast, and bacon from the breakfast platter onto an empty plate for Elsa as she sat. For some reason, the two of them got along really well. It irked me.

Elsa took a bite of her eggs. "Mmm, this is great, as always, Charm. Good job on the seasoning."

"Thank you, Miss Elsa."

"Elsa, you wandered into my room again last night," I said purposefully, sneaking a glance at Cassia to make sure she was listening.

Elsa grinned. "Sorry about that. It was a wild night. I'm impressed I made it up the steps."

I sighed. "I expect we're going to have more trouble from Mideon and his friends again very soon."

Elsa shrugged. "Those fools don't learn their lessons, do they?" Then Elsa blinked and seemed to notice Cassia's presence. "Oh, I'm sorry. Are you a new guest of ours?"

I shot Cassia a hard glance as she answered.

"I'm Cassia. I was, um, at the bar last night."

"Oh! I remember you. Are you from the church?"

"Um, yes, I am."

"You were carrying a sword."

"Ah, yes," Cassia said.

"Wouldn't that make you a templar?"

"Yes..."

Elsa took a bite of her toast. "What is a templar of the White Church doing in a tavern?"

"Don't be impolite," I said. "She isn't asking your business."

"I'm not a templar," Elsa said.

I shot Elsa a look.

Elsa smiled and held up her hands. "Fine, fine. I'm not one to pry or judge."

Cassia smiled and seemed relieved. She had to know that if she inadvertently spilled my secret, it would put her in my bad graces. "Those men seemed quite dangerous," she said, trying to make conversation.

"They'll be back," I said with dread, my thoughts turning to the effect another fight could have on my business.

"Let them come," Elsa said with a wicked smile and pushed back several strands of wavy dark hair that fell from her temples as she took another bite of her breakfast. "It's nothing a fist in the teeth won't solve."

I rubbed my forehead. I wasn't worried about Mideon's strength, but I was worried about his influence. Mideon was a superintendent's son. And not just any superintendent—the superintendent of Southbank.

Southbank was the city ward that contained the neighborhood of Kerrytown, where the Tipsy Pelican Tavern was located. If he wanted to, Mideon could cause a lot of trouble for a tavern business in his father's territory. All I wanted to do was perfect my brew, run my tavern, and have a few laughs without having to deal with arrogant perverts, church templars, or elder dragons. Was that such a tall order to ask for?

Bang, bang, bang! Someone slammed a fist against the front door. "Open up!" roared a gruff male voice.

Apparently, the order was very tall.

"Now what is it?" I growled and got up to open the door.

Standing on my doorstep was an overweight man with a thinly trimmed mustache. He wore a fine, stately coat over a white collared shirt that pulled tightly around the fat of his neck. He reminded me of a turkey.

"Bring me the owner of this trash heap of an establishment, boy," the man sneered as he peered past me. He would only be able to get a look at the barroom, not the women, who were seated deeper in the tavern.

"That would be me," I said.

He turned his eyes to me, clearly caught off guard. "You?" the man said with a hint of disgust. "You can't be older than twenty."

"If I had to guess, I would say you're in your late seventies."

The man turned red. "I'm fifty-two years of age, you ill-mannered lad!"

My guess was still closer to the mark than his. But I didn't tell him that.

"Interesting," I said. "You're the first person I've ever met who's told me their age before their name."

"That's because you made a false assumption of my age!"

"You guessed mine first. I thought you would appreciate the gesture."

His color was taking on a new shade of purple. "I am Proctor Remis Tumblee. I represent the interests of Lord Mideon Greengrass!"

Oh, this just gets better and better, doesn't it? I thought. My luck truly had turned bad. Worse yet, he'd said "Lord" Mideon Greengrass. So the rumors were true. Mideon was not only the superintendent's son but also the nephew of an actual baron.

I'd thought it a lie Mideon had spread to scare people, but if his people were openly calling him a lord, then it was likely real. With the right permission, a nephew could inherit lordship from his uncle in name, even if he didn't receive lands. That meant Mideon's father was the younger son of a noble house, but it seemed he had the sense to take the role of superintendent and give up his family's noble identity when his older brother inherited the family fortune. But even without the wealth and liegemen to back up Mideon's new title, it was still going to be plenty of trouble for me. This Remis character was exactly what I'd been afraid of when Elsa put Mideon and his two men to sleep in the middle of the street the night before.

"I see," I said loudly, letting my voice echo into the tavern and unable to keep the sarcasm out of it. "Lord Mideon's man, you say. Here at my tavern. Who would have thought you'd come?"

"Your employee has disparaged the honor of Lord Mideon Greengrass." He drawled the word *Lord*. "I am here issuing a formal notice by Superintendent Greengrass to have that tramp removed from your employment!"

"And if I don't?" I asked.

"Is that your answer?"

"Is it really one of Mideon's men?" Elsa called from the dining hall.

"Yes," I called back. "I'm handling it."

Elsa entered the barroom and strode over, a dangerous expression on her face. "It's my business. I'll—"

"No, you won't," I said, shooting her my own dangerous look that stopped her advance.

I hadn't given her a look like that before. She was stunned. It had been a while since I'd had to pull one of the Stormblood's gazes, though this was a very mild one.

"He asked for the owner, which isn't you," I told Elsa and turned back to the man. "Are you certain an apology won't do? She's quite well liked by the patrons here. I'd hate to lose her."

"I will not apologize to that pervert!" Elsa said.

Remis scowled at Elsa. "If you do not fire this woman, you will suffer the consequences!" he said, his voice turning shrill.

"Which are...?"

"Don't test me," the man said, getting in my face. "You will not survive it, boy."

Elsa came up to him, readying a fist, which I caught in my hand before she could swing it, thereby saving Proctor Remis a dentist appointment.

"How about this," I said. "Give me until a little after sundown. I'll need to find a replacement in that time and assuage my patrons."

Elsa looked at me, her face dropping. "You can't be serious!"

Remis's lip curled with glee at Elsa's reaction. "Very well. But if she is not removed from your employment by then, you will not be a tavern owner for long. That I promise you."

I nodded. "Tell Mideon to come after sundown. I'll do it in front of him so he can see it with his own eyes."

CHAPTER 6: PREP WORK FOR A BUSY AND EVENTFUL NIGHT

"**H**eru!" Elsa exclaimed after I closed the door. It wasn't like the time when she'd been ready to walk out because I didn't listen to her and do her bidding. There was real worry in her eyes.

"Relax," I said. "I'm not firing you."

"Then why did you...?"

"Who's supposed to be coming tonight?"

Elsa's upset expression turned to confusion.

"Were you already blacking out by then last night?" I asked. "Herwin is supposed to be bringing Galston the Gallant to the tavern."

"Oh, I do remember some mention of that."

"If Mideon sees us palling around with Galston and Herwin, maybe he'll leave us alone."

"I don't see why you're so worried about him," Elsa said. "That idiot couldn't find a sock in a sock drawer."

"It's not Mideon I'm worried about—it's his father. He could close down the tavern for any reason he wanted."

"On what grounds?"

"He could have one of his health inspectors come in, throw a dead rat on the floor, and say the place was too dirty to serve food. My license would be revoked, and the tavern would be shut down the next day."

"Oh," Elsa said, the indignation in her features dissipating. "I didn't realize…"

"It happens all the time to businesses that have angered the officials or the nobility."

It was strange to see that Elsa had not thought this through. She was smart and strong but surprisingly lacking in understanding of some common norms.

"But," I continued, "if Mideon sees us with the winner of the Tournament of Heroes, and if Herwin—who I don't think Mideon noticed last night—can put on a big show of being a count's son, then we'll have a chance of being left alone."

"I see," Elsa said, looking down at her feet. "Sorry, Heru. I didn't consider how far he'd take it."

"Don't worry about it. The guy deserved a beating. But as a general rule, let's avoid knocking out nobles on the tavern's front steps in front of a crowd, okay?"

Elsa smiled. "I'll try my best."

We spent the rest of the afternoon preparing for the night. Elsa mopped the floors, reset the furniture, and threw out the old broken table then replaced it with a new one from the storage room. I set to work on my newest batch of beer in the tavern's basement. The grain and hops had already been prepped. Now I was adding mashed pumpkins for flavoring. I'd been experimenting with pumpkins for a couple of months, and I hoped that this latest recipe would become my next beer at the tavern. But it wouldn't be ready for another couple of weeks.

Charm prepped food for the night, making several meat pies and putting a new pot of stew on the stove. Even Cassia offered to help. She said she wanted to work to pay back the night she stayed at the tavern, since I wouldn't take her money. I was feeling guilty about the night before, and I told her it wasn't necessary, but she wouldn't take no for an answer, so I put her on food prep with Charm, who seemed annoyed with Cassia's presence at first but was appeased when the templar turned out to be a capable kitchen hand.

There was little conversation as we worked on our respective tasks. But it felt nice. It had been a year since I opened the Tipsy Pelican Tavern, and in the past couple of weeks, the place was starting to feel like a real tavern with regular customers.

All of that could come to an end, depending on how the night went with Mideon returning for more trouble. I put up the Open sign outside the door at four o'clock in the afternoon as I always did. Our first patron was an older gentleman named Cormith. He sat in the corner of the bar, ordered a mug of Honeydew, and drank it in silence.

A few minutes later, a couple of young builders who looked like they'd gotten off work early came in and ordered some of the same. I smiled to see their refreshed faces as they drank down their first mouthfuls of the chilled brew.

I didn't serve many types of beer at the tavern yet. Only two in fact. Other than the Honeydew Lager, I also offered Red Harvest Ale, which I bought from a large distributor. Purchasing Red Harvest was more expensive than making my own beer, but it saved me time and made it easier for me to manage my inventory.

A big problem with making my own beer was figuring out how much I needed over the course of a few months. If I made too much, I'd have a bunch of useless stale beer sitting in my storage room at the end of the season. If I didn't make enough, I wouldn't have anything to serve the customers until the next batch, which usually took two weeks of brewing from start to finish.

By adding Red Harvest, I could control how much of my Honeydew Lager was being served. If business was good and I began running low on Honeydew Lager, I could just discount the Red Harvest, which would switch customers over to the cheaper ale, evening out my inventory.

The good thing about buying from a large distributor was that I didn't have to wait a month to refill my stock. Once I made the order with Munet, my go-to guy at the Tree and Stump Ale Company, a barrel of Red Harvest would be delivered to the tavern's doorstep in just a few days.

Over the past year, I'd pretty much mastered managing my inventory. With business picking up in the past month, I figured it was time to add a third beer, which I'd wanted to do since the day I'd opened the Tipsy Pelican Tavern. Most taverns in Kerrytown carried at least four or five different beers on tap, and some even a dozen or more. But they also had the patronage to support their taps. My customer base was small compared to the others. The tavern house itself was large, but I'd only opened the front barroom to the guests. And that area had only recently begun to fill up now that the tavern had been running for a year.

However, the Tipsy Pelican Tavern was becoming known for its house-brewed beer. The Honeydew Lager was a big hit, and if my upcoming pumpkin beer did well, too, I'd be able to open the larger dining hall, which at the moment was mostly unused except for breakfast and lunch among the staff. Then I might even save up enough to hire a good musician, who could play some songs a few nights a week.

I watched as more customers came through the tavern doors. More young men and boys with half a foot into adulthood. They all sat at the bar so they could chat with Elsa. She was a big reason the tavern was becoming more popular. She and the beer. It was a good combination.

Once, I asked if Charm would be interested in working as a barmaid as well. Although she rarely came out of the back of house during business hours, she always drew the attention of anyone who caught a glimpse of her and would certainly be popular among the guests.

But when I presented the question, she gave me a cold look and said, "If Master orders it, then Charm will have no choice but to do as she is asked."

I took that as a no, so she stuck with food prep, which was just as well. I did not have another cook—I was awful at it myself—and she did an excellent job. We served simple dishes that could be made in large portions. Mostly stews and pies. They were hearty and inexpensive meals that went well with the beer.

"Master Arch, you lucky bastard," said one of my regulars, who'd just walked in. "How did you land another beautiful barmaid?"

"Huh?" I said, looking up dumbly. *Another barmaid?* Then I saw to whom he was referring.

Cassia was not wearing her sword and church tunic but a stunning shoulderless dress as she served drinks. She looked a little embarrassed by the attention and seemed uncomfortable in the outfit, pulling at its seams.

Where did she get that dress? I wondered. *And good gods does it fit her well.*

Then Elsa winked at me, and I realized it was one of hers. Of course, it was. Bless her incredible taste.

"Oh, that's Cassia," I said. "She's helping out for the day."

"Only for the day?" One of the men turned to her as she poured him a mug of Honeydew. "You should just stay and work here. Master Arch won't let you down!"

I looked away, afraid of the sting I'd feel if I met her gaze. I'd already let her down—more than once if you counted what happened in the storage room.

Cassia smiled shyly. "It's a very nice tavern, but I'm afraid I won't be able to stay long."

I ducked into the corridor to escape the conversation. "How's the stew going?" I asked Charm as I entered the kitchen.

"It is warm and welcoming, Master." Charm leaned in to smell the stew. "The opposite of how Master treated the young templar last night."

I scowled. "Oh, give me a break."

"Charm sees that Master is beginning to have a habit of taking advantage of desperate young maidens."

"I hope you're not including yourself in that, because I'm pretty sure you only qualify as an old gran—"

The ladle she'd been holding flew through the air at my face. I ducked just in time, and it bounced off the pantry behind me.

"Good Celeru! Did you just throw a ladle at me?"

"Ah, Charm's hand slipped. Apologies, Master."

"Uh-huh. Then see to it that nothing else 'slips' from your hand," I said with annoyance, touching my hair to check for any drops of soup that might have splashed from the ladle.

"That will depend. Sometimes Master's words cause Charm's hands to spasm."

"That sounds like a threat. In fact, I'm pretty sure it is a threat."

"Not at all, Master. It is only because Charm puts great weight in Master's opinions that they have such an effect on her body."

I'd always been a good fighter, and I'd been known to have a good quip or two, but I was no match for Charm when it came to jests. Sighing, I picked up the ladle and brought it to the sink.

"I wish there were something I could say to cheer you up," I said as I scrubbed the ladle with soap.

Charm eyed me with one of her half-lidded stares. "There are no words Master can offer Charm that will make her happier. Only actions."

"I'm not getting into that argument again, Charm," I said, meeting her eyes. "That matter is settled."

She was staring at me intently, but I did not look away. I could afford to lose the small battles but not the big ones. Never the big ones.

After a moment longer, she dropped her gaze and turned away, taking the stew off the stove. I dried the ladle and handed it back to her. We didn't speak anymore as I put food on plates and served the customers.

Time passed quickly, and soon the sun was setting. Bran, Dalian, and Amberly had arrived, but Herwin and his guest of honor were nowhere to be found.

"Looks like the boy couldn't pull off the deed and skittered," Dalian said as I poured him a mug.

Bran put down his own mug, finishing a gulp, foam glittering in his beard as usual. "He's a good lad. I bet he and the champion are just running late."

Just then, the doors swung open, slamming against the wall. The whole tavern turned, eager to lay eyes on the champion of the Tournament of Heroes.

But it wasn't Galston the Gallant. Mideon stood in the frame of the door, with a dark smile on his face. And this time, he'd brought six men with him. They were each holding clubs.

CHAPTER 7: THE BEAR MAN AND THE TAVERN KEEPER

Nobody in the tavern moved. There must have been real fear in the hearts of my patrons. I could tell many were ready to bolt for the door, but the doorway was blocked by a massive bear of a man, who had to duck when he stepped into the tavern.

But I also saw that many of my patrons were clutching their stools and chairs, readying for a fight. Bran, Amberly, and Dalian had their hands on the backs of their chairs, ready to throw them forward at a moment's notice and come to my aid.

Bless their hearts, I thought, *but couldn't they pick something other than my furniture as weapons?*

"Where's the owner?" spat Proctor Remis, his turkey neck shaking with the sound of his shrill voice.

He moved his way toward Mideon, who stood at the center of the room. The rest of their minions were behind the two of them, wearing stone-cold faces as they held their clubs. Mideon's men were battle-scarred with cuts across their faces and arms. These weren't day laborers Mideon had gathered for some roughhousing or even trained guardsmen borrowed from his nobleman uncle. These were gang members—rough men who spent their lives fighting with tooth, nail, and blade in the back alleys of the city.

The fact that Mideon was able to call upon men like these spoke volumes about his character. But it was no surprise. I'd already gotten a pretty good idea of the man in the previous interactions I'd had with him.

Forget the fact that they could destroy the tavern. If things really got out of hand, my patrons would get maimed. And nothing killed a business like injured customers.

Elsa's face turned white. She was a good fighter, but even she couldn't deny the danger these men posed to our patrons. I stepped past the tables and met Mideon and Remis in the center of the room.

"You," Mideon said. "Yes, I remember you. Gustkin, wasn't it?"

"Please, call me Arch," I said merrily. "What can I get you folks to drink?"

"We aren't here to drink, Gustkin," Mideon said. "We are here to ensure that tramp gets what's coming to her!"

Some grins cracked on the hard faces of the men. I was weighing my options, and none were looking any good. *Where the Abyss is Herwin?*

I was certain Herwin would bring Galston that night. It was his only chance to win the respect of the three builders, though I still had no idea why the lordling desired to do so.

"I apologize," I said. "I had a bit too much to drink last night, and my memory is suffering. Which lady were you referring to again?"

Buy time. That was all I could do at that point.

"Don't play the fool with me! It's that harlot right there!" Mideon stabbed a finger in Elsa's direction.

"Oh, you mean Elsa." I scratched my head as if still struggling to remember. "But what exactly is it that you want from me?"

"I want you to fire her!" Mideon screamed, his veins bulging at his neck and temples. He glared at Proctor Remis for assistance.

"We had an agreement, boy!" the lawyer said, his own fury rising. "You promised it would be done in front of my client tonight!"

"What? Who are you?"

"We spoke this afternoon!"

"This afternoon?" I said. "The only person that came by in the afternoon was some old man in his seventies."

Remis' face turned a pure shade of red. "Y-You ingrate!" he screamed, the shrill back in his voice. He turned to Mideon. "This boy is playing us for fools! We must teach him a lesson!"

Two of the men with clubs behind them took a step forward in anticipation of their boss's orders.

I raised my hands. "I'm just kidding guys, just kidding. I remember everything. You want Elsa fired, right?"

"That's right," Mideon hissed.

"Hey, Elsa," I said.

Elsa looked at me and paused before she said, "Yes, Heru?"

"You're fired."

She blinked. Then she smiled. "Okay."

"See?" I said. "That wasn't so hard. Now, what can I get you folks to drink?"

"She's. Still. In. Your. Tavern," Mideon said through clenched teeth.

I raised my eyebrows at him as if confused at why he was stating the obvious. "Yes?"

"I want her out!"

"Well... my tavern is open to *anyone*," I said, eyeing the men Mideon had brought. "Even former employees. It's not my place to tell—"

"Out!" Mideon screeched. "I want her on the streets! She must pay for what she did!" Mideon could barely finish his words. His whole body was shaking with rage. The guy really didn't know how to control his emotions. He pointed a quivering finger at me. "Y-You dare to make light of me? I will tear your tavern to the ground!"

Mideon had to know he couldn't drag Elsa out in front of twenty witnesses, superintendent daddy notwithstanding. The city guard didn't sit well with abductions and the beating of civilians. The men he'd brought were mainly there for show, despite the true danger they presented to my tavern and customers.

But Mideon was losing his temper. And who could say what a foolish man in anger would do? My time had run out.

Just at that moment, I sensed some movement through the open door behind Mideon and his men. "Oh, excuse me. There appear to be more guests trying to enter the tavern. We'll have to continue this discussion later. Please find a seat!"

I quickly stepped past Mideon and Remis before they could protest. "You'll have to bunch together a bit," I said to their group. "It's going to be a busy night!"

I passed the rest of his men, ignoring their looks. One of them tried to trip me, and another snatched at my arm. I expertly weaved through them with minimal movement, as if I hadn't noticed their attempts.

But the bear man blocking the door didn't budge a hair as I approached. He was almost Amberly's size in height but even wider and made of solid muscle. The bear man dropped his eyes down at me without lowering his chin, as if eyeing a worm he was ready to squash.

There wasn't a lot of intelligence in those eyes, but there was plenty of violence, as if he hoped that I'd resist Mideon just so he could have an excuse to cause pain. His shoulders spanned the entrance from one side to the other, and his legs were spread slightly like a shieldsman ready to defend against a barrage of invaders. His face was as square as a brick, and his muscles protruded against dark tattoos. Old scars covered his knuckles—the kind you only got from years spent fighting with bare fists. A cruel smile formed on the bear man's face as I reached him. He was looking forward to what would happen next.

Outside, I could hear the excited voice of Herwin and the deep murmur of another man.

"Excuse me, good sir," I said, placing a palm above the bear man's right elbow. My movement was deft—not too fast but not slow either. "Don't be blocking the entrance. Someone might run into you. We wouldn't want anyone to get hurt, now, would we?"

To anyone watching, the bear man would have appeared to move out of the way as if politely guided by my touch, taking two short steps to the side. But his second step fell a little unsteadily, as if he had to put down his foot to keep himself from falling. I doubted the people in the tavern noticed what had really happened, but the bear man stared at me with unbridled surprise. Then the surprise passed as the realization that he had just been forcibly pushed aside dawned in the mostly hollow space between his ears. He bared his teeth and let out a scream of red-hot rage.

As I passed him and stepped through the entrance, I saw his attack from the corner of my eye. My senses were more heightened than usual, and in my perception, the movements happened slowly. The bear man turned on me, clenching his big paw into a fist the size of a roast chicken. In a single motion, he swung it forward with all his musculature, pushing his strength through it like a battering ram, straight into the back of my head.

Or at least, it would have landed in the back of my head. But right at that moment, I stepped to the side to make way for Herwin and his guest, gesturing them into the tavern, as any hospitable tavern keeper would.

The bear man's fist shot through the air, elongating where it had expected to connect, passing where my head had been and making a deafening slam into the stoic face of Galston the Gallant, Champion of the Tournament of Heroes.

CHAPTER 8: THE BEAR MAN AND THE CHAMPION

If the bear man's fist was a roast chicken, the head of the tournament champion was a solid slab of obsidian. The fist might as well have been a gnat that flew into his face. Galston didn't even blink.

"My goodness!" I exclaimed at the bear man with all the indignation of a haughty noble. "I've told you for the last time, Gerlanda! There is no fighting in the tavern. You, sir, are banned!"

Whatever name the bear man's unfortunate mother had given him, it was certainly not Gerlanda, but the bear man did not appear to have registered what I'd called him. I could think of two reasons why he looked so shocked. Firstly, he just punched Galston the Gallant with all his strength. And secondly, he'd just punched Galston the Gallant with all his strength *to no effect*.

"Are you listening to me, Gerlanda?" I said again with mock outrage. "I'm not just cutting you off from the bar! You, sir, are banned from the tavern!"

I quickly turned to Galston. He was a large man of a stocky build, perhaps in his late twenties or early thirties. And though his demeanor was calm, it carried weight and gravity.

"Are you quite all right, sir? I am so sorry for this man's behavior," I said, bowing and gesturing for Galston to enter the tavern. "Please, let me get you a drink. On the house, of course."

Only then did the bear man notice me. As if suddenly reminded of what he originally set out to do, he stepped out of the tavern and raised his giant fist again, but this time, it was properly aimed at me. But the fist never made its way past his own chest, because Galston the Gallant took Gerlanda's head with one hand and drove it down into the cobblestone pavement, splitting the ground.

Herwin's mouth was wide open, as were the mouths of Mideon's men inside the tavern. Everyone was silent.

"I'm afraid words are not enough for some men," Galston said, his voice deep and strong. "You must be Master Arch. Lord Herwin has been telling me about your Honeydew Lager for quite some time. I thought I'd come and see if it lived up to his praises."

"Of course!" I said, smiling. "I'll pour you a mug from a fresh barrel. I promise you won't be disappointed. And again, I do apologize for Gerlanda's behavior. We'll just let him sit outside for a bit to cool down."

If you can call having your head in the ground and your ass in the sky "sitting," I thought.

"He's a good man when he's not drunk," I continued. "But I'm sad to say, those hours of the day are rare."

Galston nodded as he stepped into the tavern. "I know the type."

Herwin followed after Galston, eyeing Gerlanda as he passed. I grabbed him by the shoulder and pulled him close. "Herwin, you came in the nick of time. I owe you one. If you ever need a favor, you let me know."

He looked at me, surprised. "I'm not sure of your meaning, Master Arch."

"You'll see once we step inside."

But when we did, Herwin glanced around, blinked, and gave me a confused look. I, too, looked and understood. Mideon's imposing, armed men were no longer armed nor imposing. Instead, they were all sitting at tables along the walls with straight, prude postures and their weapons tucked away, as if they had just arrived to attend a tea party.

Elsa was even serving drinks to a couple of them, who—save for the scars and tattoos—might have looked like nothing more than kindly patrons and connoisseurs of fine drink. Even Mideon was seated. The ghastly expression on his face was mirrored by Proctor Remis, who sat across from him.

Such was the effect of the champion of heroes accompanied by a lord, who Galston himself identified. Things had turned out even better than I expected. But the tavern was quiet as a morgue. I gave Amberly a meaningful look that he quickly understood.

He slapped Dalian hard on the back and burst out in raucous laughter. "I get it now! The chicken ate the squirrel! My gods, you really have to work for that joke!"

There were some nervous chuckles, then some of the other patrons began laughing. Then even Mideon's men were laughing. And just like that, the tavern sounded like a tavern again.

"Elsa!" I said. "Two mugs of fresh Honeydew Lager for our new guests, please."

"Right away, Master Arch," Elsa said with a curt bow reminiscent of a royal butler, and she darted off into the back room.

I did a double take and wondered who this woman was and what she'd done with the drunken temptress. Then I looked around for some empty chairs for Herwin and Galston but found that all the tables were taken now that Mideon's men were seated. Bran, Amberly, and Dalian, who were watching, immediately pushed out two chairs from their table. Their expressions were razor-sharp as if they were guiding me to place Galston at their table with their sheer force of will.

"Champion Galston, I'm afraid all our tables are taken. You've caught us on a busy night. Would you mind sharing a table with these fine gentlemen? Bran, Amberly, and Dalian are tavern regulars and excellent for a conversation."

Galston nodded, but his face remained unreadable. He and Herwin took their seats, and Elsa returned with two pitchers of Honeydew Lager and placed them in front of the two. Galston did not immediately drink from his mug. He ran his eyes over my tavern, taking a moment to eye Mideon's gangsters.

"Interesting crowd here," Galston said as he raised the mug to his lips. His eyebrows rose as he swallowed. He stared down into his mug and took another swig. "Impressive. Not too sweet and not too bitter. A strong burst of honeydew at the finish. Herwin, you did not exaggerate."

"I told you, Galston!" Herwin said proudly. "Master Arch makes the best fruit beer in the city."

I couldn't have been more pleased. Galston's appearance and compliment meant a lot to me as a brewer.

"Keep on drinking," Bran said.

"It gets better after the second mug," Amberly said.

Galston nodded and downed another swallow.

I nudged Herwin. He looked at me, and I darted a glance at the builders. Herwin quickly bobbed his head. "Galston, please meet my friends Bran, Amberly, and Dalian. They are wall carpenters in the city and witnessed your final match at the tournament."

"Indeed?" Galston leaned over and shook hands with all three of the builders.

"We saw it from the middle rows," Amberly said with a pitch of idolization in his voice that I'd never heard escape the large man's diaphragm. "Spent half a month's wages to get the seats."

"Well worth it. More than worth it!" Bran said with a laugh.

"Say, Champion," Dalian said, scratching his scraggly white beard. "We've been having a small quarrel about the tournament that perhaps you could help us settle."

As the men spoke, Galston's eyes darted every now and then toward the bar, but at Dalian's request, he returned his gaze to the old builder and nodded.

Bran spoke first. "Which of Celeru's rules did you cast in the final—"

"Now, wait a minute," Amberly said. "Let's first clear up which rules we bet on. I can't even remember all the names you've claimed the hero used."

"I don't remember their names," Bran said. "I only know the numbers. Rule Forty-Six is my guess."

Dalian joined in. "And I say it was Hellish Hand!"

I left their table and went over to Mideon, who'd been watching the entire interaction with unhidden disbelief.

"My apologies, Lord Mideon, for cutting our conversation short," I said with the utmost grace. "Let us continue. You were saying...?"

As I said Mideon's name, Galston and Herwin looked over to register the other lord in the tavern. Herwin frowned and whispered something into Galston's ear.

"Er, yes. About that..." Mideon eyed the lordling and the hero.

"But first, let me take your order," I said. "You've been sitting for so long, and you haven't even had anything to drink. I really do apologize. What can I get for you?"

"Ah..."

"Maybe I suggest a glass of our finest brandy for your lordship?"

"Yes, that seems—"

"Excellent. For your men as well?" I asked.

"Yes."

"Eight brandies, coming right up!" I headed toward the back.

"Master Arch," Galston said, raising a finger.

I stopped beside him and leaned over. "Sir?"

Galston hesitated before he said, "Who is that woman, if I might ask?"

"Ah, that's El—" I began, but I saw him looking at the bar again. Only Cassia was behind it, serving a bowl of stew to one of the customers now that things had settled down. "Oh, that's Cassia. She's, uh... a new hire."

"She is a striking woman," he said.

"That's Master Arch for you," Herwin said. He'd apparently overheard our dialogue. The builders, on the other hand, were still arguing over spells. "All his staff are stunning. You should see the one who does the cooking."

"Good patronage keeps good staff," I said. "Please, let me get you two refills."

I went to the bar and grabbed several glasses and two new mugs. Then I filled the former with brandy and the latter with beer. Cassia came by with a load of dirty mugs and placed them in the sink behind the bar as I poured.

"That was masterfully handled, Archibold-don," Cassia said quietly.

"Shhh, don't call me that."

"Master Arch, then?"

"Arch is fine. They call me Master Arch because I own the tavern. But I don't think you really see me as a tavern keeper."

Cassia smiled. "No, I'm afraid I don't. But *Master* is also an honorific for those who have mastered a discipline."

"Well, I've lost the mastery over mine. By the way, I think I just found a hero who would be interested in helping your cause."

"You don't mean Mr. Galston?"

"Of course not," I said in mock surprise. "I mean Mr. Galston." I grinned at the look she gave me.

"He's a capable man," Cassia said. "But I do not think he's a match for an elder dragon."

"Can't hurt to ask. Get a big group of eager fighters, and you might stand a chance. He seems to have taken an interest in you."

"H-How could you know that, Archibold-don?" Cassia said, reddening.

"Arch is fine," I told her again, grinning. "Here, take the Honeydew to the hero and Herwin. I'll bring these brandies to Mideon and his friends."

Cassia gave me a flushed look but did as I asked. We stepped back around the bar, each carrying a platter of drinks.

"All right, here it is," Amberly said to Galston. "Bran here thinks it was Rule Forty-Six that you cast in the final moment. And my good but mistaken friend Dalian says it's Hellish Hand. But I say it was sixty-six, Saffron Spear. But then the missy there, bringing the beers, said that it couldn't have been Rule Sixty-Six."

Galston seemed suddenly attentive now that Cassia had been referenced in the conversation. "The young lady saw my match as well?" He looked over as Cassia placed a fresh mug of Honeydew Lager before him and Herwin.

"Apparently," Dalian said. "She says the arena would have been destroyed if you had used Sixty-Six."

"Perhaps we could request her opinion?" Galston said.

Cassia looked at them, unsure of what they were talking about.

"Miss Cassia," Herwin piped up. "Could you tell us which rule you think Galston used in the final Tournament of Heroes?"

"I believe it was Rule Seventeen, Paralyzing Palm," she said.

"The effects were massive. It could not have been such a low rule," Amberly said.

"Seventeen?" Dalian said. "That's far too low."

Galston nodded, smiling. "The young woman is correct." He raised his hand to her. "Pleasure to make your acquaintance, my lady."

Cassia blinked, surprised by the offer of a handshake. She took it. "The pleasure is mine."

I chuckled to myself as I served the brandies Mideon had purchased. I brought them to his men first, giving each a polite smile and an unwavering eye as I placed the drinks before them.

"Lady Cassia," Galston said. "I hope you don't mind me saying so, but you remind me of a young woman I fell for in my hometown when I was just a boy."

Cassia blushed. "Oh, um, thank you, sir."

"But more than that, you appear to have magical training. Forgive my rudeness." Galston looked down as he held her hand. Suddenly, his eyes glowed with a blue aura. "Gods. You've awakened two gates."

All three builders looked over, the news deepening the surprise that had appeared on their faces when Cassia correctly guessed Galston's spell.

"No, I..." Cassia began.

"Incredible," Galston said. "Even I did not have my Second Gate awakened at your age."

The whole tavern went silent. Then the information sank in across the various tables.

"Did the champion say she opened two gates?"

"He did! Incredible!"

"Two gates! Even the duke has only a handful of men with two gates open in his employment!"

"I bet she would have placed in the top ten in the Tournament of Heroes if she'd competed!"

"She's stronger than most of the high guard in the kingdom!"

And that was when I decided to slap the final glass of brandy in front of Mideon. "Your drink, sir. Now, let us continue our conversation from earlier. You had a pressing matter, I believe?"

CHAPTER 9: THE MEDI GILHANNA

Mideon looked at me with wide, uncertain eyes. He glanced at Galston, then at Herwin, then at Cassia. A moment passed as he seemed to wrestle with his thoughts. I could guess what they were.

"Ahem," I said. "The pressing matter?"

Mideon returned his eyes to me. There was still anger in them, but the outrage was veiled and hidden. "No pressing matter. I mean, I was just saying..." He frowned, downed his brandy in one swallow, and stood. "How much do I owe you for the drinks?"

"Ah, let me see. You did order the finest brandy in the house. That's six shimmers each, and with eight men, that'll be forty-eight shims."

He stared at me in shock. Forty-eight silver shimmers were equivalent to a season's salary for a city guard and more than a full gold brilliance. I gave him my most oblivious and friendly tavern-keeper smile.

He looked again at Galston and Herwin's table then dug into his pocket and counted the coins. Then he made his men each dig out a shim to cover the cost. He handed me the collected coins and gave one final glance at Elsa before leaving.

Elsa came to my side at the door, and we watched Mideon head down the road with Remis, both men walking quickly and without speaking to each other. Behind him, his men peeled Gerlanda off the pavestones, dragging him away.

"I think I have a new appreciation for you, Heru," Elsa said.

"No need for that. Just appreciate my furniture."

Elsa smiled. "Will do." Then in a smaller voice, she said, "Thank you."

I shrugged. "No need for that either."

I looked back into the tavern, finding the tables still mostly filled, and it was not even past midnight. Galston had some color in his face and was speaking animatedly with Cassia, Amberly, and Bran. Dalian had fallen asleep in his chair and was snoring loudly. The sight of it all brought a smile to my face. Then I noticed Elsa was still turned toward the door beside me. Her head was tilted downward slightly, and her eyes were hidden in her hair. I guessed she still had something on her mind, so I waited.

"I-I don't know how you put up with me," Elsa said, her voice still quiet. "I'm always breaking your tables and drinking your good brandy. And this time, I nearly got the tavern shut down because I couldn't handle a little attention from a noble."

I shrugged again. "It was more than a little attention. In any case, I wouldn't worry about it. Come on. I'm buying Herwin and myself a fancy drink. You can have one too."

I walked over to Galston's table and pulled a chair next to Herwin, who was sitting across from Galston and Cassia and chatting with the builders. I clasped him on the shoulder. "Master Herwin! What are you drinking?"

"Oh, Master Arch," Herwin said, a little surprised. He raised his mug. "The Honeydew Lager, of course."

"That's no drink for the hero of the night!"

"The hero?"

Bran smiled. "You came at the perfect time tonight, Herwin. Master Arch was in a tight pickle."

"You were?" Herwin said.

"Oh yes. Mideon was here. You saw him, didn't you?"

"Yes, I of course, but he didn't seem—"

"That's because you showed up with Galston," Amberly said. "They were going to wreck the place. I was readying for a brawl."

"Holy Celeru," Herwin said, blinking.

Elsa came to our side. If she'd been crying, it was impossible to tell. She looked radiant as ever, her smile tinged with the usual measure of energy and playfulness. I began to wonder if it was a role that she played to mask something else.

"We nearly didn't make it," Herwin said. "But I knew everyone was eager to meet Galston."

"That's why I owe you a favor," I said. "But you can call that in at another time. Tonight, we'll drink some fine brandy to celebrate our good fortunes. Elsa, bring over the bottle of Gilhanna."

That wiped the smile off her face. "Uh... Heru, we finished the Gilhanna last night."

"What?!" I exclaimed, looking at her. "That's what we were drinking? That was our best Elvish brandy!"

But that was indeed the bottle we'd drunk after Elsa knocked Mideon flat on the street. I had chalked up the excellent taste to Elsa clutching my arm, but in fact it was because of its elven making.

Elsa turned a little pink. "It seemed like a worthy occasion at the time."

"Good Celeru, I don't even remember enough from the night to savor the taste of it."

Elsa looked down guiltily at the floor. "Sorry."

"No matter," I said, sighing. "I've got a better bottle in my room under the bed. Could you go and fetch it? And bring three glasses." I looked over the people sitting at the table. "On second thought, bring seven glasses. If Dalian wakes up, we can fetch another."

Elsa came back a few minutes later with a tray of glasses and a tall green bottle with shining engravings. There was a look of surprise on her face as she whispered in my ear, "Heru, this bottle... it-it's a Medi Gilhanna!"

"Sure is," I said, taking the bottle off the tray and scratching at the wrapping.

"It must be worth hundreds of shimmers... no, hundreds of gold brilliances!" Her voice was still a whisper, but it was filled with excitement.

"Uh-huh. Good thing I hid it under my bed, or it'd probably be gone, too, eh?"

Elsa blinked. Then her cheeks flushed. "I would never—"

"Oh, relax. I'm just teasing you. Grab a seat." I carefully poured seven glasses, making sure not to spill a single drop.

Galston caught sight of the bottle, and his eyes widened. "Gods, is that what I think it is?"

"Might be," I said, pouring out the last glass.

Herwin perked up and looked down at the clear purple liquid as I put the first glass in front of him. "What is it?"

"It is a king's treasure," Galston said.

This got looks from all around the table. Amberly licked his lips, Cassia gave me a curious look, and even Bran seemed interested.

"Don't worry. Everyone at the table is getting a glass."

"We couldn't," Galston said. "This... this bottle could buy you a new tavern."

"I've always believed good brandy is for drinking, not selling," I said. "My friend Herwin here has saved me from a dire plight, the most celebrated warrior in the city is gracing us with his presence, and at this table, we have my most loyal patrons and two lovely ladies. What better occasion is there than this for a good drink, eh?" I leaned over the table and placed a glass before Galston.

"You're too kind, Master Arch."

"Just means you'll have to come by more often, Champion," Amberly said with a big smile.

Galston nodded as if a deal had been made.

"How'd you come by this sacred drink?" Bran asked, receiving his glass.

"I could tell you, but then I'd have to charge you."

Bran held up his hands. "Please, keep the secret to yourself. I don't think I could afford it in a lifetime."

That got some chuckles from the table, Cassia laughing the happiest. It was a bright and pure laugh. She seemed to be in good spirits, which for some reason made me happy.

Amberly was shaking Dalian. "Wake up, you old fool. You're going to miss the drink of the century!"

But Dalian continued to snore, slumped in his seat.

"Guess, he'll have to wait until next time." I finished serving all the glasses, placing the last one in front of Elsa. Then I raised my own. "To friends, old and new. To the Tipsy Pelican Tavern. And to Herwin for saving the day!"

Herwin smiled and turned bright red. But everyone else joined in on it.

"To friends, the Tipsy Pelican Tavern, and Herwin!" said the others.

We clinked glasses and each took a sip. It tasted wonderful because it was indeed the best brandy money could buy but also because of the company I had to share it with.

***

At about two o'clock in the morning, the last patron left the tavern. Galston had given Cassia a big hug on the way out. Bran and Amberly had given Galston a big hug on the way out. Somebody had tried to give a big hug to Elsa but got thrown through a table. Then she came to me and apologized profusely, which was a first. Other than that, the night ended on a much quieter note than the one before.

As we cleared the tables and did our cleaning, Cassia approached me. "Arch-don, I was wondering if I could speak to you about my lodging here. The inn I've rented is quite far…"

"Sure," I said, placing dishes on top of one another. "Thanks for helping out today."

"No, not at all. I was, um, speaking to Galston tonight…"

"I saw. He's taken a liking to you."

"He asked me if there was anything I needed, and I did mention the dragon."

"Did he agree to be your hero?"

Cassia pouted. "He did offer to help," she said. "He said he could ask around to gather a group, as there are other awakened in the city, though he does not know their number of gates."

"There you go. Get a few hundred, and you'll take out that dragon, no problem."

"A-A few hundred?"

"Well… you know. To be on the safe side. But that's good news, no?"

"Yes. So, um… I thought I'd stay in the city for a while longer to recruit awakened adventurers."

"Uh-huh…."

"And, um, well… seeing that I'll be staying longer now, I was wondering if I could rent the room from you."

"Oh sure, no problem. Stay as long as you like."

"What fee should I—"

"Don't worry about it," I said. "I have too many rooms, anyway. And Charm and Elsa both seem to like you."

"I couldn't take your charity."

I raised an eyebrow at her. She quickly caught my meaning. It was the same as the night before when she'd said she couldn't trouble me. She had asked me to risk my life to fight a dragon. Borrowing a room was nothing.

"Perhaps," Cassia said quickly, "I could help around the tavern when I'm not recruiting with Galston."

"That'll be great," I said, smiling. Then I called to the kitchen. "Elsa, Charm, come over here."

Both young women poked their heads out.

"What is it, Heru?"

"Just come out, will you?"

Elsa and Charm came over, their hands and arms still wet from cleaning dishes.

"Cassia is going to be staying with us for a while," I said.

There was no surprise on their faces. They just looked at Cassia with encouraging smiles, and I knew right away that Cassia had spoken to them first about it.

I ran a hand through my hair. "I see that I am the last person to learn about things, as usual."

"That's what happens when you're the heru," Elsa said.

Charm wiped her hands on her apron. "Those who make maidens undress cannot be easily trusted. It is necessary to first seek advice from others."

"Huh? Who made who undress?" Elsa asked.

"*Okay*, moving on," I said. "Let's all welcome Cassia to the Tipsy Pelican Tavern!"

"Welcome!" Elsa gave Cassia a hug.

"Welcome," Charm said, giving Cassia a small bow.

"Welcome!" I said, grinning. I really was in an unusually good mood.

"Thank you." Cassia looked as if she were genuinely warmed by the greeting.

Sometime later, I climbed the stairs to the second floor with the half-finished bottle of Medi Gilhanna and two glasses. I stopped before Charm's door and knocked lightly.

"Come in," she said. Charm was sitting on her bed, reading a book against lantern light. "What is it, Master?"

"Brought you a drink," I said, placing the two glasses on her nightstand. "Figured you wouldn't have wanted to partake earlier with the crowd."

"I do not need any now either, Master."

"Oh, come on. This is good stuff, even by your standards." I poured two fingers into her glass and one into mine.

I thought she was going to sulk again and turn down the drink, but to my surprise, she raised the glass to her nose and sniffed. Then she took a small sip and gave a slight nod. "This is quite fine."

"Hey, don't be rude. We need to cheers first." I raised my glass and considered a toast then thought better of it. She clinked my glass with hers, and we each took a sip. "Good, right?"

Charm nodded. "How did Master come by it?"

"A gift from Emdark's daughter."

Charm nodded again and took another sip. After a moment, she said, "My body feels warm, like I am beside a fire and a musician is playing a song I like."

I smiled. "Told you it was good stuff."

After we were done, we sat in silence for a little while. Then Charm said, "I wish to sleep now."

I stood and took the glasses and the bottle back to my room. I considered having another glass by myself but then pushed the thought away. There would be another occasion to drink the Medi Gilhanna, I told myself. I made sure the cork was tightened and stowed it back underneath my bed.

I lay down under my covers and reminded myself of the good things that had happened. Many pitfalls had been avoided, and in my book, that was a win on any day.

I couldn't have been more wrong.

CHAPTER 10: JUST ON A STROLL TO THE MARKET (ARC 2)

C harm was making breakfast when I entered the kitchen. "Master is up early this morning," she said as she chopped several mushrooms.

"Finally had some good sleep."

"Because Master's conscience has cleared?"

I shot her a look. "Why shouldn't my conscience be clear?"

Charm did not return my gaze and kept cutting her vegetables. "No reason, Master. Certainly not because Master declined the young maiden's request for aid after making her undr—"

"Stop right there!" I said, pointing. "Good Celeru, when are you ever going to let that go?"

Charm did not reply, but the corners of her mouth curled upward slightly as she continued cutting mushrooms.

"Good morning."

We both turned and saw Cassia pushing past the curtains of the kitchen entrance. "Are you making breakfast, Charm? Can I help?"

Charm nodded and laid out grapes and apples for Cassia to wash in the sink. I leaned over the stove and checked the pot. It looked like a vegetable stew and smelled good, but we ate stew for dinner three to four days a week.

"No eggs today?" I asked.

"The tavern is out of eggs," Charm said. "And bread. And bacon. And many other things."

"Aren't we supposed to get deliveries today?"

"In the afternoon, Master. The tavern is properly supplied for the customers, but breakfast and lunch ingredients for staff has run out."

"Mmm... guess I'll head to the market after breakfast to pick up a few things."

I set the table while Charm and Cassia finished making the stew. Elsa came down as we were getting seated. She hadn't changed out of her evening dress, which looked like it had been slept in. In contrast, Cassia was wearing her white church robes, which gave an interesting variety to our evolving little group.

"Arch-don," Cassia said. "Would you mind if I joined you at the market today? I've yet to see much of the city."

"Sure. I won't be going far, but I can show you around to help you get your bearings. You can also help me carry the pumpkins."

"Pumpkins?"

"I've been experimenting with a pumpkin brew for a while now. I'm hoping to get the recipe right in time for the Summer Festival."

"What's wrong with the Honeydew?" Elsa licked stew off her spoon.

"Nothing, it's just that I already entered it in the contest last time. The recipe has changed quite a bit since then, but I'd still like to try something new."

"What is the Summer Festival?" Cassia asked.

Elsa smiled. "It's the biggest festival of the year in Meritas. Lots of food, performances, and people. One of their events is the Brewmaster's Best Ale Cup, the most important contest for any ale brewer."

"How do you know about it?" I said to Elsa. "We hadn't hired you yet last summer."

"I went last time," Elsa said. "Even tried some of the alehouses, though I mainly stuck to the harder drinks on offer. We might have even passed by each other and not known it."

Unlikely. If anyone passed by a woman who looked like Elsa, they'd remember. Especially me, given my current state, anyway.

"Is there a prize for winning the contest?" Cassia said.

"I hear it's a big shiny trophy," Elsa said.

"Forget the trophy," I said. "If you win, the foot traffic to your tavern will triple from the notoriety."

"There are less than three weeks left, Master," Charm said. "Perhaps Master should consider entering the Honeydew Lager. Boreas already won last year with his Cherry Purple Ale. He won't submit the same one, and none of his other beers can compete against the Honeydew."

Boreas was the most well-known independent brewmaster in the city. He'd taken home the trophy the year before. The festival had happened a couple of months after the Tipsy Pelican Tavern opened. I'd only just gotten started, and I entered a version of the Honeydew Lager that wasn't quite ready. I placed second in the contest. They gave me a ribbon. This year was going to be different.

"Boreas is expecting the Honeydew. We need to surprise him. In any case, I want to add the pumpkin ale to the menu. We've been running for too long with only two beers on tap. It's time we added a third."

"Can we afford that, Master?" Charm asked.

Pumpkins weren't expensive, but the brewing process along with unfinished stock could add up quickly.

I smiled. "We sure can—now that we've received a handsome donation from our good friend Lord Mideon."

Elsa wrinkled her nose.

"Charm did notice forty-eight silvers in addition to the usual night's returns in the coffers last night," Charm said. "But Charm doesn't see how he and his men could have drunk that much. They left quite early."

"He purchased our best brandy," I said. "For himself, Proctor Remis, and the six men he brought. It's a shame he didn't bring more."

"Master poured him the Medi Gilhanna?" Charm said.

"You didn't!" Elsa stood. "A glass of that is worth far more than forty-eight silvers!"

"I meant our best brandy we offer to customers."

"Which brandy is that?" Elsa said, relaxing.

"Well… it would have been a regular Gilhanna until someone finished it all in one night."

Elsa shrank back in her chair.

"Does that mean Master served him the house brandy?" Charm asked.

"Yup. Currently the house brandy is the best brandy. Don't worry about it—they were so busy staring at Galston that I doubt they even tasted what they were drinking."

"Mideon had to get his men to cough up the coinage to cover the bill too," Elsa said, smiling again.

"Goodness…" Cassia said. "They left without any trouble but not before Arch-don emptied their pockets."

Elsa chuckled. "That was quite the trick, Heru. Though we did wash those profits down the drain by drinking a Medi. Not that I'm complaining. It's the most wonderful booze I've ever tasted."

Charm nodded.

"Hope you savored it," I said. "I won't be breaking it out again anytime soon."

"Oh, I certainly did," Elsa said. "Say, how did you come by that bottle?"

"A gift from a very old friend. And when I say old, I don't only mean the years in our friendship."

Elsa took a moment to grasp the meaning. "You're talking about an elf… but only a noble elf would—"

I waved her comment away. "Enough about brandy. We've got other matters at hand to discuss. Such as ale—pumpkin ale to be exact—which we are adding as the third tap after the Honeydew and the Red Harvest. Even after accounting for production costs, we should have a nice chunk of coin left that could be put to use for the tavern."

"We could hire a musician," Elsa said. "Perhaps even open the main hall for room to dance."

"I think it's a bit early to hire a musician," I said. "We still don't have enough regular customers to fill the main hall. But maybe we can get some more tables for the barroom. We seem to be running low."

"Or that," Elsa said with a sigh.

"It would be nice to expand the tavern's kitchen set and the menu," Charm said.

I was surprised to hear this. Charm had not asked for anything or shown much interest in the business since I opened the tavern. Perhaps she was finally getting settled.

"Yeah, that's a good idea," I said. "We could add some other items to the food menu."

Charm gave a small nod.

"How about you, Cassia? Any suggestions?" I said, and Elsa and Charm looked at her too.

"Oh... I wouldn't know. I've just arrived."

"You're part of the tavern now," I said. "No need to be polite. If you've got an idea, then spill it."

"Um…" Cassia put a finger to her lip. "Well, perhaps some decorations around the tavern? It's a little bare at the moment."

"That's a wonderful idea, Cassia," Elsa said. "We could get a dartboard."

Charm nodded. "Some art would be nice."

"All right, then, it's settled," I said. "Our next steps in expanding the tavern are a new menu, a new ale, and decorations!"

Cassia smiled cheerfully and gave a little clap, and Elsa joined in too.

CHAPTER II:
CLOSING THE GATES

After breakfast, I grabbed several cotton bags from the storage room and headed toward the market with Cassia. She'd changed out of the white church robes into another dress that was likely lent to her by Elsa.

"You don't have much clothing for casual occasions, huh?" I said to cover my tracks when Cassia caught me staring.

"Oh, um yes, I hadn't expected to stay in Meritas for long and only packed for the road. Elsa let me borrow this dress."

"Which church were you serving at before you came to find me?"

"The Catagolion."

I whistled. The Catagolion was the head church of the Order. It was located far north on the other side of the kingdom in the city of Yestereaster.

Since the last king of the royal line had been killed nearly a century before, the country of Adentris was governed by four dukes, each commanding a major city. But of the four cities, Yestereaster was the largest, the richest, and the most powerful. The White Church played no small part in adding to that power.

The fact that Cassia was stationed at the Catagolion meant that she was not just any templar but an important one. Not unexpected, of course. They wouldn't have sent some fresh-faced girl to find me, though Cassia did kind of fit that description at first glance.

"Must have taken you a month to get here," I said.

Cassia nodded. "I traveled for two months. I first visited the Elven Forest to ask High Lord Emdark for your location."

"And how is the traitorous elf king?"

"Tr-traitorous?"

"He was supposed to keep my location secret on pain of death. I guess he's still kicking, then."

"H-he is well. He sends his regards."

"Uh-uh. Well, if you see him again, tell him to send more than regards—ideally, some Medi Gilhanna."

"I wondered if he had given you that bottle," Cassia said.

Actually, I hadn't gotten it from him, but I didn't tell her that.

"I don't believe I will be returning to the Elven Forest soon," Cassia said when I did not reply. "But if I do, I will, um... pass on your message."

We arrived at a wooden bridge, and I pointed at the canal that ran beneath it. "See the canal here?"

Cassia nodded.

"It marks the separation of the wards," I said. "This side we're on is called Southbank. It contains the neighborhood of Kerrytown, where the tavern is located."

"Is the ward on that side called Northbank?" Cassia asked as we crossed over the bridge.

"You would think so, but no. They call it Keeper's Garden."

"Why is it called Keeper's Garden?"

"No idea. The names seem to be ancient. Meritas has twelve wards total. Don't worry about learning them all. They'll come naturally the longer you stay in the city."

Cassia looked around. I could tell that she was examining the structures of the buildings. They were a bit shabbier than those in Southbank, which contained relatively affluent neighborhoods like Kerrytown with many shops and taverns and restaurants. Keeper's Garden was not known to have any gangs, but the crime rate did run a little higher than around the Tipsy Pelican Tavern.

"It's pretty safe around here, but watch your purse," I said, which I then realized was completely unnecessary. As an awakened of the Second Gate, Cassia could easily take care of herself, even against the most dangerous criminals in the city.

"Are there any markets back in Southbank?" Cassia said.

"There are, but the one here is bigger and cheaper. Plus, I thought you wanted to look around."

"Yes, I did," she said quickly. "Thank you for taking me."

We arrived at a bustling open market five minutes later. Shopkeepers beneath colorful tents were selling wares of all kinds, from fabrics to oranges to swords.

"Wow," Cassia said. "It reminds me of the markets in Yestereaster."

We bought duck eggs, salted bacon, a fresh loaf of bread, a brick of cheddar, tomatoes, and of course, several pumpkins. I opened my wallet and dug out the money to pay for the pumpkins, finding a lot more coins than I'd expected. It was strange. I wondered if there was a sale going on in the market that day. Then I looked up.

"These pumpkins are so adorable," Cassia said with a light chuckle as she inspected a bright-orange one in her hands.

"Thank you, miss," said the shopkeeper, an old man with a wide-brimmed straw hat. "I raise them with the utmost care. Please, take that one with you."

"Oh, thank you, sir," Cassia said. "But I believe we have enough."

"No, no, consider it a gift. Your compliment is payment enough."

Oh, so that's why everything is cheaper, I thought. Cassia was such a pure presence that no one wanted to swindle her. They gave her lower prices just because she was likable. The few times I took Elsa shopping, I also got lower prices. That was either because the shopkeeper wanted to win her favor or because she had won an aggressive bout of haggling.

"Could we have that one instead?" I pointed at a pumpkin that was a little smaller but riper in hue. Better for the brewing process.

"That'll be two coppers for you," the old man in the straw hat snapped, his face suddenly stone-cold as he eyed me.

"What? You charged her only thirty glints for the first one of the same size!" Thirty glints was less than a single copper.

"I name my prices as I like, hmph."

"You know what? We have enough for today, as the lady said," I said, giving up.

"Thank you, we'll be sure to come back again," Cassia said to the old man.

His face broke out in a big smile. "That would be lovely, miss. I look forward to seeing you again!"

Good Celeru, it isn't fair.

"You really get along with everyone, don't you?" I said as we headed back toward the tavern.

"What do you mean?" Cassia said.

"Never mind. Here, switch with me. My bags are lighter."

"I'm fine, Arch-don. I can carry weights several times heavier than this."

"Oh, right." Watching her slender figure, I'd forgotten again. With her Gate of Breath open, she would tire hours after I did, even if she carried a far heavier load. Sometimes I missed my gates. It was strange to feel my muscles turn sore after only a short amount of exertion.

"May I ask you a personal question, Arch-don?"

"Sure. Dunno if I'll answer it, though."

"What caused the closing of your gates?" She hesitated. "Are you... ill?"

I laughed. "No. They're closed because that's the way I wanted it."

Cassia turned to me, shocked. "But why?"

I looked ahead as we made our way through the city streets. They were moderately busy and filled with other shoppers and citizens going about their day. There were parents with their kids and couples on dates. Cassia had asked a simple question that lacked a simple answer. I considered just brushing it off, but then I thought better of it.

"You know what it's like to awaken a gate, so perhaps you can catch the hint of understanding," I said, looking at her. "Let me first ask you this—what difference did you notice when you opened your first gate?"

Cassia considered the question. "My body felt incredible. Like I was light as a feather, and I could run and move as quickly as I wanted. When I told my body to do something that should have been impossible, it could do it. And I wouldn't get tired. I felt entirely connected to myself. I don't really notice it now—I suppose I've gotten used to it—but I remember feeling an immense difference when it first happened."

I nodded. "And what about when you opened the second one, the Gate of Spirit?"

"It felt like my mind opened. I became much more aware of my surroundings. Attuned to my thoughts and the actions of everyone around me. Before, I would get tired from studying or training back at the academy—not just physically tired but mentally tired—but now I can keep going for hours on end. The biggest difference is the effect on my control of magic. Before I opened the Gate of Spirit, casting a spell was like trying to hold running water in the palm of my hand. Now it is as if I have a basin. I can't imagine what it would be like to open the others."

I nodded again. "When you open a gate, you are moving to a new level of consciousness. After the Seventh Gate, the world gets pretty wacky."

"Erm, wacky?" Cassia said.

"Things look different. Feel different. It's not a bad feeling. If anything, it's a great feeling. You can sense things you could never imagine. I'm not sure how to describe it..." I paused, gathering my thoughts. "Take wind or moonlight, for example. It was like they had emotions, and I could... touch them. I know that doesn't make a lot of sense. How can moonlight have emotions? And how can you touch an emotion, let alone moonlight's? But that's what it was like. For animals and people, it was even stronger. I could feel what others felt in their hearts just by looking at them. I could sit for weeks in one position, just tapping into all the things around me, and experience some of the strongest and most vivid sensations imaginable."

Cassia was watching me, her eyes filled with awe. "That's incredible."

"It is. But at that level of consciousness, you don't really feel human anymore. You are so connected with the earth and the natural auras of all things that you really do start feeling like a god."

"My goodness. It sounds as though you've experienced what Nahael and Celeru themselves must have felt as they awakened the Gates of Greater Ascension."

I shrugged. "Maybe. They both got farther than I did. The problem for me was that I'd lived most of my life that way. I opened the Seventh Gate over two hundred years ago. Then I stopped aging, and that level of extreme awareness became normal to me, just like the First and Second Gates have become normal to you. So I wanted to see what it was like to be like other people. Like most people. Because the thing about getting used to something is that it becomes boring, no matter what it is."

It wasn't the whole truth. There were some other reasons I'd closed my gates, but I hadn't thought them all through yet. And I wasn't in a rush to go down that snake pit.

Cassia was silent for a few minutes, watching the road in front of her as we walked. Then she said, "I'm sorry for asking you to give that up to defeat the elder dragon. I wasn't considerate of your position."

I shrugged again. "You've got nothing to be sorry for."

She was quiet again. After a moment, she said, "Can I ask you one more question?"

"Sure, but only if you stop prefacing your questions with questions."

Cassia's cheeks turned a little pink. "Which spell did you use to defeat Demon Lord Izirath?"

"Oh, that?" I said, grinning. "That's a secret."

Cassia gave me a disappointed frown.

"My turn," I said. "What made you join the church?"

Cassia looked away, sadness filling her expression. She opened her mouth to speak, but she was cut short because someone ran into her.

Or tried to. Cassia noticed him coming and stepped out of the way like it was a reflex.

It was a kid. He stumbled and fell flat on his face. He looked about twelve years old. He had short dark hair and a dirty shirt. He sprang up immediately and turned to us with tears in his eyes.

"Please, you must help me! It's my mother. She just fell and stopped moving. I don't know what to do!"

CHAPTER 12: TEMPLAR CASSIA HIGHTOWER

"Dear Celeru!" Cassia exclaimed. "Take us to her."

It was the first time I'd ever heard her use the god's name as an exclamation. And judging by the look on her face, we were going to be late for lunch.

"Follow me." The boy led us back down the main road and onto a side street. "Everyone I asked just ignored me," he said, wiping away tears.

"Don't worry," Cassia said. "We'll help you."

I said nothing, knowing that there was no way out of this, and resigned myself to my fate. We made one more turn and headed down a secluded alley.

"It's just down there," the boy continued. "She was fine one minute, then she suddenly collapsed. I didn't know what to do..." His voice trailed off in a whimper.

"You did the right thing," Cassia said.

But when we reached the end of the alley, we found a dead end and no woman. Instead, there were three older boys a couple of years younger than Cassia and me, each holding chains and bats.

"Well done, Simon," said another boy, who was sitting on the roof above. He had a sharp nose and a thick head of dark hair that he wore in braids.

The boy called Simon was no longer crying, and he had stepped away from us. However, unlike the other boys in the alley, his eyes held no ill intent. Behind him, two larger boys appeared, with dark grins on their faces.

Cassia turned to Simon. "Where's your mother?"

"Oh, come on!" I said to Cassia. "Even if you didn't see this happening from the beginning, you should understand the situation now!"

"What do you mean?"

"What do I mean?" I pointed at the large boys blocking our escape. "This was a trap. They're going to try to rob us."

"Oh," Cassia said, looking at the boys.

"Sounds like you've been down this road before," the older boy on the roof said, looking down with his braids swinging. "That makes things easier. Hand over all your valuables, if you please, and we'll let you go about your merry day."

"You can't be older than fifteen," Cassia said sadly to the boy. "Where are your parents?"

I just sighed and shook my head.

"Don't talk to me about parents. Hand over your valuables, or you're going to get hurt. I'd hate for anything bad to happen to a pretty girl like you." The boy gave an imitation of a malicious smile, as if he meant to do something nasty. But he was too young and inexperienced. Malicious smiles took time and practice, or at the very least, true evil.

"Come on, Cassia, let's go," I said, turning around. "Maybe Charm won't murder us if we hurry."

"Hey! Are you listening? Hand over your valuables this instant!" the boy with the braids said. He'd lost his cool already.

I turned my head back to him. "Oh, shut up, you little brat. You're not scaring anybody."

"I don't understand," Cassia said, seemingly to not have heard anything. "How could your parents let you run off like this? You should be in school."

The older boy and I stopped scowling at each other and looked at her as if she had to be kidding.

"They're orphans," I said.

"What country is this lady from?" the older boy asked.

I shrugged. "Come on, Cassia."

"Hey!" the boy with the braids said, leaping to his feet on the roof. "You take one more step, and I'll have my bruisers beat you to a pulp!" The two boys blocking our exit stepped forward. One of them was taller and larger than me.

"But they can't be orphans," Cassia said. "The White Church operates in this city. Orphans are given room and board in the church until they're seventeen and can find employment."

"So, they missed some, or these kids didn't want the church's help."

That, of course, was unlikely. Who would turn down a clean bed, a hot meal, and schooling for a life on the streets? I'd seen church orphanages. Most were quite hospitable and well-run. The only times kids didn't want to stay was when there was a problem with the orphanage's administrators or if a local gang had snatched the kids up. This case looked like the latter.

The leader boy had his hand clenched in a shaking fist, apparently having reached a breaking point for being ignored. "That's it! Jo, punch that one in the gut!" He was pointing at me.

The biggest kid came at me, and I dodged him easily. "Come on, Cassia. We don't have all day to fool around with these twerps."

"Jo! I said punch him!" The leader boy was screaming at the top of his lungs.

Jo took another swing at me. He missed and hit the wall behind me. He screamed and began to cry as he clutched his broken knuckles. It sounded like he'd shattered his hand.

"This is wrong, Arch-don," Cassia said, a crease forming at her brow. "These boys shouldn't be here."

"How dare you ignore me! We are no simple street gang! We are part of Lord Ashbane's syndicate! Don't you dare defy us, or you will face the fury of the syndicate!"

I looked up at him, giving him a minor measure of the Stormblood's glare. "What did you say to me, you little turd? Did you just threaten me?"

The kid nearly fell off the roof as I stared into him. He didn't say another word, tripping on tiles and scrambling to his feet as he turned and ran. The other kids didn't know what had happened, but with their leader gone, they, too, turned and ran for it.

"Let's go, Cassia. Charm is going to kill me." I headed out of the alley.

Cassia didn't say anything. She followed me to the main street, and we made our way back toward the tavern.

***

"If Master would prefer to skip a meal, he should inform Charm before he leaves so she knows in advance not to wait for the groceries."

"We got held up, Charm. I wasn't trying to make you wait, honest."

While Charm and I quibbled, Cassia had been sitting at the dining room table, her eyes far away, lost in thought before she got up and went upstairs.

"Ah, Charm understands. Master was busy flirting with Miss Cassia, so he forgot the time and decided to let his dutiful servant starve."

"It wasn't my fault! Cassia got tricked by some street urchins and—"

"Yes, Master truly is a gentleman and a hero. He easily blames his companion for his misdeeds."

"I wasn't blaming—I was just explaining what happened!"

"Don't worry," Charm said. "Since Master seems to prefer skipping lunch, Charm will just remember not to make his for the rest of the week."

"No, that's not what I—"

Out of the corner of my eye, I saw Cassia come back down the stairs, wearing her full templar's wardrobe and sword, and leave the tavern. I turned and watched her.

"Is Master listening?"

"Sorry, I've got to run."

"Will Master be back for dinner?" Charm asked.

"Uh..."

There was a bright glare in Charm's eye.

"Maybe?" I said.

"Master, Charm's hand is about to slip," she said, raising her knife.

I jumped through the tavern's front door just as the knife flew into the door frame. *Good gods, she's really going to kill me someday,* I thought as I jogged down the street.

I saw Cassia a block ahead and caught up to her. "Where do you think you're going?"

"I'm going to the church," Cassia said. "Something isn't right. After Nahael's Edict, all orphans in Adentris were promised homes by the church. The church here is not poor. They must not be aware of these children. I will go inform them."

Although gangs did recruit or even kidnap orphans from time to time, it was extremely rare in large cities. The White Church generally steered clear of affairs outside of its domain, but if they found out that a gang had orphans among their ranks, the church would send out their personal guard—the White Guardians or, in the more egregious cases, their White Templars—to put an end to the gang. There had yet to be a gang that could match the power, zeal, and training of the White Church's emissaries. So generally speaking, in a city with a White Church, orphans weren't worth the effort for the criminal underworld.

"Ah, I see," I replied. "In that case, you might want to know that you're going the wrong way."

"Oh," Cassia said, turning to me. "Which way is the church?"

"The cathedral is north. Come on—I'll take you."

"Are you certain you wish to guide me? Do you not have to make preparations for the tavern this afternoon?"

"It's probably best to let Charm cool off for a bit. We'll be back before dinner, right?"

"I believe so," Cassia said.

"Okay, good. Let's hasten our pace."

Though I had never been there, I knew the church was located in Quel Hills, a ward about thirty minutes by foot from the tavern.

We arrived at around one o'clock. I was feeling the hunger of my empty stomach by then, since we had skipped lunch. That was another one of the bodily troubles that came with having my gates closed.

The cathedral was in a monastery, a massive white structure with four tall walls that surrounded multiple white buildings. We headed inside, and Cassia quickly found an administrative deacon.

"I am Cassia Hightower. I need to speak with the head of your orphanage."

"Hightower?" the deacon said. He was a young man carrying a heavy load of scrolls underneath his arm.

"Yes."

"As in *Templar* Hightower?" the young man said with widening eyes focused on Cassia's templar's robes.

"Yes."

"Right away, sir. I mean, yes, ma'am. I m-mean..." The deacon stuttered as he tried to figure out the workings of his mouth. After a moment, he said, "I'll be right back. Please wait here, Templar."

The deacon ran off, frantic. I guessed Cassia was a big deal in the church. I knew templars were held in high esteem among the clergy, but judging by his reaction, you'd think it was the archbishop herself visiting. And this was Meritas, a city Cassia had never set foot in before coming to find me.

"I sure wish I had that effect on the clergy," I said. "Usually, they just hassle me for favors. What's your secret?"

Cassia blushed a little. "I'm sure they would react quite dramatically if you revealed your identity to them."

I grinned at that.

A minute later, the deacon ran back, his hands emptied. "This way—please follow me."

We were led farther into the monastery and taken into an office. Behind a desk sat an elderly, overweight man.

"This is Brother Erwel," the deacon said. "He is in charge of the orphanage."

"Brother Erwel, I am Cassia Hightower," Cassia said in a tone I hadn't heard before. "I come to you with grave news. My companion and I were attacked by a group of orphan boys in the Keeper's Garden Ward."

Unlike the deacon, Brother Erwel did not seem impressed by Cassia's presence. "Are you certain they were orphans?"

"Yes. They looked at most fifteen years of age, but possibly even younger—and unsupervised—and they admitted to me as much."

"That seems very unlikely, Templar Hightower," Brother Erwel drawled. "Meritas does not have street orphans. Not since Nahael's Edict."

"These boys must have been overlooked. Or they are being controlled by a local crime lord."

The old man shook his head slowly. "Perhaps they were troublemakers with inattentive parents. Just because a child is alone on the street doesn't make them an orphan."

"That could be a possibility, Brother Erwel," Cassia said with patience, "however, they admitted to being orphans and part of a gang."

"Mmm," Brother Erwel said. "And did you consider the possibility that they were lying?"

Cassia looked at me as if asking for help in explaining the situation to this man. I gave her a shrug and a grin that said, *Hey, this isn't any of my business. I'm just enjoying the show.*

"May I see your books?" Cassia asked.

"See our books? Is this an official inquiry?"

Templars had the right to investigate the church. This was another clause in the edict created by Nahael to rid the Order of any possible corruption. It worked, to a degree. Templars were also forced to obey bishops and the archbishop. But Brother Erwel was no bishop, and he could not deny her.

"It is not an official inquiry," Cassia said. "Not yet in any case."

"Is the bishop aware you are here?"

"Not to my knowledge. I ask you again, may I see your books?"

I could tell Erwel was grappling with his options. No doubt, he felt that the bishop would not allow this, but because the bishop hadn't given an order to prevent it, he was forbidden to deny Cassia.

In the end, he must have decided it wasn't worth putting up a fight. He opened a drawer in his desk and drew out a book. It was a registry of all the orphans in the city. Cassia began reading, turning the pages quickly.

"Deacon Obi, please inform the bishop that a templar is visiting us," Brother Erwel said. "We want to ensure that she is properly welcomed."

"Yes, Brother Erwel." Deacon Obi exited the room.

Cassia must have caught the meaning behind this because she picked up her pace as she scanned the pages--she would only have time to search through the pages until the bishop summoned her. By then, it was hard to say how the bishop would react. He could help her with her inquiry, or he might force her to drop it. Either was possible because nobody liked having a templar rummaging up their ass.

Cassia flipped through the pages quickly.

Five minutes later, there was a knock at the door. A friar entered. "Bishop Tamblion calls for Templar Hightower. The bishop awaits you in his grand hall."

Cassia put down the book and followed the friar out. There was a cold fury in her clear blue eyes that even put a small tremor in my heart. It appeared that she did not like what she'd found in the registry.

CHAPTER 13: THE BISHOP OF MERITAS

"Arch-don, I'm afraid this may take longer than expected," Cassia said as we made our way toward the bishop's grand hall. "You may wish to return to the tavern. I wouldn't want to hold you up."

"Oh, I'll tag along," I said. "There are few things I enjoy more than a bishop slapping."

Cassia simply nodded, whereas the friar we were following turned his head and gave me a dark scowl. I winked at him. We were taken down several corridors until we reached a large sculpted-marble door. I could hardly imagine the cost to make a door like that.

The friar pulled it open and ushered us through. Inside was a space that looked like a king's throne room. The walls were decorated with golden ornaments, and the floors were covered with velvet carpets. Even Cassia seemed unnerved by it. The room was not the norm for the audience quarters of a White Church bishop.

The bishop himself sat on a high chair of marble with gold trimmings. He was a man in his late fifties or sixties. He had a finely trimmed beard and dark-blue eyes. He also wore a big silly hat and long white silk robes. Beside him were two guards, and in addition to them, two more stood beside the doors we had entered.

"What is this I am told about a templar tearing through my monastery without even a greeting or an introduction?" Tamblion spoke as if he could have been addressing anyone in the room.

Cassia bowed. "I apologize, Bishop Tamblion. I am Templar Cassia Hightower. I went to your Department of Lost Children to inform them of an orphan gang in the city."

"Were you sent by the Chamber to inspect our monastery?"

The Chamber of the White Church was the official administrative body that governed all churches and sects of the Order. The head of the Chamber, the chamberlain answered directly to the archbishop.

"No, however—"

"If the Chamber has not sent you, then why are you here making trouble? Are you so absent of duties that you must come here to find error with my church?"

"I was here on other business," Cassia replied. "Now I am here on behalf of the orphans."

"What other business?" Tamblion said, peering at her.

Cassia didn't even look at me. "I cannot say."

"So, you claim to be on a secret mission, with no introduction from the chamberlain, and you decided to stroll into my church and start giving orders?"

"I am not giving orders!" The patience in Cassia's voice was spent. The fury in her eyes raged. "I have seen the registry of lost children.

Your orphanage has fewer than fifty orphans. For a city of half a million people, it should be ten times that number at least!"

"So, you believe that there should be more orphans? That more children should lose their parents?"

"Of course not! I am saying that proportionally, there should be more orphans than what is in your registry for a city of this size."

"Well," Tamblion said, his voice turning deeply sarcastic. "I do apologize that the people of Meritas are more willing to adopt young innocents than those of Yestereaster. I apologize that more mothers and fathers aren't losing their lives so that your need for proportions can be met."

Cassia's hands made balls that shook at her side, but she kept control of herself. "How do you explain the orphans I came across on the street?"

"I don't," Tamblion said. "I haven't seen these orphans you have conjured up. I know that my people have done Celeru's great work in taking care of the children in need in this city. I don't need some outsider meddling in my affairs."

Cassia looked like she was at a loss for words. It was as if she couldn't believe someone in her order would be like this.

I couldn't help but chuckle. *What a joke.* Tamblion was a little man dressed in a fancy costume, acting like he was better than everyone else. I'd met so many of these types over the years, and here was yet another one.

"How dare you laugh in my quarters!"

I looked up. "Who, me?"

"Yes, you!" Tamblion snapped. "Have you no respect?"

I shrugged. "You've got me there. I really don't. I mean, it's clear as day. You're entirely corrupt, though I have no idea what you have to gain from not running your orphanage. Maybe you just use the money that would go to them for your ridiculous hats."

"How dare you insult me! I am the bishop of Meritas! You do not have the right to speak to me in such a way!"

"And yet I did."

"Who are you? Tell me your name!" Tamblion demanded.

"I'm just a guide showing the templar around the city."

"What is your name, I said!"

"Oh, don't worry your tiny mind about it."

"Give me your name!" The bishop was standing now, his cheeks bright red with rage. "I will have your employers know you insulted the bishop himself! Your name! I demand it!"

"Demand away. Meanwhile, I'm going to fart in your church."

He didn't seem to like that too much. I could tell because the old guy looked like he was beginning to froth at the mouth. "I-I will have you arrested."

I laughed. "For what? Farting? Is that also in Nahael's Edict? 'No farting allowed. All farters are to be arrested on the spot!' Sounds like the type of silly rule you people would have."

The bishop was bug-eyed and stammering, so angry he could barely speak. Cassia was caught trying to keep the peace between a bishop of her order and "the hero of our time." I could see the turmoil in her eyes. Both the bishop and I were figures she couldn't risk displeasing.

"Guards! Arrest this man!" Tamblion hissed.

"Is that how the Order of the White Church spends its time nowadays? They arrest citizens for gassing up fancy rooms?"

"For all I know, you are a spy!" Tamblion said, shaking his finger at me. "You do not share your name, yet you stand in my halls."

Cassia was looking very worried, and I didn't like that the bishop had his hand raised at me. If he were a mage, that would be the equivalent of having a drawn arrow or a raised sword. A classic fighting mistake was to let your opponent take aim before you did. But I doubted he had much magical prowess. He looked like he had trouble just getting out of his chair.

"Fine, fine," I said, sighing heavily. "I will tell you my name."

Tamblion seemed mollified by this. He grinned in the way the boy with the braids couldn't. "Speak."

"My family name is Rew."

"And?"

"No, that's it. You can call me Mr. Rew."

"Rew? You expect me to accept that? I want your full name, boy!"

"No. I don't want to give it."

"You will give it, or you will not leave this place!" the bishop screeched.

"Ugh," I sighed again. "Fine. My given name is Sella. S-e-l-l-a."

"You will pay the consequences for insulting me, Sella Rew, now that I have your name, I will soon know your place of employment and—" He suddenly stopped, realization dawning in his eyes. He'd just called me "Celeru," the name of his patron lord, savior of humanity.

I howled with laughter, slapping my leg. My stomach even started to hurt. The silly little trick worked as well as the last time I'd used it.

The bishop was white, his rage having moved from red-hot to deadly. "Apprehend this man! At once!"

The church guards on the sides of the room drew their swords and moved forward.

"Stop!" Cassia said, drawing her own sword. "Anyone who lays a hand on him will be cut by my blade by order of Archbishop Katharis herself!"

The guards paused in their advance. Even the bishop hesitated. "You dare invoke the archbishop's name for your selfish purposes?"

Cassia drew from her robes a chained pendant made of white stone. "This is the emblem of the archbishop! It grants me the power to act under her will. Those who disobey me in this matter will be disobeying the archbishop!"

The guards looked uncertain of what to do. Their master was the bishop, but the archbishop was the head of the church. No matter what, they had to obey her. And with the emblem, Cassia was clearly an emissary of the archbishop. They couldn't just ignore it.

"How do I know that is real?" the bishop said.

Cassia looked at him in disbelief. Even I was surprised that the man would question even this.

"I've never met you before. Customarily, the archbishop would send a letter ahead of any emissary sent to Meritas working on her behalf. And she did not. You could be an imposter for all I know."

"My mission was secret," Cassia said. "That is why no letter of introduction was sent."

"So you say. Arrest them both," the bishop said to his guards. "We'll contact the Chamber afterward and see what is what."

The guards began to move forward again.

"Hold, father. I recognize this templar," said a voice from the shadows. From behind a doorway, a man dressed in shining white plate armor—the official armor of a church templar—stepped into the light of the hall. He had a strong jaw, piercing eyes, and flowing black hair that fell just past his ears. I didn't recognize him, but it was clear that Cassia did.

"High Templar Darren Tamblion," Cassia said, nodding.

"Templar Cassia Hightower," Darren said, smiling.

There was visible relief on Cassia's face. She lowered her sword and sheathed it.

"Father, there is no harm in investigating the templar's claims," the younger Tamblion said. "If there are indeed orphans in the city being taken in by gangs, we should do our best to rescue them."

The bishop considered his son's words as he glared at me. "Very well, my son. Then I will let you lead this task."

Darren bowed to his father then turned to Cassia. "I will come to you with my findings once I have the matter thoroughly investigated. Will these terms suit you, Templar Hightower?"

"Yes, of course," Cassia said with notable relief.

"Where are you staying in the city?" Darren asked.

"Um... I'm currently residing at the Tipsy Pelican Tavern in the ward of Southbank."

"The Tipsy Pelican Tavern? I've never heard of it. Very well, I'll find you there once I've done my rounds."

Cassia bowed to him. "Thank you, High Templar."

Darren bowed back then shot me a look. I gave him a shrug, and then we departed.

***

We made our way through the streets back toward the tavern. The sun was setting as we walked. Most of the regulars had probably arrived by that point. I wondered how Charm and Elsa were faring without me there.

Cassia looked tired and drained by the run-in with the bishop. She also looked sad. I guessed even she couldn't deny the bishop's poor behavior, and he was one of the most powerful men in her religion.

"Do you think that templar will do a good job?" I said.

"He must. He is bound by Celeru to find the truth."

"How do you know each other?"

"He was at the Templars' Academy in Yestereaster for a time while I was there. He was many years ahead of me."

"And?" I said. "What was he like?"

"I didn't know him well."

"But you heard rumors…"

"Rumors?"

"Everyone has rumors about them in a close-knit community. His father's a bishop, and he's a high templar. He must have had a fair cut of the rumors."

"Well," Cassia said uncomfortably. "Some of the other girls said he was a… womanizer."

"I'm not surprised about that. With a face like his, it'd be hard not to be. Did you have a crush on him too?"

"No, of course not!" Cassia said. "Arch-don, you really must stop teasing me."

"Oh, must I?"

Cassia looked at me with her brow furrowed. Then she relaxed. "Thank you for coming with me today."

"Don't worry about it. I had a great time. Just help me fend off Charm's wrath when we get back to the tavern. We're going to be so late."

Cassia chuckled. "You really are afraid of her, aren't you?"

"You have no idea."

CHAPTER 14: THINK OF THE CHILDREN

Amberly threw his tree trunk of an arm around me when we got back. "Master Arch! I can't believe you've been hiding this lovely young lady from us all this time!"

"Huh?"

I glanced up and saw that Charm was helping Elsa with the customers. She was in the middle of filling a mug. The look she gave me could have frozen a fire spell.

I swallowed. "Oh, uh... yes, Charm is our cook."

"What a waste!" Herwin exclaimed. He was well embedded between Bran and Amberly. "She's too much of a beauty to be hidden in the back of the house!"

"Well, what do you say, Charm? Would you like to work at the front of house, from now on?"

Charm's eyebrow twitched. In that little twitch, I could guess exactly what she wanted to say: *Charm is only here because, for the second time today, Master was late. Because of his impropriety and tardiness, we were left shorthanded and unprepared. Therefore, Charm is standing here, pouring drinks to these drunkards. Master is well aware that Charm is uninterested in being the object of attention among the customers. Now Master is taunting Charm about having her do this permanently? I will murder you in your sleep, you insect.*

I coughed violently. "Ah-ah! Well, unfortunately, a good cook is hard to come by, so I can't pull her away from that duty. But now we have Cassia helping with serving. Isn't that right, Cassia?"

"Oh yes, Arch-don. Let me wash my hands, and I'll take over for Charm," Cassia said, catching the murderous gaze Charm was giving me.

"Thank you, Cassia." *You may have just saved my life.*

Surrounded by patrons, Elsa looked stunning as ever and was already several drinks in.

I quickly threw on an apron, scrubbed my hands with soap, and joined the women to attend to the customers. My rounds took me back to the builders. Herwin looked like a new member of the crew, although his finery didn't quite match Bran and Amberly's simple shirts and work trousers.

"No Galston today?" I said, taking Herwin's mug to refill it.

"Ah, he had other appointments today," Herwin said. "But he said he would be sure to come again."

I smiled. "That's good to hear. A man like him will make things livelier."

"That's very true. He's a good man!" Bran said happily.

"Where's Dalian?" I said, looking around for the third builder.

"Ha," Amberly said. "He's upset we didn't wake him when you were pouring the Gilhanna. I tried raising him that night, but he was out like a candle."

"Don't worry," Bran said with a cheerful grin. "He'll come around eventually."

The rest of the night went much smoother than the previous two had. Mideon didn't return, and there were no theatrical confrontations, which some of the patrons seemed to find disappointing after two nights of heart-pumping excitement. But I was happy for things to be back to normal again.

Better yet, word had gotten around that Galston had visited, and the tavern's barroom was nearly full by the height of the night. There were several new faces, along with many customers who hadn't come by the tavern in some time.

Elsa was in a chipper mood and got several of the new patrons blind drunk. Charm was still sour as a raw lemon, though it was probably not noticeable to anyone besides me. Cassia did a fine job with the customers. However, she wore a distracted expression throughout the night.

Later, after we'd cleaned up and gone to bed, I heard a knock at my door. "Arch-don? Are you asleep?" It was Cassia.

"Not yet," I said, sitting up in bed. "Come in."

Cassia entered, wearing her sleeping gown. My nineteen-year-old brain suddenly was sending me certain signals that I had to push away in order to focus.

"What is it?" I asked.

"I'm having some trouble sleeping… may I sit?"

"Yes, of course," I said, feeling my pulse rise.

She took a seat at the little desk in my room. *Right. Of course. She sat in the chair.* That made sense.

"I feel uncertain about those orphans we ran into today," Cassia said.

"You don't believe the pretty templar boy will take care of it?"

"I believe he will, but perhaps… I don't know. I am afraid he will not be as… diligent as he could be."

"So, you want to help find those kids?"

Cassia nodded.

I shrugged. "Then do it. We don't open until four o'clock in the evening. Plenty of time to do your searching."

"I'd like you to come with me."

"Why's that?"

"Because I might need your help."

"My help?" I said, incredulous. "You have two gates open, and you're a templar. I haven't seen your swordplay yet, but I bet it's good. I think you'll do fine without me."

Cassia bit her lip. "Then perhaps I have ulterior motives…"

My ears perked up to their maximum ability. As did my teenage senses. "Ulterior motives?"

"I want you to come because I think it will remind you of the merits of helping others. Even if it's just a few orphans."

"The merits of helping others?"

Cassia nodded. "There is great joy in aiding those in need."

"Cassia, you do realize that there are orphans all over the world that have it worse than those kids. There may be fewer in the major cities where the Order of the White Church operates, but the church isn't everywhere. And not just orphans. There are all sorts of atrocities committed every day—even in Adentris, where things are generally better than the rest of the world. And don't get me started on our neighboring countries. Go farther south across the Primordial Sea, and you'll find that slavery is still a popular trade."

"That doesn't mean you shouldn't help these orphans."

"Nor does it mean that I should. True, their lives are hard. But there are people out there suffering far worse than them. Why do these kids get my help and not the others? Because they're near me? So, I'm helping them out of convenience? You want me to rescue some orphans then go back to being a tavern keeper, thinking I've done something good? Because I won't, Cassia. I'm no hypocrite. People who only do good when it is convenient are just fools that believe themselves virtuous, but that doesn't mean they actually are virtuous."

"I disagree, Arch-don," Cassia said, her voice even. "You're right that there are people suffering everywhere, but every little bit counts. Perhaps some people do good in order to think that they are good, but I believe they also do it because they believe it to be the right thing to do. It can be both."

I shook my head. "When you've lived as long as I have, you see the truth of things. No matter how much good you do, injustice will exist. And oftentimes, the very people who claim to be doing good become the ones to create new injustices. That's the way of life."

"If you truly believed that, you would not have become the Hero of Our Time." Her voice cracked, and she stood, gripping her hands together. "You are a good man, Archibold Stormblood. I know you are."

"Sure, I've done a few good deeds, but I only did them because they were necessary and there was no one else to do them. If a demon lord with the power to wipe out humanity appears, or a mad king bent on enslaving the whole continent shows up, sure, I'll lend a hand. But these other things? The smaller things? You will never be rid of them."

Cassia dropped her eyes, looking disheartened.

"You go ahead and help those orphans," I said. "You can stay at the tavern as long as you like even if you don't show up to work nights. We have plenty of rooms, anyway." I fluffed my pillow and lay back down.

Cassia was quiet for a long time. Then she said, "If you help me find the orphans, I will wear any of Elsa's dresses of your choosing for an entire week. Assuming she lets me borrow them, that is."

I sat up and swallowed. "A-Any of them?"

"Yes."

My head swam with the possibilities. There was a thin-laced white dress that even Elsa had only worn on one or two occasions because it had drawn *too much* attention.

"I-I don't know…" I said. "This doesn't seem like a fair trade for me."

"That even includes the white dress that Elsa saves for special occasions," Cassia said.

"Y-You know about that one?"

Cassia nodded.

"The one with the laces and the ample cleavage?" I had to be sure. As someone who'd negotiated the borders of nations and the rights of millions, I knew to never make a crucially important deal unless I was certain of the details.

Cassia nodded again.

"Th-This… this is *blackmail*!" I said, feeling myself swaying.

"Umm… I'm not sure you know what that word means, Arch-don."

"For a whole week?"

"For a whole week," she repeated.

***

"Is Master saying that he's going to leave and return late again and have Charm tend to the bar, where she does not belong?"

Charm had her eye of destruction on me again as we stood in the kitchen. She had just finished beating a bowl of eggs for breakfast when I gave her the news. For some reason, she picked up a knife. I didn't know what business a knife had with a beaten bowl of eggs, but I wasn't deterred. Not when the stakes were so high.

"Listen, Charm, there are orphans to be saved. Poor little kids without homes or parents! It's my duty as a citizen of this city to do all that I can to rectify this horrible situation. Cassia and I hope to return before sundown, but yes, it is possible things might run late. I'm sure you can understand and make a small sacrifice and tend to the tavern while I'm gone for this noble cause! Think of the children! Isn't that right, Cassia?"

"Erm, well... yes."

Charm gave me one of her half-lidded stares filled with suspicion as if she was thinking something didn't add up.

"Well, we must be on our way," I said quickly, guiding Cassia to hurry out the door. "Thank you, Charm! I will pass along your blessings to the children!"

CHAPTER 15: THE MIND OF A STRATEGIST

Cassia and I left the tavern and headed toward the ward of Keeper's Garden.

"I hope Charm won't be upset with us if we're late," Cassia said, looking back at the tavern.

"Ah, don't worry about her. She's been in a sour mood lately."

Cassia looked at me. "How come?"

"Huh? Oh…" I tried to think up a reasonable response. "Well… let's just say she hasn't been thrilled with my decisions as of late."

"I see," Cassia said in a way that suggested she didn't understand at all. "You two seem quite close. Have you known Charm for very long?"

"Not that long."

It seemed like Cassia wanted to ask more but couldn't figure out how to proceed without being rude. That was the thing about being a polite person—it limited your options.

So instead, she asked, "Have you any ideas of where we might find the orphans? I don't think they'll be in the same spot as before."

I shrugged. "I'm not much of an orphan stalker, but I've got a few ideas."

Cassia turned to me. "I was not suggesting—"

"I know, I know. It was a joke."

She let out a breath. "I've never met someone with your sense of humor."

"Good. I like being one of a kind." I grinned.

Cassia shook her head, but by the curve of her lips, I could tell she was enjoying the banter. Before I could make my next quip, I sensed a presence behind us. I didn't turn to look. I could tell that Cassia sensed it as well.

"We're being followed," Cassia said.

"We sure are."

I wondered for how long. If my gates had been open, I would have felt it the moment anyone even looked at me. But with them closed, it was impossible to know. I only picked up on the presence because it had come close enough to be noticed by normal human senses.

"But who could it be?" Cassia said.

"Maybe the church doesn't want us to find those orphans."

"Do you really believe the church would do such a thing?"

"Sure, why not? I've seen them do plenty worse."

"But—"

I held up a hand. "I've seen them do good too. But they're people like anyone else. There are always good ones and bad ones, and generally, there are more of the latter than the former."

Cassia frowned.

"But it might not be the church," I said. "It might be the gang those boys mentioned, worried about someone sniffing around. Or it might Mideon and his band of morons. We seem to be collecting enemies lately."

"What should we do?" Cassia said.

"Nothing. At least not right now. Let's see what they do first."

Strangely, as we entered the ward of Keeper's Garden, the presence disappeared. I didn't know whether it had left or was doing a better job of concealing itself. Once again, I missed the power of my gates. With them open, catching someone on my tail would have been child's play, even if that person was located a thousand paces away and only viewing me through a glass scope.

But my gates were closed, and Cassia had not reached the Gate of Perception. So we made our way through the city and continued our search for the orphans. I led us down several alleys and boroughs that would have been good locations for street rats, but we found no children unaccompanied by adults.

"It's possible we scared them off the other day," I said.

"I was thinking the same. Are there any other wards where they might be?"

"Yeah. This is still one of the nicer areas of the city. Not the best but certainly not the worst. Yumentown and Addenwood Row are the poorest wards."

"Then let's go there," Cassia said with a determined look in her eyes.

"Mmm, sure, but let's eat first."

"Eat?"

"We already skipped breakfast," I said. "I'm starving."

"But..."

"Come on. I'm buying."

Cassia was hesitant to pause the search. But I was hungry, and unlike the old days, I needed food to maintain my energy. So we found a noodle shop on the side of the road and stopped for lunch.

I paid four coppers for two bowls of steaming-hot noodles and two mugs of tea. The food came out quickly, and I dove into mine. Cassia ate hers as you'd expect—slow and proper.

"This is great," Cassia said after taking the first bite.

I nodded. "Not bad for a copule coppers."

I killed the bowl before Cassia could even finish half of hers. Food had been different when I had my gates. Not only had I been able to deeply taste the ingredients, but I could also sense the effort and energy the chef had put into his craft. I'd had to stop eating meat, as I'd pick up on the pain and suffering the animal had gone through when it was slaughtered.

Without my gates, food was still good, albeit in a simple and primal way—satisfying the need for sustenance. I hadn't experienced that for the two hundred years my gates were open. Also, I'd begun to eat meat again.

After lunch, we walked to Addenwood Row, the closest of the two wards that the orphans were most likely to be stationed in. Cassia's expression changed with the scenery. The buildings got poorer and more desolate. The streets grew dirty. The clothes on passersby became ragged and torn. And the wrinkle in Cassia's brow deepened as we went.

"So much poverty," she said.

"Not everyone can live in golden, marble throne rooms," I said, unable to hold myself back from another dig at the church.

Cassia frowned. "I was also surprised at the bishop's quarters."

"What's to be surprised about? As the great philosopher Maternes said herself, 'Foolish merchants trade spices. Clever merchants start religions'."

Cassia shook her head, but she didn't say anything. There were several religions on the continent of Visseria, but the Order of the White Church was the richest and most powerful, stretching the farthest, beyond Adentris and into its surrounding countries.

The children we came across in Addenwood Row were unsupervised. They ran through the streets, playing, waving sticks, and chasing each other, but they didn't appear to belong to gangs. They were poor, wearing unclean and torn clothes. They were children whose parents had to work during the day and couldn't afford the time to care for them.

For hours, we walked and didn't see anything, and the sun began to set.

"This is taking too long," I said. "It was a lot easier when they came to find us."

"Perhaps they recognize us and are in hiding."

"No. We're walking around with too much awareness on our faces. Bad targets. You know what a good target is? A girl walking alone with a big purse, looking lost. That's what we need." I gave Cassia a look.

"Oh... yes, I suppose I could play that role."

I stepped into a shop, purchased a cheap bag, and filled it with dirt in an alley. Then I handed it to Cassia. "I won't be far behind. Also, you now owe me eight coppers. For the bag."

Cassia took the bag and returned to the street. As she walked, she stopped and looked around with a confused expression. Then she started moving forward in one direction, hesitated, and turned to move in another. She played a lost pedestrian perfectly. She seemed like an outsider, someone who had wandered into the wrong side of town.

Five minutes later, she was stopped by two men. They were tall and brutish, wearing leather greaves and short knives at their backs. I was far away enough that I couldn't hear their voices. I didn't have to be this distant, but I had hoped to find the presence that had been following us earlier by staying out of sight. However, I hadn't sensed anything since it disappeared.

The two men led Cassia into a secluded alley. By the time I arrived, both men were hunched over on the ground. One was clutching his back and the other his shoulder. It looked as if both had bounced off the wall behind them when they tried to lay hands on the lady.

Cassia was standing over them. She watched me as I jogged down the alley. "It was as you said would happen. They tried to rob me. But they don't seem associated with the orphans."

"That's okay," I said. "They're from around here. They'll know."

I kicked the big bald one in the shin. He yelped with pain.

"Where are the orphans?"

"Orphans? I don't know about any—"

I kicked him in the shin again.

He howled. "I swear, I don't know!"

I kicked again. Hard this time. Same shin, same spot. The big man opened his mouth for an ear-piercing scream, but I covered it with my hand, shoving him against the wall.

"Arch-don," Cassia said, clearly unsettled by my forcefulness.

"Don't worry," I said. "If this doesn't work, we can break their legs next."

Cassia and the two men all looked at me with the same expression of horror.

"What about you, Two-Leg?" I said to the smaller man, who was still clutching his shoulder. "You know where the orphans are? Or do I need to give you a new nickname?"

"N-no, sir, Two-Leg is an excellent name, sir. I do know where the orphans are."

I gave Cassia a winning smirk. She didn't return the smile.

"Most of them stay in the Yumentown Ward currently, good sir! They move around often, but last I'd heard, they were living under the Gray Stone Bridge!"

"They better be," I said. "You and your friend are to stay here for the next hour. I'll stay behind to watch you from a tower while my lady friend goes on ahead. If you disobey my command, I'll change your nickname to No-Leg. Do you understand?"

The man bobbed his head rapidly.

"Good." I took Cassia lightly by the arm, and we walked back down the alley toward the main road.

Cassia leaned close to me and whispered, "Why an hour?"

"We don't know if he's friendly with the orphan gang. We don't want him to run ahead and tell them that we're coming, do we?"

"Ah, I see," Cassia said, turning to me. "You really do have the mind of a strategist, don't you?"

I felt Cassia's chest accidentally brush against my arm. Suddenly, everything went quiet, and all I could think about was her body at my side. Then the moment passed as our bodies parted.

I looked back at her. "Huh? Did you say something?"

She gave a little sigh.

CHAPTER 16: NICE AND TIDY

The Gray Stone Bridge was in the center of Yumentown. It crossed over a moat and connected the slums to an old prison that was no longer in use by the city. Though I'd never been to it, I'd heard the story of the place a couple of times in the tavern. That was the thing about taverns. If you spent enough time in a good one, you could learn all sorts of things.

The prison had been abandoned after a fire broke out during a riot among the inmates. Nearly half of the prison guards were killed during the revolt, and most of the inmates escaped. One story claimed Yumentown had once been a semi-wealthy ward, but after the inmates were let loose onto the streets, the ward succumbed to crime and ruin. Another story said that it really had little to do with the inmates, and the ward collapsed into poverty due to the poor management by its superintendent, an official who had also been responsible for not properly fireproofing the prison before the riots.

In any case, what was left was a husk of a building and a moat that had dried out over the years. The bridge itself was nothing remarkable, relatively small as bridges went—about the width to fit a single carriage or wagon and a length that could be walked across in a minute. Originally, it had been the fastest way to escape the prison. If prisoners swam the moat, they'd be slowed by the water and shot with arrows by the guards on the walls.

But now there were no guards, and there was barely any wall either. The place looked deserted and untouched since the fire. Nowadays, the prisoners of Meritas were sent to Mandrol Down, a massive dungeon far north of the city gates.

We stepped to the ledge of the moat and saw a few tents beneath the bridge. We didn't see any bodies, but we did hear voices. Possibly children's voices.

I sighed. "They're not going to be too happy to see us."

"What should we do?"

"Surround them. I'll jump down on one side and you on the other."

"And if they try to escape?"

"Ideally, they won't until they hear what we have to say. But you'll have to catch any that try to run."

Cassia walked to the other side of the bridge and stood at the ledge. She nodded to me when she was ready, and we both jumped from the ledge and into the empty moat. Cassia simply leaped and landed on her two feet. With the Gate of Breath open, it was an easy maneuver.

The same was not true on my side. I was still getting used to my body and its lack of abilities. Having made several mistakes in the beginning, I'd become extra careful. Instead of jumping down directly, which was a twenty-foot drop, I took several steps along the wall of the moat before making a final jump and rolling against the ground to break my fall. I managed it successfully without any harm to my body, but it came at the cost of dirtying my clothing.

The young boy Simon, who had run into Cassia the day before, was keeping watch. He spotted me first, then he turned and looked around until he saw Cassia behind him. Immediately, he began beating the cover of the tent beside him. "Kien! Kien, get out here! She's here."

The leader boy with the braids stepped out, as did six boys from the other tents. He saw Cassia first then turned and scowled at me, seeing that he was surrounded.

"What do you want?" he said.

"We're just here to talk," I said.

"We have nothing to talk about," Kien said. "You'd better get out of here or we'll finish what we started last time."

I smiled. "You're going to finish running away, you mean?"

Kien scowled. For some reason he seemed quite confident despite our last meeting.

"We just want to know why the White Church hasn't adopted you," Cassia said in a voice the opposite of mine, all warm and kind. We had an interesting unintentional dynamic going.

"The White Church?" Kien said, twirling a lock of braided hair.

The other boys said nothing.

"The White Church has a mandate to look after orphans," Cassia said. "Have they not found you?"

"We aren't orphans," Kien said. "We're part of Gendro's crew."

Gendro? I thought. *That's a different name from the other day. Didn't he mention a Lord Ashbane or something?*

"We'd like for you to come with us to the White Church," Cassia said.

"And if we decline?"

"Look at where you're living," Cassia said. "You have no homes. No shelter. No one to look after you. The White Church will take care of you until you're adults. Then you'll be free to live as you w ish."

"We've got Gendro to look after us," Kien said.

"Cassia, let's stop wasting time. Grab the kid and let's go."

Kien looked at me with fear in his eyes. "Now!" he said under his breath, and all the boys turned and darted away from us, toward the foundation of the prison.

There was a door beneath the prison that I hadn't noticed earlier, leading to the cellar. Now their encampment made sense. If there was a staircase inside that took them to the upper level, they would be able to enter the prison, climb up one level, and escape over the bridge. Otherwise, it was a lousy spot, easily ambushed by other gangs.

Cassia looked at me. "Should we not chase after them?"

"I guess."

I could see that Cassia wanted to run after them, but she didn't speed up as she followed me into the prison, and I took my sweet time walking in. We came out to the other side and saw that the upper floor had caved in. It looked more like an arena than a prison, with tall, dilapidated walls surrounding the open center. The ground was covered by dark rubble, and above us was a clear blue sky.

Several staircases led farther down into the depths of the prison. I wondered how many levels below there were and if the prison had another exit. But the orphans had climbed upward and were watching us from the walls and the edges of upper floors that had not entirely fallen. They were no longer running from us.

"Ha! You're surrounded now," Kien said, looking not dissimilar from when he was positioned on the roof the first time we met.

"Not a bad trap," I said. "We had you surrounded, and you managed to flip it around. There's only one problem. I saw this coming a league away."

"That's crap," Kien said. "You wouldn't have come in if you'd known."

"You think a dragon steps around an ant trap? Best you come down now. Or we can come up. Either way…"

"No one's doing anything," said a new voice.

An old man came out from the crevices of the broken cells far across from us. He was flanked by several large men. In fact, at least two dozen men were standing all around us, glaring down from the levels above and coming out of the floors below. Each marked by ink and scars to let you know what kind of men they were. You might say they looked dangerous.

"You must be Gendro," I said.

"Indeed, I am." The old man wore a vest of leather armor and matching leather gauntlets. "And who are you?"

I shrugged. "Don't worry about it."

"I am Cassia Hightower, Templar of the White Church!" Cassia said, stepping forward. She was ready for a fight. "These orphans belong in a home. Not in your gang!"

"This is their home," Gendro said, widening his arms. "You shouldn't have come here, girl. We don't take kindly to unannounced visitors." He turned to the man on his right. "Take her."

"What about the other one?" asked a henchman.

Gendro gave me a sour look. "Dump his body in the cana—"

Before Gendro could finish his sentence, Cassia had begun a summoning. This was going to be interesting. I'd yet to see her fight.

"Celeru forgive me," she muttered, then she raised her palm at the men across from her. Her halos expanded, spinning in great rings around her body.

With the release of her aura, I could see the rings without casting the Spell of Seeing. Being able to detect another spellcaster's halos was the first mark of a skilled mage. The second was the ability to taste another's aura. Tasting an aura had nothing to do with taste buds. A discerning food critic did not make for a good mage. But the sensation was as if you had flavor on your tongue. The stronger your mage senses, the better you could pick up the flavor of the halos around you. Cassia's halos tasted like freshly fallen snow.

"Rule of Ruin," Cassia said. "Rule Twenty-Three, Wild Win—"

Before she could finish her incantation, another spell had been conjured. Several bolts of lightning shot down from the sky. I recognized this to be one of Nahael's Eleven Spells of Retribution. *Thunderous.*

I then tasted the aura of this spell too. Unlike Cassia's, it held a mildly sweet, leathery flavor.

The walls, filled with Gendro's men, exploded with light and static. Many soon joined us on the ground level, making hard thumps and convulsing on the floor with sparks of lightning. At the western wall stood a man in plate armor, flanked by two more wearing church whites.

The orphan boys still clutching to the walls nearly fell over as they found the three men behind them. The one who had conjured the spell was none other than High Templar Darren Tamblion. The remainder of Gendro's men charged toward him on the upper level. A few who were mages began chanting their own spells.

Cassia finished casting her spell, and gusts of wind blew down the mages and the rest of Gendro's men. Gendro turned and began to run. He was on the second floor, and I had no idea how he planned to escape. The moat exit was behind Cassia and me, and Darren had the bridge above blocked. It looked like he wasn't thinking too hard and had jumped through a window.

"Levi!" Darren called, and Gendro froze midair.

Despite his scrambling, Gendro floated back into the arena. Darren released the spell, and Gendro fell to the ground on the first level.

I was surprised that the High Templar could use elven spells. Now, that was impressive.

Darren jumped down and landed lightly before Gendro. He gave Cassia a nod. Then he looked at me with a question in his eyes, as if wondering who I was and why I was still with Cassia.

Finally, he looked down at Gendro, who was struggling to his feet. "You have been found conspiring against the duke and the White Church, kidnapping orphans, and enslaving them for your evil deeds."

Cassia came forward. "How did you find them?"

"We went to our orphanages and found that Gendro's men had been around, stopping children from entering our halls. It's our mistake that this wasn't reported earlier. The ones that held this information back will be disciplined accordingly."

"But are there more?" Cassia asked. "Is it only this handful?"

"From what we've seen, yes," Darren said. "These are the only ones. But of course, there may be others. We'll find out once we take Gendro to the City Watch for questioning. But don't let it trouble you. I'll see this to the end. If other children are being held captive, they will be found. I swear it."

Cassia nodded with visible relief. "Thank you."

"There's no need," Darren said. "I'm only doing my duty, as were you."

"Indeed," she said.

The city guards soon arrived and took Gendro and his men away, while Darren and the two church guards walked the orphans toward the monastery. Simon and Kien gave me one last look before they turned and were led away by the High Templar.

"Well, that ended nice and tidy," I said. "Looks like the church were the good guys after all."

"Yes, it did," Cassia said with a smile. She looked happy and proud that her church had done the right thing.

I let her have the moment and didn't tell her I didn't mean my words.

CHAPTER 17: PERFECT, PERFECT, WHOLESOME

"And then the templar arrived. A bunch of magic was thrown around. And the orphans were rescued," I said. "You guys should have seen it. I was heroic, leading the charge into the prison."

"Our Heru is a hero," Elsa said, smiling. "Who would have thought?"

"This is true?" Charm said to Cassia. She had been giving me one of her suspicious looks as I recounted the story.

"Err, yes," Cassia said. "Arch-don was very helpful."

"We are the saviors of orphans, Charm. Aren't you proud?"

Charm said nothing and went back to cleaning the bar. By the time we'd returned, it was already past midnight, and there were only a couple of patrons left. It was also Ruday, and most people had to return to work the next morning. The Tipsy Pelican, however, was closed on Awndays. The first day of the week tended to have less foot traffic so it served as our rest day.

"Hey, by the way, Elsa, would it be all right if Cassia borrowed some of your clothing?" I said, trying to keep my voice steady and not reveal any eagerness in my expression. "She didn't bring any casual clothing. She'll probably need to borrow some clothes for about a week until she can get some of her own."

"Oh yes, of course," Elsa said, giving Cassia a once-over with slow, seductive eyes. "No problem at all. It'll be fun to dress you up."

I always knew I could count on you, Elsa! I thought.

Cassia made an audible gulp. Charm shot me another suspicious look and finished wiping down the bar.

We said our goodnights, and the ladies took their baths while I waited my turn. I lay on my bed, exhausted. It had been some time since I'd had this much activity in a day. For the past year, most of my time had been spent at the tavern. But I had to admit I'd had fun running around with Cassia. Although that probably wasn't what she wanted me to experience when she'd asked me to go with her.

After my bath, I went to bed, thinking about the boy, Simon. I remembered his eyes as he was led away, and his expression kept returning to mind. I pushed the thought away and let sleep take over my tired body.

That night, I dreamed of my father. I suppose it should not have been a surprise.

"Come, son. Come watch the stars with me."

We were on the lake again. The water under our feet was entirely reflective, and I could not see what was beneath.

He looked at me with a kind smile. "You did well today. Why are you troubled?"

I said nothing for a long time. "I'm not. Why should I be?"

"Good. That's good."

Then a gong sounded, sending shock waves across the water.

"What the Abyss is that?" I exclaimed.

The gong sounded again. Louder this time.

I woke up and found Charm standing over me at my bedside, holding a pan. She hit it with the spatula.

"I'm awake, I'm awake!" I said, sitting up. "Good Celeru, it's the middle of the night!"

"It's morning, Master," Charm said. "And Master forgot to buy lettuce last time!"

"What?" I looked up and saw daylight entering through the window. Gods, that night of sleep had felt like seconds.

"While Master was gallivanting with Miss Cassia, he forgot to purchase lettuce for our Awnday sandwiches."

Charm always made sandwiches on Awnday. They were delicious. Rye bread, ham, tomatoes, mustard, figs, and lettuce. So she had a point. They would be less tasty without the lettuce.

"Ugh... all right, I'll go to the market today," I said, rolling away from her. "Jeez, you don't have to—"

She hit the pan with the spatula again.

"What?"

"It's nearly noon, Master."

"Already?" I groaned. "All right, all right, I'll go now."

I heard some murmurs from Elsa's room as I exited my own and stepped into the hallway. I wondered if she was talking in her sleep until I heard Cassia's voice there too. I desperately wanted to knock and see what was going on, but I was already late, so I headed downstairs and exited through the front door.

It was a beautiful day as I walked to the market. The sky was clear of clouds. The streets were not busy. Even the shopkeepers at the market seemed to be in a good mood and charged me lower prices than usual—not as cheap as when Cassia came with me but cheaper than what I would typically get. I purchased more eggs and plenty of lettuce and then made my way home. As I stepped up to the tavern's door, I could hear the voices of the young women.

"No, no, leave that button unbuttoned."

"B-But this is too much," said Cassia's voice.

"This is how the dress is worn," came Elsa's reply.

"Ah, I don't know about this. I feel naked."

My ears perked up to gate one thousand.

"That's how you're supposed to feel. Exhilarating, isn't it? What do you think, Charm?"

"Sexy."

Wait. Did Charm just say that?

I stood before the door, not sure if I should wait to see what happened next or jump in headfirst.

"See?" Elsa's said.

"Ah, I'm sensitive there," Cassia said. "No, I can do it myself. Miss Elsa! Ahh!"

Then the door burst open, and Cassia rushed out. She was wearing Elsa's white dress, the special one. I nearly dropped the produce. She looked absolutely amazing. I had the desire to thank Celeru's divine grace for my good fortune.

She looked at me, blushing. We opened our mouths at the same time, but nothing came out.

Control yourself, nineteen-year-old Archibold, I told myself. *And stop staring at her chest. That perfect, perfect, wholesome chest. Get a grip. You are the Stormblood! Your heart is a stone. A hardened stone. A hardened stone made of lust! Stop that! Get it together, man!*

My concentration on Cassia's wonderful figure suddenly broke. I felt a prickling at the back of my neck, and I turned. Cassia turned with me.

The presence that had been following us the day before when we searched for the orphans had suddenly returned. Then with the same speed, it disappeared, just as it previously had.

"Arch-don..."

"This time, we squash him like a bug," I said.

Elsa came out of the door just then. "Cassia? Oh, hey, Heru—"

I threw her the bag of groceries and dashed off with Cassia. "I sensed him two blocks this way," I said, leading her south and around a corner.

"Two blocks? Are you sure?"

"No, but it's the right direction. Wear your scariest face, Cassia. Fear makes people forget what they should be doing."

Sure enough, a dark shape parted from the shadow of a wall and ran as we approached the end of the street. We would not have noticed him if he hadn't moved, but he undoubtedly saw my look of murder and lost his nerve.

"There!"

"I won't let him escape!" Cassia rushed forward with incredible speed.

I was about to follow her, but I saw something soft bouncing at her chest and nearly tripped. Then I was running at her speed, at her side again... so I could get a better view. The full power of my youthful body brought me to the same speed as an awakened who had opened the Gate of Breath.

"Arch-don, watch where you're going!" Cassia shouted.

"Huh?" I looked up just in time to avoid running straight into a wall. "Thanks."

Okay, that's enough, nineteen-year-old Arch. This was not the time to be ogling templars with fantastic cleavage. Plenty of time for that later.

We raced through the street, weaving through people. Then we both skidded to a stop.

"Where did he go?" I asked.

The presence had disappeared. It was there, and a moment later, it had vanished as if it had never existed.

Cassia cast the Spell of Seeing, and her eyes filled with aura, but she shook her head. "I don't sense him."

The Spell of Seeing could sense auras through walls, but it couldn't see past high-tier concealment spells. Whatever spell the stalker was using, it was certainly of a high caliber. If I'd still had my gates, it would have been as easy as finding a horse in a shoebox. The Fifth Gate, the Gate of Perception, could see through nearly all misdirection, auras, and spells. But in my current state, I could sense nothing.

"Hmm..."

I picked up a pebble and threw it against the wall. The stone ricocheted and hit the opposing wall then hit another, making zigzags, bouncing eight times between the area around us.

Cassia's eyes widened. "Incredible."

"Told you I was a pebble-tosser," I said and threw another.

The pebble bounced between the walls, hitting new points that the first one had missed. On the seventh point, it bounced off air and not a wall. Something invisible was there. The pebble slid off it, revealing a wavering mirage.

I only caught a glimpse before the invisibility returned, and he ran again. He was a short bald man, and he wore the white priest's robes of the church. But once he was on the move, we could track him by his footfalls and the wavering colors of his spell. Only when he stopped was he difficult to find.

We followed him several more blocks until, once again, he disappeared. I reached down for another pebble and noticed that the sewer lid had been opened.

"Great," I said as I lifted the lid, stink rising from the hole. "He went down there."

Cassia jumped in without hesitation. I sighed and followed. We landed on a walkway beside the underground canal that acted as both a flood drain and the city's sewer. It smelled awful. But I could sense the invisible man's presence again. We followed him down several stretches and around several turns in the walkway.

"I didn't even know all this was down here," I said, marveling at the underground passage system.

"Look!" Cassia said.

Up ahead, the walkway opened, and light flooded the tunnel. We crossed the entrance and stepped into a massive atrium made of brick and stone. At the center, a man-made waterfall fell from a hole in the high ceiling. This water was not sewage. It ran off into a pool that led back to the canal that we had just come from. The rest of the atrium's flooring was flat and paved with fine white stones, and tall white rocks protruded from the walls. The entire place was practically pure white.

"What the Abyss is this place?"

"This..." Cassia said, looking at the markings of the ceiling, "is a church."

"You are correct," said a voice. "It's the church beneath the church."

We both turned and saw the invisibility drop from the bald priest. But he wasn't the one who had spoken. Behind him, a man stepped out from the shadows of a stairwell and into the light that radiated from the ceiling of the atrium. It was none other than High Templar Darren Tamblion.

CHAPTER 18: THE CHURCH BENEATH THE CHURCH

"Before the time of Celeru and Nahael, the Elder Gods reigned in Visseria," the High Templar said as he stepped across from us. "It was the time of Amvoldin, Salapsis, and Izirath. When the Order of the White Church was founded by Nahael nearly three thousand years ago, it was considered a pagan religion by the peoples of that age—pagan and forbidden by punishment of death. So the Order operated secretly, building underground places of worship."

Darren smiled up at the atrium. "This is one of them. It's been here for thousands of years." He turned his eyes back down to us. "But what most people don't know is how the church was able to find the funding for such endeavors. Have you heard the Tale of the Two Brothers?"

"High Templar Tamblion," Cassia said in a tone that suggested she didn't have time for long, meandering history lessons. "The man standing next to you has been following us for days. We must apprehend him for questioning."

"Cassiaaa…" I rubbed my temples. Sometimes she was incredibly capable. And other times, she was dense as granite.

Darren continued his story as if he hadn't heard her. "Celeru had seven disciples, and of them, two were brothers—Nahael and Inias. We all know Nahael founded the White Church and died fighting his brother when Inias turned against the Word of Celeru. But what is never spoken of openly is that Nahael's greatest act was not done alone. He created the White Church with Inias as equals."

Darren's voice grew louder. Stronger. More forceful. "Without Inias, the White Church could never have become what it is today. Inias was the one who made sacrifices and cut deals to secure allies among the elites that would give the White Church the ability to practice its faith."

He stepped forward. "Inias sold his skills as a warrior-mage to any that would pay his fee. He killed many men. Some were his enemies. Some were his friends. And some were simply innocents that were in the way of the wealthy and powerful. But in return, he gained the funds necessary to build secret churches across Visseria. These churches spread the Word of Celeru. These churches made the Order what it is today."

Cassia was frowning. I wondered if she'd heard this version of history. I certainly had. It wasn't exactly a secret among the faithful, but it was rarely spoken of—and even then, it was done in hushed tones. Inias was the black sheep of the Order, the one who had nearly brought the whole thing down. But what Darren said was also true. Inias, who had reached the Eleventh Gate of Awakening before he was brought down by his brother, was an original founder of the Order of the White Church.

Darren opened his hands. "This atrium is his. For hundreds of years, the followers of Celeru would practice their worship secretly in the Churches of Inias. Without them, the Order would never have existed here in Meritas."

Cassia had been watching him closely and finally seemed suspicious. "Who is that man in the priest's robes, High Templar?"

Darren shot Cassia a look as if annoyed that she'd ignored his story. "This is my servant Drimdelon. I had him watch you."

"Why?" Cassia asked.

"Oh, come on, Cassia!" I exclaimed, unable to hold myself back anymore.

Everyone turned to me.

"Remember Simon—the kid who ran into you?" I said. "Remember what he said to the leader kid under the bridge when he saw you? He said, 'She's here.' He didn't say, 'Why is she here?' or 'What is she doing here?' or even 'Aahh, they found us!'"

"What are you saying?" Cassia asked, still not understanding.

Darren's mouth made a thin smile.

"And Gendro?" I said, turning to Darren. "Who in Celeru's magnificent ass is Gendro? The kids said they were part of Lord Ashbane's syndicate, not this make-believe Gendro fella."

The wrinkle in Cassia's eyebrows was deepening. "You believe there is someone else behind this?"

"Yes, there's someone else!" I was getting heated. I never got heated. I pointed at the priest. "That bald idiot has been following us since we left the church that day. Why else would he follow us again after we'd already caught the bad guys and saved the kids?"

Cassia's face was stricken as the realization hit. "To ensure that we believed what we saw." Her body was shaking. Her fist clenched, and her knuckles turned white. "To ensure that we would not continue the search for the orphans."

"I would have preferred to avoid a confrontation with you over this, Cassia," Darren said. "I hoped you would give up after the capture of Gendro. But it seems your companion saw through my little ploy." He looked at me. "Tell me, stranger, who are you?"

"A pain in your ass."

Darren scowled, as did the bald priest. "My father was right to want you arrested," Darren said. "I should have let him."

"How could you?" Cassia said, still shaking. "Where are the orphans we rescued yesterday?"

Darren smiled. "They're back where they belong. Part of a growing underground enterprise. It was bad luck that one of them targeted you. If that boy hadn't run into you that day, none of this would have happened."

"What I don't get is why you bothered with the big show with Gendro," I said.

"My mistake," Darren said. "It cost me too. I paid good money to have Gendro take the fall. But it was important that Templar Cassia reported the issue was taken care of when she returned to Yestereaster." Darren ran his hand back through his hair. "No matter. This way works too."

Cassia trembled with anger. "How could you? You're of the Order. You are to serve and protect and aid the people... you monster."

Darren's reserve broke, and his expression turned ugly. "You do not know the position I'm in! You couldn't stand the pressures that I face. But I will succeed. The Church of Meritas will overtake the Catalogion in Yestereaster. We will become the seat of the Order. My father's wishes will be fulfilled! He will be a better archbishop than Katharis! But to do that, it takes coin. Don't you see? I'm only doing the same as Inias—making sacrifices for the greater good of the church. Those orphans have no one to need them or miss them. Their lives are put to much better use by helping me strengthen the church. Each is worth a dozen gold brilliances on the black market! You would have done the same in my position."

High Templar Darren Templion sounded as if he wanted Cassia's approval. Or if not approval, at least her understanding of what he was doing. He stared at her, his eyes large and pleading, begging for her to acknowledge him.

It didn't happen. Cassia said nothing for a long moment, and then she looked up at him, her eyes wet with disappointment. "You are no templar," she muttered. "You are the Fallen."

And I felt immense power rushing from her gates—more than I thought possible for a mere spirited. Cassia had finally come face-to-face with corruption and hypocrisy in her church. I no longer felt the need to rub the situation in her face, which was what

I'd intended to do and the true reason I'd agreed to tag along. I'd never given up my dislike for the Order, and from the moment Simon bumped into Cassia, I knew there was a high probability things would end in confrontation. But seeing her standing there, ready to risk her life, I did not feel my typical scorn for the Order, which was unexpected.

Anger washed over Darren's face, but it was quickly masked by his handsome features. He sighed and shook his head, with a disturbing smile. "It really is unfortunate. I don't enjoy killing young women." He slowly ran his eyes over her body and licked his lips. "Especially incredibly beautiful ones. I would not have thought a templar such as yourself would wear such a provocative dress. Back at the academy, I'd always thought you a good girl. Oh, how wrong I was, wasn't I? A shame. If this were any other time, I would have bedded you."

Cassia didn't shrivel from his gaze or turn away in discomfort. She met his eyes and said, "You, Darren Tamblion, are a bad human being."

Darren's face flushed, and I found myself smiling broadly. The insult seemed to have struck deeper than any other could. Darren's eyes deadened. He drew his sword.

"Drimdelon," Darren said to the bald priest. "Kill the boy. I will take care of the girl."

It took me a moment to realize that by "boy," he was referring to me. Despite having spent a year in my new life as a bona fide teenager, I was still getting used to being seen as barely a man in the eyes of strangers. Although my appearance hadn't changed in the past two hundred years, I'd never been called a boy during that time. Even the unawakened could unconsciously sense my power when my gates were open. But with them closed, I probably seemed as much of a threat as the pudgy-faced baker's son down the street from the tavern.

As I was contemplating these thoughts, Darren and Drimdelon burst forward from their positions. Darren had his sword raised and was already swinging it down as he closed the distance to Cassia. Drimdelon looked to be a mage, yet he moved like a charging barbarian, coming at me at an incredible speed.

"Celeru, forgive me," Cassia said quietly as if she were truly sorry for what she would do next. "Rule of Ruin Twenty-Six, Spectral Sword."

Cassia's halos widened enough that I could see them without the Spell of Seeing. Once again, I tasted fresh snow. A long red blade of aura appeared in her hand just as Darren brought his sword down.

Cassia swung up with a perfect grace that was practically blinding in her white dress and parried Darren's attack, sending him falling back. Before he could counter, she jumped backward in a single leap, appearing before me just as Drimdelon arrived.

The priest was not expecting her. With her sword-free hand, she buried a fist into Drimdelon's stomach in a powerful thrust that sent him flying across the atrium and into a wall, cracking the limestone tiles as he bounced off it.

Drimdelon fell to his knees, the air escaped from his lungs. He propped himself up on one foot and tried to stand before twitching once and collapsing to the ground, motionless. And just like that, Drimdelon was out of the fight.

I studied Cassia, reassessing her. I knew she'd opened two gates, but this was the real thing. No wonder Deacon Obi had nearly crapped his pants when he heard her name.

"Darren Tamblion," Cassia said in an unwavering voice. "You have acted against the Word of Celeru and the Order of the White Church. By the powers granted to me by Nahael's Edict and the archbishop, I hereby renounce your title as High Templar." She pointed her strobing red sword at him. "Face your judgment."

Darren chuckled. "Do you really believe you will leave this place alive?"

With a sudden force, I felt Darren's power. I'd sensed it before, but now he was releasing it in a massive thrust. His halos exploded from his core in great rings of energy, and I knew right then and there that we were in a perilous situation. As strong as Cassia was, her halos were minuscule compared to Darren's, for he had opened the Third Gate of Awakening, the Gate of Radiance. At his level, he was at equal standing to Galston the Gallant, Champion of the Tournament of Heroes. It was likely Darren and Galston were the only two people in the entire city who had awakened the Third G ate.

Each gate made the awakened several times stronger than an awakened of a previous gate. This was especially true of the Gate of Radiance. Although each gate granted the awakened an increase in magical aura, the Gate of Radiance increased one's halos severalfold.

Cassia's halos were a fraction of Darren's, and mine were a fraction of Cassia's.

Back in the old days, we used to say that it took three breathers to defeat a single spirited, and five spirited to defeat a single radiant. But here in this room, there was only one spirited to fight the radiant.

"He has awakened the Gate of Radiance," Cassia said with widening glowing-blue eyes, having cast the Spell of Seeing. She turned to me. "Arch-don, perhaps with your assistance, we will stand a chance."

I looked over at her and grinned, picking at an itch in my ear. "Hmm? What are you talking about? Our agreement was for me to help you find the orphans. We found them. And you already took care of our stalker. This issue with the high templar... well, that's the church's problem." I balled the wax and flicked it. "I'm on vacation, remember?"

CHAPTER 19: A TRUE TEMPLAR

Cassia's shoulders slumped, but then she took a breath and straightened herself again, determination taking over her features. "You're right. You have fulfilled your agreement with me, Arch-don. You should escape now. I don't know if I'll be able to defeat him."

I gave Cassia an incredulous look. "Escape? Are you kidding?" I chose the large white rock protruding from the wall to the side of me and hopped on top of it for a better view. "This is going to be a great fight!" I said as I sat down. "A church templar against a church templar—I wouldn't miss it for the world."

Darren laughed. "What a fool you have there, Templar Hightower. He wishes to watch you die. And when you're dead, he will be next."

I could tell he was happy that I wasn't leaving. Even as a radiant, it would likely take him some time to kill Cassia. If I had gotten away, I could spread the word about his corruption.

Cassia looked at me then got into a fighting stance. "If you won't leave, then I must not lose."

"That's the spirit," I said.

"You have no chance," Darren said. "With your ability, you can only cast low-tier rules. I bet you haven't even broken thirty."

Cassia grimaced. He was right, it appeared. But being able to use Celeru's rules up to thirty was already an impressive feat without the Third Gate open. Rules beyond twenty required significant halos. Technically, it was possible for someone without the Gate of Radiance to cast a high-level spell, but they'd likely blow out all their halos on just the one. However, the likelihood of such a scenario was low because spells, especially high-level spells, were very difficult to master. And you couldn't practice much if you didn't have the halo reserves to draw on.

Another problem was that as the spell difficulty increased, so did the risk to the caster's body. Celeru's Seventy-Seven Rules of Ruin turned one's halos into destructive energy—a dangerous thing to hold within your body before releasing. Even with the Gate of Radiance open, this posed limits to which spells a caster could use as it required superb aura control.

Apparently, Darren had exquisite mastery. "Rule of Ruin Forty-Five, Desert Doom," he said with a scythe of a smile.

The ground around Cassia morphed into black sand. She jumped half a second before the spell struck, but the sand rose from the ground in sharp black pillars, attempting to pierce and swallow her.

"Grace of Seraphel, Red Armor!" Cassia called out just before one of the pillars struck her and knocked her to the ground. The pillar did not impale her, hitting instead the gleaming crimson light that covered her body. But it looked as if she'd still taken damage from the fall and the blow.

Red Armor was an old fighting incantation created by the Takklan, one of the great warrior tribes. I was surprised she knew it. Even I didn't have that one in my arsenal, mainly because it wasn't the type of spell I'd needed in the past.

Cassia struggled to her knee, wincing at the reddening bruise on her abdomen that peeked through a cut on the dress.

"You cannot win!" Darren roared as he rushed forward again with his sword.

She met him halfway, colliding, sending sparks of red and orange as steel clashed against spellblade. The taste of both their halos was intermixed on my tongue, but the flavor of sweet leather was overwhelming.

Cassia was holding him off, but I could already see the difference in ability between them. Darren had barely broken a sweat, and his halo reserves were enormous. Meanwhile, Cassia was wasting her precious energies maintaining her summoned sword and armor. If she'd come with her own physical weaponry and armor, she would have stood a better chance. Instead, she was wearing Elsa's thin-laced white dress that was coming apart at the seams. Probably the opposite of what you'd call the ideal protective garment, but gods, was she stunning to watch fight.

As they clashed and drew apart again, Darren raised his hand for a summoning. "Rule of Ruin Forty-Six, Bane's Blade."

A black sword appeared in his open hand, taller and thicker than the steel sword in the other. It was another high-level Rule of Ruin. This was starting to become dangerous for Cassia. Darren held two swords now, but the conjured one made of aura was far more deadly. It could cut through both Cassia's Spectral Sword and the Red Armor in one swing.

"You really shouldn't be giving him time to cast spells," I said, putting some weight into my voice and letting it echo across the atrium. "Each time he does that, your chances of winning go down. You'll need to avoid that sword at any cost now. I bet he can make three swings with it before he loses it and has to summon another."

Even with Darren's Gate of Radiance open, Bane's Blade took incredible power to hold on to. But because it could cut through just about anything, casters didn't usually need to keep it around after one slice.

"Understood." She rushed forward.

The first swing came, and she ducked just in time. The sword singed the ends of her hair as it passed above her—the strands unable to keep up with her speed.

The next swing came from the top. She stepped aside in the nick of time, but the black sword caught her Red Armor at the edge of her shoulder, shattering it and tearing the dress's strap, leaving a thin thread that, by some divine miracle, held together.

I was suddenly on the edge of my seat. My increased attention on the fight was because I was worried about Cassia's well-being. That was the reason. Nothing to do with the diminishing dress.

The third swing, she could not dodge fully. She swung her Spectral Sword to block. It didn't block. The Bane's Blade cut right through it. However, her Spectral Sword slowed down the swing, giving Cassia the time to step out of the way.

Three swings. The blade dissipated. She'd survived.

"Amazing," Darren said. "I'm impressed that you've lasted this long. But your time is running short. You can't have more than a third of your halos remaining." He still looked immaculate in his shining plate armor, while Cassia, in contrast, was bruised and panting, wearing a dress that was falling apart.

She was winded, but with the Gate of Breath open, she wouldn't tire just yet. However, Darren was right about her halos. They were deteriorating rapidly. She would have to make the next two spells count if she were going to have a chance of winning.

"Think about what advantage you have now," I said. "Whatever it is, you'll need to maximize it at the right time."

I didn't spell it out for her, partly because Darren would hear and partly because she should figure it out herself. After all, it was obvious that Darren was underestimating her. I bet that she had something up her sleeve that he wouldn't expect from her. A person with her abilities always did—a special trick or a well-honed technique—and I was telling her that she needed to save it for the right moment. It was her last chance.

Cassia paused then nodded once without turning to me.

"Rule of Ruin Forty-Si—" Darren started.

He didn't finish because Cassia reached him in an instant, sending her fist at his face. He dodged, but she succeeded in preventing him from finishing the incantation. She swung again. He brought his steel sword down. She stepped out of the way and tried to close the distance again.

"Rule of Ruin Fort—"

Again, Darren's incantation was cut off as Cassia reached him in time. She was learning. Their physical abilities were nearly equal, as they both had opened the Gate of Breath. As long as she could prevent him from casting, she could match him.

"Damn you." Darren swung at her again with his steel sword. He went into a full melee now, forgetting his spells. She couldn't keep up without a weapon of her own.

They broke apart. Both began casting at the same time.

"Rule of Ruin!" they bellowed in unison.

"Twenty-Eight, Ferocious Fist!" Cassia charged forward, one fist balled and turning red with aura.

"Forty-six, Bane's Blade!" Darren finished, and the black sword reappeared in his open hand.

But he didn't have enough time to attack with it. He would have to swing with his steel sword first. So he did. But it was a weak swing. His footing wasn't right—he'd put too much attention on the spell and not enough on his positioning. And this time, instead of dodging his attack, Cassia caught the steel sword in her right ha nd.

"No!" Darren exclaimed.

This was her hidden move. *She could catch a freaking sword with her bare hand.* It stopped in the crevice between her thumb and her index finger.

Darren tried to bring around the Bane's Blade in his other hand, but he was too late. Cassia shot her crimson fist forward, pushing all her strength and power into that single swing. Darren couldn't dodge it in time. She aimed at his face, but he jumped upward at the last minute. The fist landed right in his armor's solar plexus.

The armor shattered. Cassia's fist broke through, launching him backward. He flew thirty feet and crashed thunderously into the wall of the atrium.

Cassia panted heavily, looking at the hole she'd made in the wall with Darren's body. She dropped to one knee, shaking with fatigue. That was the rest of her energy. She'd put everything into that punch, and it had been a good one too.

I clapped. "Wooo, way to go!"

"I nearly thought I was done for..." Cassia began shivering. Then she smiled weakly at me, and the tension in her shoulders released.

"But you pulled through," I said with a smile of my own. "You did good."

Her eyes became alert again. "We must find where they took those orphans, Arch-don."

"Yes, yes," I said, standing from my seat on the rock. "Let's see if we can wake up Drimdelon and get some answers."

But then came the sound of a wall cracking. We both looked up and saw that it was coming from the hole. A hand reached out from the darkness and caught the edge of the cratered wall.

Darren Tamblion stepped out. He was bare-chested, his armor completely destroyed. His body looked like it was chiseled out of stone. It was made of hard, lean muscle and not a measure of fat. A dark circle was forming around his chest, but he was standing. And he was laughing uncontrollably.

"Impressive! Very impressive! Had that not been armor blessed by the archbishop herself, you would have defeated me. I am humbled, Cassia Hightower! I have misjudged you, and I apologize for that. But now you will die."

CHAPTER 20: TOO NAIVE

Cassia let out a sharp breath as she pushed herself back to her feet. She wavered, taking a step forward, then backward, barely able to keep her balance. Her eyes closed, and her breathing slowed. I realized that she was trying to call up the last reserves of her strength.

Even in this moment, when she had thought she'd won and found herself mistaken, she did not spend an extra second on despair. Already, she was preparing to counter. Though I respected her courage, I knew that she stood no chance... unless she was to open her Third Gate.

It was in these times of intense pressure that a gate was most likely to be opened. The Gate of Breath is commonly opened during moments of hard training, but more often than not, gates are opened when one is near death. My gates had been opened in this very way. I'd faced down my own destruction, and instead of letting my mind be lost to fear, I turned that heightened awareness and focus on awakening.

Now that my gates were closed, I wondered if I could do it all over again and regain the power I'd once had. I doubted it. One needed not only courage to open a gate but will as well—the strength to accomplish something beyond simple need and hope. If I were to open my gates again, it certainly wasn't going to be anytime soon.

However, if Cassia could awaken the Gate of Radiance, she'd have a chance against Darren. Yes, only a chance. Even if she did open the Third Gate, she still would not possess his level of spell knowledge, and she was still more injured than he was. But perhaps a chance was all she needed.

Just as power increased severalfold with each additional gate, so did the difficulty of awakening. Out of all the awakened who opened the Gate of Breath, only half managed to open the Gate of Spirit in their lifetimes. Of the spirited, less than one in ten would ever open the Gate of Radiance.

But for some reason, I had come to believe that it was just a matter of time for Cassia. And perhaps, the time had come.

I cast the Spell of Seeing and let my halos fill my eyes as I set my gaze upon her. After a moment, I saw it. Beyond her two opened gates was a third. An image formed in my mind that looked like a door slightly cracked, bright light leaking from the edge of its frame. However, the door remained closed.

But as Cassia stood there, breathing, concentrating, I saw that the light from the crack along the gate's edges grow brighter. She, too, had realized that to survive this fight, she had to evolve and become stronger. She was awakening her Third Gate.

Cassia breathed. Her face was calm and focused, her eyes still closed. And slowly, bit by bit, the crack in the door widened, light flooding through...

Then it suddenly snapped shut.

I blinked, my halos leaving my eyes, and I saw that in a flash of speed, Darren had appeared before her and buried a fist into her belly. Cassia spat blood as Darren finished out his punch, sending her bouncing across the stone floor until she rolled to a stop several paces away.

"Can't have you doing that," Darren said with a cocksure grin. "You've already been more than enough trouble."

Cassia trembled as she clutched her stomach and tried to push herself upright. But her arm gave out, and her cheek slapped hard against the ground, her head facing me. Her features were filled with pain and fatigue as she looked out at me.

"Arch-don..." Cassia croaked from the floor, unmoving. "R-Run."

Darren stepped before her and opened his hand. "Rule of Ruin Forty-Six, Bane's Blade."

The guy clearly had a favorite spell, and my guess was it was his most powerful one. But the fact he could call Bane's Blade three times in such a short period was stunning. Even with the Gate of Radiance open, that was an impressive feat. I certainly hadn't had such ability during the short time I was at the same gate, back in my youth.

The dark aura extended from his hand and condensed into the shape of a long blade made of oscillating black energy. Darren glared down at Cassia's fallen figure with a manic grin as he raised the black sword high over his head for the final blow.

"Ah-ah-ah."

Darren's body stiffened. Then he looked around, as if confused by the chiding voice, until his eyes landed on me. I was wagging my finger from the top of the rock. His brows furrowed in disbelief.

"That's far enough," I said.

The confusion on Darren's face held for a second longer before he broke into a mocking smile as if interested in seeing how this would play out. "Excuse me?" he said, almost polite.

I hopped off the rock. "That was a great fight," I said as I strolled over. "I enjoyed it thoroughly. Both of you did great. Darren, your spellcasting and halos are something to be marveled at." I looked over at Cassia as I came to a stop before them. "Cassia, you nearly managed to beat him with one gate less. That's incredible. But your problem was that you let him drag out the fight. The longer a fight goes on between opponents of different strengths, the greater chance for the weaker fighter to lose. What you should have done was run a distraction then hit him with everything you had in one go at the very beginning. But don't feel too bad. Your mistake was a classic one."

Darren narrowed his eyes at me. Perhaps it was the tone of my voice or my comment about the mistake that disoriented him. He let go of his spell, the dark sword evaporating in his hand, and turned his body to me as if I was a threat.

"I think it's time you told me who you are," he said, his tone cool and dangerous.

"Ah, don't worry, I have no intention to fight you and rescue the injured young lady here like a majestic moron with delusions of heroism. I'm just a tavern keeper—a businessman in other words—and I'd like to make a deal."

"A... tavern keeper?" Darren said in disbelief.

"Not just your average tavern keeper either. I brew my own ales. That's how seriously I take my business."

"Is this some kind of joke?"

"No joke. That young lady there," I said, pointing at Cassia, "is one of my barmaids, whom I'll be needing back, by the way. She's on her way to becoming a favorite among my patrons. If you kill her, it'll affect my business, and that's the last thing I want."

"You really are a fool, aren't you?" The smile returned to his face, his shoulders relaxing again. "I'm going to kill the both of you."

"Ah, but that's the last thing *you* want."

"Oh? And how do you figure that?" His expression was pure arrogance.

"The archbishop sent Templar Hightower to Meritas. It'd be mighty strange if she suddenly disappeared right after openly inquiring about orphans in your church, wouldn't it? Don't you think the archbishop would start a big investigation to find out what happened to her favorite templar?"

Darren frowned.

I smiled. "If you thought Cassia was a hindrance, you just wait till you have an official inquiry from the Chamber crawling up your ass. Bet they find some issues with your church right fast. But I think we can come to a satisfactory agreement. You let her leave with me, and I'll make her promise that she'll never bother you or your father again."

"Arch-don..." Cassia said.

Darren laughed. "I don't think you know this one well enough. She'll never give up the search for those orphans. Not unless she's dead."

"Oh, don't worry about that. I can be very persuasive. You see, Cassia here needs a favor from me. A very big favor that she won't get if she doesn't obey my orders."

"Arch—" Cassia began in absolute shock, immediately realizing I was referring to her original assignment to get me to save the kingdom of Lareinti by defeating an elder dragon. "You can't make me choose—"

"Oh, but I can!" I snapped. "This is the way of the world, Cassia. This is what happens when you are weak. You make hard choices, or you die, and this is the one you have to make now. You either forget about those orphans, or you can say goodbye to my help in the future and die right here and now. Which will it be?"

"I-I..." Cassia looked at me with wide eyes. I was asking her to choose between the lives of a few orphans and the lives of hundreds of thousands in Lareinti. I could see her mind fighting against itself, trying to understand, trying to come up with a solution, trying to find the right path.

"But..." Cassia began with a pleading voice. "But it's wrong. No life is more important than another's."

"Don't be naive!" I said, pointing at her accusingly. "This is the reality. These are the choices the weak must make every single day. There are no happy endings!"

Darren was watching our exchange with a widening smile made of cruel pleasure, like our argument was becoming an enjoyable show to him.

"Look at him!" I said, drawing my finger to Darren.

Cassia turned her eyes miserably to him.

"This is the kind of people that fill this world," I continued. "If you don't overcome your naivety, you will never be able to defeat people like him! Now choose!"

Tears of frustration spilled from Cassia's eyes. "I can't—"

Darren's smug grin revealed all his perfect teeth in an expression of pure pleasure as he peered down at Cassia.

"Rule of Ruin," I began.

Darren's face dropped as he heard my words and his eyes snapped to the finger pointed at him. Recognition flashed across his face. "Impos—"

"Sixty-One, Pointed Pillar."

Blue light exploded from my index finger in a single concentrated beam of power. It punctured Darren's chest like a spear going through rice paper and continued on, cutting through the wall behind him.

The light faded instantly, leaving him staring at me like a man who'd just had a hole blown through his body, which was precisely what had happened.

"—sible," he finished. Blood poured from his chest, and he fell backward to the ground.

Cassia wore an expression that nearly matched Darren's. She turned her bewildered eyes to me.

I rested a hand on my hip. "Aaand *that* is how you run a distraction."

CHAPTER 21: SOME ANSWERS

New tears flooded Cassia's eyes. "I thought you were really going to make me choose..."

I didn't want to say anything to that, so instead I asked, "How's the belly? Can you stand?"

"I'll need a minute," Cassia whispered, pushing herself up to a knee.

She was covered in scrapes and bruises, and she still clutched her abdomen, but I could already see that her strength was returning. From the moment she'd been punched, she had begun to regain her physical energy. That was the effect of having the Gate of Breath open. She'd even gathered some aura from the cracked Third Gate. However, from what I could tell, it was completely sealed again.

I winced and looked down at my hand, chuckling to myself. Then I caught Cassia looking up, and I quickly tucked my hand into my pants pocket. Gateless casters can't use high-tier spells because they don't have the halo reserves to learn and practice mastering them. Obviously, this fact didn't apply to someone who'd once had enormous reserves and two hundred years of practice. However, in truth, I hadn't been certain I would be able to pull off the spell.

Rule Sixty-One, Pointed Pillar, was not in fact meant to be used that way, but without my gates, it was the most powerful spell I could cast. I hadn't been lying when I told Cassia a weaker fighter should hit their opponent with everything they had from the get-go.

Pointed Pillar worked by condensing all of one's magical halos into a single point. With such minimal halos, however, I could only hold the spell for a split second, and it would have been easy to miss. But with the situation I'd set up with Darren, in which I openly pointed at his bare chest from only a few paces away, it was a guaranteed hit.

That being said, it was still an extremely difficult spell to pull off without any gates. My halo reserves were entirely drained, even though I'd held the spell for only a blink. My whole body shook from the exertion. The feeling was akin to having been starved for days. If Darren got up for a second time, I'd be in the same situation Cassia had been in only minutes earlier—completely helpless. But there was no chance of that.

I strolled over to him. The High Templar's back was against the floor, his face drained of color, and his eyes were barely open slits that watched me as I stepped before him. His wound was only a hole the thickness of my finger, but it was bleeding profusely, pooling around his body.

His voice was hoarse and strained as he said, "Wh-Who are you? T-Tell me."

"I told you. I'm a tavern keeper."

"You've d-defeated m-me," he said as if he was still having trouble believing the fact.

"Of course, I did. You may be a genius at spellcraft—only a few handfuls of people in the world can cast spells above Rule Forty without letting the destructive energies tear them apart, and you've done it with only three gates. But your skill is also your greatest weakness. You put too much weight on that one thing and grew overconfident. First, you underestimated Cassia, and when you didn't learn your lesson, you made the same mistake with me. I wouldn't lose to someone with a glaring inadequacy like that. What I want to know is who taught you such powerful spells when you clearly weren't ready for them."

Darren didn't reply, nor did he speak again. It appeared he wished to but didn't have the strength for it. He watched me until his eyes closed, and he fell into unconsciousness.

Cassia limped to my side. "Is he alive?"

"For another minute or two."

Cassia fell to her knees beside him and placed her hands over his wound.

"What are you doing?" I said in disbelief.

"He's lost a lot of blood," she said, concentrating. "He'll be no threat to us."

"If you save him, it'll be his word against ours."

"Celeru gave mercy to Daiboth on the Mountain of Death. We must do the same."

I sighed. "Fine, do what you want. I couldn't care less." I doubted she'd be able to save him, anyway.

"Spell of Lesser Binding, *Mend*," Cassia chanted, and her hands began to glow with a soft green light over Darren's wound. Slowly, it began to knit together.

Once again, I found myself impressed by the templar. It was a low-tier healing spell, but healing spells were the most difficult to master—it was far easier to destroy than to put back together. Despite all my years and experience, I was no better than she was at this type of magic. Her halos were spent, but healing magic didn't depend upon the body's aura, so it was the one spell she could still cast. Nevertheless, there was a fifty-fifty chance, at best, that she'd be able to save him.

In the end, Celeru came in on Darren's side. That damn bastard—always saving the wrong people. Cassia pulled her hands away and drew a breath of relief as Darren lay unconscious but alive.

"Your aim was incredible, Arch-don," Cassia said. "If you'd hit him only half an inch to the left or right, I wouldn't have been able to save him."

Oh great, I thought. *So it's my fault he pulled through.* I had, in fact, been aiming for his heart, but in my sorry gateless state, I couldn't properly control the spell, and my finger shook at the last moment, missing my intended mark.

"You knew you could defeat him from the beginning, didn't you?" Cassia said. Coming from anyone else, her words would have been an accusation given that I let her get beaten first, but she sounded as if she were in awe and praising me.

I shrugged. "I had a hunch. Met plenty of his type of personality before. But you can never be sure. And anyone who is sure will make the same mistake this idiot made."

Cassia smiled warmly at me, her eyes bright and blue, and it made me feel uncomfortable.

"So, uh… what would you like to do now?" I said.

Cassia nodded, shifting her focus, and a new look of hardened determination overcame her features. "Now we speak to the bishop."

"Figures." I looked between the two fallen men. "I don't think Darren's going to be waking up anytime soon. Guess we'd better get the other one to talk."

I kicked Drimdelon in the shin. He snapped awake with a yelp, saw us, and quickly searched the atrium for a view of his master. When he located Darren's unconscious body lying at his side, his face turned pale.

"Oh good, you're up," I said, leaning over him with a darkening smile. "The lady here would like some answers, Two-Leg."

CHAPTER 22: RECKONING

"**I** am Templar Cassia Hightower, and I stand before you on behalf of the archbishop!"

The two guards standing in front of Bishop Tamblion's doors looked uncertain of what to do.

"This man, here, has confessed to several crimes that implicate the bishop and his son, the high templar." She turned to the guard on the right. "You will send whoever you have to the atrium below the church and bring Darren Tamblion to the hospital wing. He is in critical condition." Then she turned to the guard on the left. "You will call the City Watch and the monastery guard and bring them here at once."

The guards were still watching her, dumbstruck. I couldn't say that I blamed them. She was quite the sight to behold, covered in wounds and grime while wearing a battered dress that somehow was still holding together by the thinnest of threads.

"I said, *at once,*" Cassia said in a way that was all the more dangerous because it was delivered quietly.

The two guards snapped to, suddenly terrified, and dashed off without a word. I grinned, kicked open the doors, and threw Drimdelon—who I'd been holding by the back of the neck—into the room.

Sitting on his throne was Bishop Tamblion. His face scrunched together with fury as he saw us enter. "How dare you enter unannounced! You!" he said, glaring at me. "I warned you! Guards! Arrest them!"

But the guards only gaped at Cassia. She looked like someone who not only had just walked out of battle but was ready to do more, and no one was going near that, especially since she was the only person in the room who had opened two gates. As I mentioned before, it was said that it took five spirited to defeat a radiant, but it would take a dozen unawakened to defeat a single breather.

The bishop glanced around at his men, growing ever more furious. "You will obey my authority!"

"You no longer have any authority!" Cassia said. "This is Drimdelon, a priest of your church and a servant of your son! He has admitted to selling orphans on the black market to criminal gangs."

"This is ridiculous. Nonsense! Lies!" Bishop Tamblion screamed. Then he turned his eyes to me. I was leaning against the wall, with my hands in my pockets, and grinning widely. "You!" The bishop pointed at me. "This is your doing. I know it! You are a spy, a troublemaker, here to disrupt my courts!"

"Oh, I'm much more than that," I said, grinning even wider. "I'm the guy who tried to kill your son."

Horror spread across the bishop's face. "What did you say?"

"Oh, don't worry. The good templar here decided to spare his life. But if it were left up to me, I would have finished the job."

"Where is he?" the bishop screeched. "Where is Darren?"

I only chuckled to myself.

"I've already sent guards to retrieve your son," Cassia said. "He will be taken to the hospital wing of the monastery and cared for. In the meantime, there are other matters we must discuss, Bishop."

The bishop completely disregarded her. "You heard him!" he screamed at his guards. "He's confessed to a crime! Arrest him!"

"Your son tried to murder me in cold blood," Cassia said, not batting an eye.

Once again, she didn't raise her voice. She was not impolite, cold, or angry. She said her words with disappointment and sadness, and it silenced the entire room.

Just then, both the monastery guard—the White Guardians—and a captain of the City Watch arrived. I was surprised by their speed, but then I remembered that there was a City Watch guards tower located just beside the church—the benefits of being a wealthy and centrally located establishment.

I saw that Cassia was aware of their presence, but she didn't turn to them. "Darren Tamblion sold orphans on the black market. Then he hired gang members to deceive me by making it appear as if they were the perpetrators. Darren brought the orphans back to the church with the intention of returning them to the syndicate he'd sold them to after he killed me. Luckily my... friend and I stopped him before this could be done." Cassia gestured to Drimdelon. "This man is a coconspirator of these crimes." Then she pointed at the man with the pointy hat. "And so are you, Bishop Tamblion."

The bishop turned white as Cassia said these words. "You lie!" he shouted after wavering for a second too long.

I pushed Drimdelon forward. He looked back at me with terror in his eyes before he limped forward toward the bishop, wincing with each step. "Master Tamblion... I'm sorry. I am so sorry." The bald priest began to cry. "I did everything that you and Master Darren told me to do. But they've beaten him and forced me to tell them everything."

The bishop glared at him, rage spilling from every pore of his body. "I do not know this man! I've never seen him in my life!"

Cassia turned to the church guards in the room. "Summon all administrative staff of the monastery. I shall appoint new leadership in the interim while this matter is resolved."

The guards quickly dispersed.

"What? You have no power to command anyone here!" The bishop was so red in the face that he was starting to look like he shared ancestry with a tomato.

Cassia glanced back at him. "Until the city and the archbishop have decided what to do with you, you will be confined to a cell."

"How dare you! First you arrest my son. Now you dare issue me commands. I am the bishop! I answer to no one!"

"You answer to Celeru!" Cassia said, sounding angry for the first time. "You have broken your vows." She turned to the captains of the White Guardians and the City Watch, who had arrived in time to hear the entire exchange. "Take him away. I believe both our organizations will want him for questioning."

The captains nodded to each other and moved toward the bishop. The bishop smiled as if he didn't believe they would dare touch him. It looked exactly like the smile Darren had worn before someone poked a hole through his chest. Then, as soon as hands lifted Tamblion up off his throne and dragged him away, he began to wail.

"Looks like you'll be losing the fancy hat," I whispered to him as he passed.

The monastery staff she'd summoned had begun to arrive, and they watched wide-eyed as their bishop was carried away in a screaming fit by armed guards.

Cassia stepped before them. "I am Templar Cassia Hightower," she said in a clear and even voice. "Bishop Tamblion and High Templar Darren Tamblion have been stripped of their positions for crimes against lost children."

A wave of shock fell over the church staff.

Cassia continued. "The image of our order will be tainted by their misdeeds. People will fear us and doubt us. And they will be right to. But we must prove that there is still goodness here. We will readily admit our failures. We will condemn them. And we will seek forgiveness. And all the while, we will work to better serve our communities and the Word of Celeru."

If anyone thought her ragged, barely clothed appearance to be scandalous, none showed it. Instead, they seemed mesmerized by her words. Emboldened. And hopeful. Cassia looked dazzling and radiant. She issued new commands and appointed new leaders for the church while they awaited directions from the archbishop in Yestereaster, who would be informed as soon as the messaging hawks had reached her.

Brother Erwel, who'd been in charge of the Department of Lost Children, was suspended and taken away by the guards for questioning. Cassia put Deacon Obi in charge of the department for the time being.

Next, she met with the captains of the City Watch and the White Guardians. Though the captain of the White Guardians had done as she instructed and arrested the bishop, the crimes had happened under his command, and he, too, was suspended. His lieutenant was appointed as the new captain to aid in overseeing the investigation. She then asked the new captain to station several guards around the orphanage to ensure the safety of the orphans until the investigation was concluded.

By the time she'd done enough to tide things over until the next day, the sun had set, and stars had taken to the night sky. Once again, we were going to be late returning to the tavern.

***

"Thank you for waiting," she said as we walked back toward the tavern together. "And thank you for everything else."

I shrugged. "I had fun."

Cassia gave me a look. "Fun?"

"Oh yeah. Watching you fight a high templar then watching the bishop get arrested and dragged out by his own guards—gods, I would have paid ten gold brilliances just for the news, but instead, I got to see it firsthand. It'll be a long while before I forget the look on his face when they took him away."

Cassia looked sad. "I didn't want to do it."

"Don't let it bother you. The bishop got what he deserved, though he'll probably never realize that he was in the wrong."

"That is how evil begins. When you think you are wholly right and incapable of being wrong."

"Wise words," I said. "Took me many decades to learn that one."

Cassia smiled at me. Then she collapsed. I caught her before she could hit the ground.

"I'm sorry," she mumbled. "I'm..."

"You're exhausted. Tends to happen when you have a fight to the death against an awakened with an extra gate." I put her arms around my neck, picked her up by her thighs, and carried her against my back.

She didn't protest, though she probably would have if she'd had the strength to. Then I felt something soft and warm pressing against my shoulder blades as I walked. Heat rose to my cheeks.

"You're a good person, Arch-don. Even if you won't admit it."

"Uh, what? Did you say something?" My mind was occupied with a specific sensation.

Cassia chuckled. It was a pretty sound.

"What are you laughing about—ah, don't wrap your arms so tightly around—ah! Stop laughing. Hey! Now you're just doing it on purpose!"

After several minutes, she caught her breath. "I know why you made me fight Darren on my own."

"So that you'd be exhausted, and I'd get to feel your chest against my back as I carried you home?"

Cassia chuckled again. "No. You remind me of my instructor, Lord Theodore Strongarm. Have you heard of him?"

"Yeah, I know that brat. He was your instructor?"

"B-Brat? You've met him, Arch-don?"

"He challenged me to a sword fight once."

"Lord Strongarm p-picked a fight with you?"

"This was many years ago," I said. "I guess there was a young lady he wanted to impress."

"How long ago was this?"

"About thirty years ago."

"Thirty years?" Cassia exclaimed. "He challenged the Storm-blood when he was just twenty-one years of age?"

"Please, it's just Arch," I whispered and took a look around to make sure no one heard us.

"Of course, Arch-don. My apologies," Cassia said from my shoulder. "What was the outcome, if you don't mind my asking…?"

I grinned. "What do you think? I beat his ass. Probably overdid it a little."

"I see..." Cassia said as if she'd come to an understanding. My guess was that Theo hadn't had many kind words for me over the years.

"I saw him fight again in the Tournament of Masters in Yestereaster some years ago," I said. "He was quite good, a lot better than when we had our match anyway."

"He's the best swordsman alive today, Arch-don!" Cassia said with a bit more energy, and I felt her leaning over on my back to make the point. "He won that tournament!"

"Mmm," I said, not wishing to have a debate on the subject.

The Tournament of Masters was held at Yestereaster every five years and brought together the winners of city tournaments from across the continent of Visseria. Even foreign countries like Lareinti sent their top warriors to the tournament. The winners of the Tournament of Masters were certainly capable fighters but not necessarily the best in the world. After all, not every great fighter attended the tournament.

Cassia laid her head back on my shoulder. "Master Strongarm used to do the same thing you did when I trained with him."

"What's that?"

"He made me fight tough opponents and gave me pointers as I fought them. You were teaching me how I could defeat someone several times stronger." She leaned against my back, and I felt her lips brush against my neck as she spoke. It sent tingles down my body. "Thank you," she said quietly.

I nearly forgot to respond, but then I said, "Pff. I was just thinking aloud like you would if you were watching a game of kickball. You shouldn't read goodness in everything I do, especially when it's not there."

But she had dozed off while I was talking.

"Damn it. That's not fair, Cassia. You've gotta at least give me a chance to reply." I sighed, and like the first night we'd met, I felt as if she had somehow defeated me.

CHAPTER 23: THE LAKE AND THE STARS

Since the Tipsy Pelican Tavern was closed on Awndays, the tavern was quiet and dark as I approached with Cassia sleeping on my back.

"My gods, Cassia!" Elsa exclaimed when we entered the tavern. She rushed forward and put a palm against Cassia's sleeping face.

Charm came out of the back room and looked at me with questioning eyes as if she was thinking, *What has Master done to this poor girl?*

"Nothing! I was helping her!" I said.

Charm actually had the gall to raise an eyebrow at me.

"What happened?" Elsa asked.

"She got into a fight," I said. "She's all right, but she's got some cuts and bruises that need tending to. Charm, could you boil some water and get some ice?"

Charm nodded and disappeared into the kitchen.

"Sorry about the dress," I said to Elsa as I carried Cassia up the stairs to the bedrooms. "Things got a little crazy."

"Don't worry about the dress. Tell me what happened. You two disappeared. I thought Charm was going to murder both of you by the way she was cutting the vegetables tonight. Never knew she was the jealous type."

I chuckled tiredly. *She still might kill me even after hearing the story.*

I took Cassia to her room and laid her down on the bed, taking care to keep my right hand out of Elsa's sight. The burning sensation coming from my finger was giving me the sweats, but Elsa probably just assumed my appearance was from carrying Cassia to the tavern. I began telling Elsa the official version of the story that Cassia and I had agreed upon. I described how we'd followed our stalker and how Cassia had sensed him, chased him to the atrium, and then fought and defeated High Templar Darren Tamblion single-handedly. Charm caught the end of the story as she entered Cassia's room with a bucket of ice and a pot of hot water.

Cassia had been against lying and taking credit for defeating the High Templar, but I finally convinced her after explaining how much of a problem it would be if word got around that I knew how to fight. There would be questions, and if anyone discovered my identity, I'd probably have to close the tavern and go into hiding. I still had enemies in the world, and they were not the sort of people you'd want to find you while you were mortal and gateless. Plus, it was Cassia's fault that I'd gotten mixed up in the situation in the first place, so the least the white templar could do was tell a white lie.

"Um..." I said, looking at Elsa and Charm, who were tending to Cassia. "If you two don't mind, I'll leave it to you..."

"Of course," Elsa said.

Charm nodded again and dipped a clean towel in the water, while Elsa began to take Cassia's dress off.

I quickly turned, blood rushing to my face. "I'll be in my room."

I grabbed a couple of cubes of ice from the bucket and closed the door behind me. I took a deep breath and headed to my bedroom, pressing the ice to my finger. It had been hurting badly since the walk back, and I began to wonder if I would be able to keep it.

***

Sometime later, I heard a knock at my door. I sat up, but before I could answer, Charm entered. "What really happened, Master?"

"Oh... not much."

"Master defeated the high templar, didn't he?"

"Well, she nearly had it handled," I said. "I just helped finish it up at the end."

"Did Master wet the bed?"

"What?" Then I noticed a puddle in my bed from the ice that I'd taken. I'd fallen asleep with it in my hand. "Oh, that's just ice. I uh... needed to cool my head. You two got to undressing Cassia quickly, and she's a pretty—"

"Show me."

Damn. She'd noticed. I sighed and lifted my hand, showing my finger. It was dark black, burnt to a crisp.

Charm knelt beside me and took my hand into her fingers. "Blessing of Supreme Healing, *Ameliorate*," she whispered, and a pink light glowed around her hands. A minute later, my finger was back to normal again, if a little stiff.

"Thanks," I said.

"Master should not use such dangerous spells in his current state."

She was right, of course. High-level spells were not meant to be used by the unawakened. Even with the Gate of Radiance open, the spell would have done damage to my body.

"I know," I said. "I got carried away."

"Master's body is very weak."

"Yes, yes…"

"Weak like a baby kitten."

"Right…"

"That was born with brittle bones."

"Yeah, I got it."

"And a failing heart."

"Okay! Enough already, I'm starting to feel bad for the kitten!"

"Master is the kitten. If Master decides to use expert spells, he should open at least to the Fifth Gate, if not the Seventh Gate."

"That's not going to happen," I said. "I doubt I could even if I wanted to, anyway."

"Then why is Master fighting high templars while he is on vacation?"

"That's the question I keep asking myself."

"That is not an answer."

"Well, if you really want to know, I didn't have much of a choice."

"If Master is going to be a hero again, he should do it properly. If something happens to him, others will suffer too." Charm stood.

"Is that a threat?"

Charm watched me, her face revealing nothing. Then she turned to leave without another word.

I sighed once more. "Goodnight, Charm. Thank you for fixing my hand."

Charm looked at me one last time and closed the door behind her. I lay back on my bed. I didn't want to think about Charm's words or Cassia's. And as usual, it was easy not to... at least until I dreamed, in any case.

That night I saw my father again on the waters of the dark lake. "You did well today," he said.

I snorted. "Did well with what? Killing some idiot?"

"You didn't kill him. Your attack wasn't fatal."

"It was meant to be."

"You helped those children."

"No, I didn't."

"You are too hard on yourself, son. Of course, you did. Without you, they—"

"I would have made the deal," I said, cutting him off.

"The deal?"

"I would have forced Cassia to drop the issue about the orphans in return for our lives. The only reason I didn't was because I knew a bastard like Darren wouldn't have let us live."

My father stared at me.

"When I mentioned that the archbishop would come to investigate if Cassia disappeared, I saw it in his eyes. There was only a moment of hesitation, then it passed. He was going to kill us both. If he'd taken my deal, I wouldn't have fought him. I could not care less about those orphans."

My father shook his head. "That's not true. I know you."

"Oh yeah? What do you know?"

"Orphans, children who have lost their parents—it is something you care for deeply."

"And why's that?" I said, a manic grin spreading across my face.

"Because..."

"Because what?" I shouted. "Say it!"

"Because... you are an orphan too."

"Then what are you?"

My father blinked at me. "I am your—"

"No, you're not, you fool. I'm not just an orphan," I said, growing even more heated. "I'm an orphan that never knew his parents!"

"But—"

"You're just a figment of my imagination. Something I created for myself. You are a lie, but I did not create you to lie to me. I don't need you to tell me that I did something good to make me feel better about myself. I'm fine with knowing the truth. I don't care. I don't care about the templar or any of her wishes to do good. I helped her today on a whim because it was amusing to me, and that's it. It's the same reason I created you. But now I'm done with you."

"Wait," he said.

But I didn't. I waved him off, and my imaginary father vanished into nothingness.

Then I woke up. It was still dark outside my window. I stared through the glass at the stars for several long moments. My mind was filled with dark thoughts, and I had difficulty falling asleep again.

I tossed and turned in my bed before I remembered something extremely important: Cassia had agreed to wear Elsa's dresses for an entire week. Even the truly scandalous ones. This thought improved my mood, and I had wonderful dreams that I did not wish to wake from for the rest of the night.

CHAPTER 24: THE SUMMERFEST ALE COMPETITION (ARC 3)

"**M**aster Arch, it is a fine evening, yet you seem to be in a dark mood, standing here alone at your bar. Perhaps you wouldn't mind sharing your thoughts? I have a good ear to lend in times of trouble."

Galston the Gallant stood across from me with a mug of Honey-dew Lager in his hand. He'd come to the tavern three times in the last week since the news of Cassia's arrest of the bishop had spread. Each time, he had brought Cassia anti-scarring salves, potions, and other gifts while offering his services to help her in any way he could. The man was clearly smitten, but all in all, he seemed like a good guy and I was happy to have his presence at the tavern.

All right, to be honest, I was mainly happy to have his presence because his celebrity status as the winner of the Tournament of Heroes in Meritas boosted foot traffic to the tavern—and therefore sales—immensely. The tavern's barroom had been packed wall-to-wall after his first night there, when he had openly declared he would be returning later in the week.

Now he was standing next to me, asking me why I was troubled. But could I tell him the truth? Would he understand?

I looked at the tall, stocky champion with his thick bushy eyebrows shaped like lightning bolts. And there, in his dark-brown eyes, I saw a man I could trust.

"It's... it's about Cassia," I said quietly.

"Ah, yes," Galston said. "The business with the church. A foul affair indeed. I cannot imagine what it was like to watch her fight the high templar alone. But in the end, she prevailed despite the advantage of her foe." He turned to look at her with admiration.

Cassia was busy serving drinks at another table, as were the rest of the ladies, even Charm. Each was running back and forth with beers and plates of food that we had prepared earlier in the day. The sudden surge in business meant it was all hands on deck. But I was behind the bar, moping.

"That's not what I mean," I replied. "Look at her, Galston! Surely, a man of your stature would understand!"

Galston glanced at me uncertainly, then he turned his eyes to Cassia again. She was in the middle of taking orders from a young couple who had just found a table after waiting for twenty minutes. The injuries from her fight had not yet fully healed. She wore bandages beneath one of Elsa's black evening gowns. I rated it as the second best dress Elsa owned. The first one, the white dress, had taken too much damage during Cassia's fight against Darren and had to be discarded.

I'd begged Charm to heal Cassia, but she'd denied my request, stating that she didn't want Cassia aware of her abilities and that Cassia's injuries would heal on their own without issue.

"I'm not sure what you are referring to, Master Arch," Galston said as he watched Cassia. "I can see that she has suffered minor injuries, but she still looks stunning as ever in that captivating dress."

"Yes, the dress! Do you know the pains I've had to go through to get her to wear that dress?"

Galston blinked and shook his head.

I looked around to make sure Charm wasn't nearby. "Well, it was a lot—trust me. A lot, alright?"

"And so she is wearing it," Galston said, still not understanding.

"Galston!" I exclaimed with shock. "I thought you were a man of intelligence and wisdom—a man who could see the truth of things—a scholar of beauty! I could only get her to wear the dress for one week. Today is the last day of our arrangement. But now imagine if I could have had two weeks?"

"Two weeks?" Galston's great eyebrows twisted. He looked at Cassia again. Then his mouth dropped. "Dear gods... she would have healed in two more days, and the bandages would be... gone. And if she wore that dress..."

"That's right, Galston! You think her stunning now, but she's essentially been wearing the dress over a sweater of bandages this entire week! It is a crime against eyesight! Just imagine how she'd look without that turtleneck beneath the dress!"

The big man's cheeks turned pink. "Dear gods..." Galston muttered again, and he took a deep swig of Honeydew from his mug. "I can see why you are in a dark mood, Master Arch."

I crossed my arms and nodded Finally, I had found a comrade to share my pain. "Yes," I said. "If I could only figure out some way to prolong my agreement with her."

"You must think of something, Master Arch," Galston said, turning to me with sudden graveness. "I will support you fully."

I nodded back with equal gravitas. "I know. But what can be done?"

"Perhaps you could use the same method as before to secure another week?"

"I put myself at great risk last time. I do not know if—"

Bam! Someone slammed a pitcher right in front of us, making us jump.

"The pumpkin ale that Master asked for," Charm said flatly. Then she ran her eyes between me and the tournament champion. "Why does it look like Master is plotting something evil with Mr. Galston?"

Both Galston and I held up our hands innocently.

"Not at all, Mistress," Galston said. "We were merely engaging in a friendly conversation..."

"Yes," I said. "We were talking about the, uh... upcoming Summerfest competition. Isn't that right, Champion Galston?"

"Yes, yes, indeed!" Galston said. "Master Arch was just describing the competition. Sounds like a grand time. Please, Master Arch, you must tell me more about the heroic fighters of the competition. Perhaps I will enter as well, ha ha ha."

I paled but quickly recovered. "Ah, you joke, Champion. The heroic fighter will be an ale that I've concocted, as this is the Summerfest Brewmaster's Best *Ale* Cup, where the best ale will be chosen as the winner, but you know this well because I've been talking to you about it for the past several minutes, and that's why you made that funny joke, ha ha ha."

"Why yes! Of course, Master Arch, that is exactly what happened! I am glad you saw the humor of my joke. Of course, I will not be competing because it is an ale competition, ha ha ha."

Charm squinted at us with deadly suspicion for a long moment. Finally, she said, "I hope Master is preparing properly. It is only two weeks away." Then she turned away to attend to the customers.

Both Galston and I leaned over the bar and took a deep breath of relief.

"I don't know why, but that little one frightens me," Galston said. "It was as if a band of Night Cult assassins had set their killing intent upon me."

"Consider yourself lucky. We have just touched Death's Door and not fallen through."

***

The next morning, I woke early and headed downstairs to the basement of the tavern to determine my next steps. The basement was a large space with a tall ceiling and walls made of brick and timber. A myriad of channels and pipes ran up and down pillars and across the ceiling to transfer liquids as the ale passed through the various stages of brewing. The process began in the basement and ended upstairs in the storage room, where it was stored once the ales were properly fermented and carbonated.

My equipment was entirely state of the art, and some were trade secrets that I'd built by hand. But despite all my advanced methodology and brewing equipment, I was hitting a wall with my latest ale. For the past two months, I'd been experimenting with the pumpkin ale, but it still wasn't hitting the mark. The series of small batches I had made were good and improving. The ale contrasted nicely against the Honeydew Lager, offering a stronger and richer flavor. However, it was not a better beer as a whole. Something was lacking.

To win the brewmaster's competition, I needed something that would steal the show. But there were only two weeks until the festival, which was exactly the minimum amount of time it would take to brew a new batch of ale.

I needed to come up with the final recipe that day. But my latest batch, which I'd made two weeks prior, tasted unsatisfactory. The pumpkin flavor was plentiful, and the ale wasn't too sweet or too bitter. The flavor just wasn't attention grabbing enough. Simply put, it was almost forgettable. I poured myself a glass from the pumpkin ale barrel and tasted it again, hoping to find the missing element. But I couldn't figure out what the right choice would be. "Honeyflower?" I said to myself. "Or perhaps cinnamon?"

I heard footsteps coming down the stairs, and I saw that it was Charm. "Master is awake early today," she said.

"It's the last day for me to finalize the recipe."

"Charm thinks Master should not risk it and should submit the Honeydew instead."

"The Honeydew lost last time. I've got to come up with something better."

"Master has improved upon the Honeydew since then. He must not lose to Boreas."

"I know, I know," I said, still thinking. After a moment, I looked up and saw that Charm was still there. "Oh, sorry, Charm. Was there something you needed?"

"Actually, Charm was wondering if there was anything she could do to help Master with preparations for the contest."

I blinked. That was probably the first time I'd ever heard Charm offer her help for the tavern. Or if memory served, for anything.

"Uhh, here, try this," I said, giving her the glass of pumpkin ale I'd just poured.

She took it but didn't drink right away. Instead, she eyed it with growing suspicion.

"It's not poisonous!" I exclaimed.

She nodded and took a small sip. Then she nodded again.

"Well?" I said. "What do you think?"

"It is good."

"Better than the Honeydew?"

"No."

I hung my head. "I thought so too…"

"Only Boreas's Cherry Purple Ale is comparable to Master's Honeydew."

"That's the one he won with last time," I said. "But he probably has something even better now."

Charm shook her head. "He does not. Charm has done reconnaissance."

"You what?"

"Charm went to the Sword and Shield Brewing House the night Master was out gallivanting with Miss Cassia."

"I was not gallivanting! Wait… you went to Boreas's tavern?"

Charm nodded sagely. "Charm tested each of his newest beers."

"And…?" I said, leaning forward in my seat.

"None of the new ones are very good. Only the Cherry Purple is a worthy opponent."

"The Cherry Purple, huh?"

"Charm thinks Master's updated Honeydew can beat the Cherry Purple this time. But it matters not, because Charm does not think Boreas will enter the Cherry Purple as he already won with it last year."

"So, you're saying if I enter the Honeydew again, I can win?"

Charm nodded. "The Honeydew is much improved since last year."

I sighed. "You're right, but it doesn't feel right to enter the same ale twice. I won second place last year. It'd be unfair to use the same one again. I doubt any of the other brewers will reenter old ales."

"Master must not lose again."

I looked at her, depressed. *Where is this pressure coming from?* Then I remembered that Charm had always been highly competitive, even when we'd first met.

"I'll come up with something," I said. "Just wish I had a few more days."

But there really was no more time. An ale took at least fourteen days to make, and I had exactly fourteen days until the competition. I had to start brewing now.

"Is there anything else Charm can do?" Charm asked.

"I'm going to enter the pumpkin ale, Charm. You can come up with the snack to go along with it."

Charm perked up at this and nodded.

I sighed. "Guess I'll infuse it with cinnamon." I stood and got to work.

Five days later, I changed my mind.

CHAPTER 25: AN OFFICIAL TAVERN EMERGENCY OF THE HIGHEST ORDER

The problem with using cinnamon was the heat. Meritas was the southernmost city of Adentris, and its summers were scorchers. Cinnamon was a unique and novel brewing spice. However, it did not have the refreshing effect I needed for a summer ale.

I realized the mistake during a visit to the market with Cassia. Once again, we were shopping for our weekly food supplies, and since Cassia had been a big hit with the shopkeepers—which, in turn, meant a small hit to my wallet—I decided to bring her along again.

After picking up the usual supplies, we headed back toward the tavern with our arms full. Before even reaching the halfway mark, both of us were already drenched in sweat from the late-morning sun, so we decided to stop at a snack stall on the road for a rest and a bite.

Cassia ordered a cinnamon bun and a glass of iced water. I was severely dehydrated, so without thinking much, I asked for the same. After our orders came and I had downed the glass of water, I realized that I did not want the cinnamon bun at all. I had eaten the bun at this snack stall before, and I remembered enjoying it, but I could already imagine the burning taste of cinnamon against my tongue. Under the sweltering sun, that was the last thing I wanted.

I glanced at the menu and opted for vanilla ice cream instead. There were several flavors, but vanilla was the easiest to pick with my sun-fried brain. I knew what I was getting, and I knew it would be cold.

But before my vanilla ice cream arrived, I jumped up and let out a mournful, wailing scream that made Cassia jump, causing her to drop her unfinished cinnamon bun. It bounced on the ground and rolled away. Without saying another word, I took off running back toward the market.

"Arch-don!" Cassia called from behind, but I paid her no attention. Time was of the essence.

I arrived at the pumpkin tent and pointed at the shopkeeper. "You!"

"Eh?" the old man with the wide brim straw hat said, looking up from his seat.

"I need your pumpkins. All of them!"

"All of them?"

"All of them!"

The contest would require several barrels of ale. I had used a restaurant supplier for the previous batches, but an order from the supplier took three days for delivery. The old pumpkin man scowling at me was my only hope.

"You're serious?" he said, peering at me.

"As death. And I need them now."

"Fine. That'll be two shims."

"Two silver shimmers?" I said, my jaw dropping.

"That's what I said."

"There can't be more than a single shim's worth here."

The old man nodded. "There are thirty-two coppers' worth, to be exact."

"Then what am I paying another shim and eight burns for?" A silver shimmer was worth forty copper burnishes.

"That's a surcharge for me to overcome my distaste for you."

"What?" I said, surprised.

"You've been buying pumpkins from me for the past month, and each time, you've come down to the market with a new lady at your side, you scoundrel!"

"New lady..." Then I realized that I indeed had come with Charm, Elsa, and now Cassia. "Wait... this is a misunderstanding. They are simply my employees—"

"Employees? You expect me to believe a brat like you happens to run the type of business that can attract such benevolent and innocent beauties to work for you?" He jabbed an accusing finger at me. "I don't know what you've been doing to these poor women and my pumpkins, but I am against it, I tell you!"

"*And your pumpkins?* Hey, wait a minute, now. What are *you* suggesting?"

No, really, old man, I thought, *what are you suggesting? What could I possibly be doing with these girls and the pumpkins?* Although it was indeed true that I had bought pumpkins from him each time I'd come to the market with a new young woman.

"If you want these pumpkins, it'll be two shims and no less!" he spat.

"Damn old man, calling me a brat—not even a third of my age, I bet," I muttered as I dug out the coinage. I was short on the patience to argue, and I was even shorter on time.

I slapped two shims on the counter. The old man grabbed for them, but I pulled them out of reach with my fingers. "I'll give you two shims, but I want these pumpkins delivered to Kerrytown in Southbank."

The old man's eyes narrowed. "I don't do deliveries."

"For two shims, you will."

"I already told you, that's the surcharge. You want delivery, I'll take another shim."

"I'm already paying you a shim extra!" I said. "Tell you what—if you deliver them to the Tipsy Pelican Tavern in Kerrytown within the next two hours, you'll get to see with your own eyes that all three ladies are well and happy to be working for me."

The old man squinted. "They'll all be there?"

"In the next two hours, they will be." I lifted my hand off the two silver coins.

The old man frowned beneath his straw hat, then he looked down at the two coins and took them. "Very well. You'll get your delivery."

I nodded and headed toward the tavern. Then I realized that I had left Cassia at the snack stall without any money and all the bags. But before I reached the stall, I saw her heading down the street in my direction, carrying all our groceries. She didn't look tired, but sweat was soaking through her blouse.

I quickly took my half of the bags from her. "Sorry about ditching you. I had to order more pumpkins."

"Oh. Is everything okay?"

"No, not really. We've got to hurry back. There's a lot of work to be done. How much do I owe you for the snacks?"

"Oh, um... well, the owner thought you ran off on me with the bill, so he didn't charge me. I tried to pay, but he wouldn't take my money."

Of course, that was what happened. Everyone was much too nice to Cassia. I sighed. "If you only had come with me to get the pumpkins too. I really could have used your presence."

"Ah... well, then he started talking with me, and since he wouldn't take my money, I felt bad about leaving abruptly."

As if on cue, we passed by the snack bar, and the owner popped his head out, locking gazes with me. He then saw Cassia and looked back at me, frowning with distaste. I realized that I had been to his snack bar with both Charm and Elsa as well. *Oops.*

***

Charm and Elsa were cleaning the bar area when we returned to the tavern.

"Listen up," I said. "Something terrible has happened, and we are now in a dire situation. I hereby call an official tavern emergency of the highest order!"

Elsa and Charm stopped what they were doing and headed to the staff dining table. Cassia seemed a little surprised and uncertain of what to do, but she quickly joined them at the table.

I stood at the front of the table with my arms crossed. "Let the record show that all staff members are in attendance for this emergency meeting."

"There are no records being kept, Master."

"Well, they are in my head!"

Cassia looked worried. "What could have happened?"

"Don't get too excited," Elsa said. "Last time Heru called a 'tavern emergency,' it was because he couldn't find his socks."

"They were my favorite socks! And they're still missing, by the way! Anyway, that's all beside the point. I have terrible news to share with you, my Tipsy Pelican comrades!" I leaned forward, giving each of them my somber gaze to let them know the seriousness of the situation.

Elsa smiled. Charm looked as placid as ever. Cassia was filled with worry.

"The cinnamon-infused pumpkin ale cannot be our entrant to the Summerfest's Brewmaster's Best Ale Cup!" I declared.

"I guess that is an emergency in a way..."

"What is Master saying exactly?"

"That's terrible news. What's wrong with the pumpkin ale?"

"Cinnamon is not a desirable taste in the summer heat," I said. "Perhaps it could be something to try in winter, but not now."

"Will we enter the Honeydew Lager, then?" Elsa asked.

Charm nodded.

I shook my head. "No true brewmaster reenters previous brews, and neither will we."

"Master," Charm said with a hint of worry. "Ale takes at least a week to ferment and a week to carbonate. We will not have enough time to make another batch. In addition, although we have plenty of grain and hops, we do not have any other ingredients to create something new."

I grinned. "In less than an hour, the cranky pumpkin man will arrive with a cartload of fresh pumpkins."

"Heru's still going to make a pumpkin ale?" Elsa said.

"Not just me. It's all hands on deck! Every second will count if we want to make it on time. But this time, it won't be cinnamon as the final ingredient. We'll be using vanilla."

"Vanilla?" Charm said with an arched brow.

"A common ingredient that we have plenty of. The smoothness of the pumpkin will combine with the smoothness of the vanilla to create a highly desirable and highly drinkable ale!" I dropped my voice for emphasis on my last point: "And most importantly, it'll be served *extra cold*."

"Mmm, that does sound good," Elsa said.

"I'll help in any way I can, Arch-don," Cassia said, standing. "Just tell me what I can do."

I nodded. "Cassia, I want you to bring six bags of grain down to the basement. Elsa, start milling it as Cassia brings it to you. Charm, heat the oven and start the kettle fire. We'll need to bake the pumpkin first then add it to the mash."

"Let's do this!" Elsa said with an energetic fist pump. Then Cassia and Elsa disappeared into the storage room to gather the grains.

Charm rose from her seat but didn't leave right away. "Master," she said once Elsa and Cassia were out of earshot. "The problem of the brewing time is still unresolved. The competition is in nine days. At best, the fermentation will be complete, but there will not be enough time for the carbonation. The beer will be flat."

I grinned. "Don't you know who I am?"

"Master is Archibold Stormbl—"

I clasped over her mouth. "Don't say it so simply!"

"Mester 'sked m—" Charm mumbled behind my hand.

"Yes, I know what I asked! It was a rhetorical question."

Charm gave me her signature half-lidded gaze.

"I'm saying, trust me, Charm," I said, putting my hand on her shoulder. "I'm not going to make a stale ale. We're going to win that trophy."

A moment passed, and I dropped my hand as I realized I'd touched her without thinking. She was looking at me, and I thought we might have another disagreement. We'd lived in Meritas for more than a year, and she'd been unhappy with me since before we arrived.

But Charm didn't disagree or sulk. She merely took the time to stare into my eyes. Then with a nod, she said, "I trust you." With that, she turned and headed to the basement to start the kettle fires.

~MENU~

CHAPTER 26: PUMPKINS, PUMPKINS, PUMPKINS (AND GAS)

"By gods, what is this place?" The old pumpkin man in the straw hat stood at the entrance of the basement's stairwell, looking down at us.

"This place is off limits! You're trespassing!" I snapped.

"Trespassing?" said the old man, a big frown forming on his face. "I've been knocking at your door for ten minutes! I came down here out of courtesy since it seemed you wanted these pumpkins so badly at the market! If you don't..."

He stopped talking as I finished pumping water into the big mash pot from a pipe that ran up through the basement's ceiling. It was connected to the well behind the tavern and pulled a steady stream of water as I pumped.

"Gods, what dark arts are you crafting down here with these contraptions?" he said.

"They are not contraptions. It's proprietary machinery, and if you tell a soul about their designs, I'll have you sued!"

"Oh, hello Mr. Oakdigger," Cassia said after she finished a spell on the chillers that I'd asked her to help me with. "Please, let me help you unload the pumpkins."

Of course, Cassia knew his name.

"Miss Hightower, what a pleasant surprise!"

What surprise? I thought. *I told you she was going to be here, you old coot.*

"Charm, you'd better go with Cassia," I said. Charm was crouched beside me, helping me stack firewood below the kettle. "We've got to get those pumpkins roasted as quickly as possible."

Charm nodded and headed up the stairs.

"How are you doing over there, Elsa?" I said.

She was sitting at the mill, making rotations with the grinder. She let out a breath. "I can't feel my left arm, but it's done."

"You did good." I saw that the fire Charm had started under the mash pot was picking up, and the water was beginning to steam. "All right. Let's add these grains and start the mash."

An hour later, Cassia and Charm came down with steaming plates of pumpkin from the oven. By then, I had filtered out the grain and pumped the dark, boiled liquids from the mash pot to the massive kettle pot in the center of the basement. I threw blocks of timber into the fire beneath the kettle while Elsa helped me fan the flames.

"By gods! What poisons are you concocting?"

I looked up and saw the old man carrying a plate of roasted pumpkin as well. Apparently, he had stayed behind to help the ladies. *Of course, he did.*

"It's not poison, you daft old man!" I said. "It's ale!"

"Ale, you say…" The old man came over to get a whiff of the steam rising from the kettle pot. "The ladies did say you were a brewer, though I have difficulty believing it." Then he gave me a once-over. "And I never heard that the brewer has to be a naked pervert to do it."

You're the pervert, you old pumpkin weirdo. And I was only half-naked. The basement was generally much cooler than the floors above, but I was sweating from the heat of the kettle fire.

"Only my shirt's off—and you're not supposed to be down here!" I shot Charm a look.

Charm betrayed no emotion on her face but pointed a stealthy finger at Cassia, who noticed.

"We needed the help, Arch-don," Cassia said. "And I don't think he'll understand much about your brewing equipment even if he sees it."

"All right, fine, but hurry. We need to add the pumpkins. The wort's already been heated with the first round of hops and molasses."

Charm and Cassia moved quickly and dumped the pumpkins into the kettle pot. Then they went back upstairs to gather the rest. The old man dumped his, too, but not before giving me another look of suspicion. Then I began to stir the kettle in great big circles. A couple hours later, we ran the wort through the chillers that cooled the liquid thanks to Cassia's spells and then into the fermenter, a big ceramic barrel, where we added the yeast and tightened the lid closed.

"By gods, I say we've created a wonderful ale. Good job to everyone!" the old pumpkin man said. For some reason, he was still here.

"*We*? What *we*? Don't you mean 'you'?" I said.

"These are my pumpkins in this barrel, lest you forget," the old pumpkin man said with a sniff. "The heart and soul I put into farming my pumpkins played as much of a part as any of your work. In any case, I'd better be off. See you lovely ladies at the festival! I am certain our ale will win first place!"

It was rare for me to have violent outbursts, but in that body-fatigued, sweat-drenched moment, I wanted nothing more than to smash some pumpkins.

***

A week passed, and sure enough, word had gotten around about a new pumpkin-brewed ace in the hole that I had up my sleeve for the

Summer Festival Brewmaster's Best Ale Cup, no doubt thanks to the old pumpkin man blabbing his mouth off.

On the seventh and final night of fermentation, Boreas, the owner of the Sword and Shield House and last year's winner of the brewmaster's ale competition, visited my tavern. I'd been checking on the ale in the basement, and I found him in the bar after I came back up. He was drinking the Honeydew Lager.

I walked up to his table and offered my hand. "Master Boreas. How nice of you to visit."

Boreas ignored my hand and took a sip of the Honeydew. "I don't know how you can charge for this," he said, setting it down with an expression of distaste. "But I heard you've made a pumpkin ale." He made a show of looking around at the other customers in the tavern. "I don't see anyone drinking it. And your waitress wouldn't serve it to me when I ordered it."

"Oh, that's because it's not ready yet. We brewed it just last Rathday."

Boreas snorted. "A week ago? You won't have time for carbonation... so you aren't entering it in the competition." Then he looked down at his mug of Honeydew. "You are aware there's a new rule for this year's competition. Contestants are barred from submitting previous entries."

I said nothing, but I hadn't known that. I was relieved that we'd decided to go ahead and brew the new pumpkin ale.

"Good thing too," Boreas continued as he looked into his mug. "This Honeydew tastes the same as last time—like piss." He turned the mug and let it pour onto the ground of the tavern and over my boots.

"Elsa!" I called. "Can we get a refill? Master Boreas accidentally spilled his drink!"

If the tavern wasn't aware of Boreas's presence before, they were now.

Boreas smiled with his mouth only, but his eyes remained hard and empty. "No, thank you. I must be on my way. What do I owe you for the..." He took a look down at the spilled Honeydew. "Water?"

"Water's free," I said. "And the first beer's on the house for any fellow brewer."

Boreas got up and left without turning back. I watched him go. Elsa arrived beside me with a pitcher of the Honeydew.

"What an arsehole," she said under her breath. "You know, he had the gall to ask me for your recipe."

"How much did he offer you?"

Elsa smiled. "He lowballed. Ten shims."

"Guess we're moving up in the world. Last year, he offered Charm three."

"We're going to win, right, Heru?"

"You bet we are."

***

It was past midnight, and the tavern had emptied. Everyone had washed and gone to bed, myself included. But I had lain awake, waiting, and now the time had come.

I headed down to the basement and checked on three separate barrels. The first was a ceramic barrel that contained my pumpkin ale. The fermentation had been completed. Typically, the next step was to add more yeast and sugar for carbonation. But that process would take another week, and there wasn't enough time.

Instead, I'd already added the yeast and sugar to a large empty oak barrel at the beginning of the week while my beer was fermenting. This produced the carbonated gas I needed, and I now had plenty of it. But the trick was to move that gas into my uncarbonated beer in the ceramic barrel.

I first connected a pipe between the ceramic barrel and a smaller empty barrel that would come into use shortly. Thus, the three barrels were in place—the ceramic barrel containing my ale, the empty barrel that was connected to the ceramic one, and the larger oak barrel containing my gas.

I needed to condense and move the gas from the large oak barrel into the smaller one, a process that would pressurize my ale. I'd never been much of a mathematician, but I had spent several days calculating out the times and sizing when I first came up with the idea. This was my first time putting my theory to the test.

"Here goes nothing," I said, placing my palm against the barrel with the gas. "Rule of Ruin Forty-Two, Contracting Cone."

The spell worked by creating a translucent cone of magic over the target that would shrink, condensing everything and anything within it. I could shrink the cone to the size of my thumb. Of Celeru's spells, it was one of the most gruesome when used in a battle.

And there I was, using it to create carbonation. Within an ever-decreasing amount of space, the gases would become more and more pressurized. And since I was only condensing gas and not solids, the spell didn't require much aura to cast and maintain.

I couldn't see my cone directly, but I could feel it beyond the large barrel, condensing the gases I had gathered from the yeast and sugar. Then I opened the barrel and lifted the cone, which looked like a thin purple sphere. I placed it in the smaller oak barrel, which was about the same size as the sphere.

I closed the lid and tightened it, making sure there were no leaks. Then I let go of my spell, letting the gases within the sphere release and spread in the small barrel. Immediately, I could hear the connected pipes filling and pushing the gases into the ceramic barrel. With the heightened pressure, my ale began to carbonate.

CHAPTER 27: ALE, RULES, AND ADVANTAGES

C harm and I stood at the counter beneath our tent. It was only morning, and already, the festival grounds were packed with visitors. Hundreds of stalls and tents covered the great square of Lumitra Ward, which had been cleared for the festival.

It was the second day of Summerfest. The Brewmaster's Best Ale Cup was one of the first events of the day, and it would last until the evening. The competing brewmasters' tents were given prime real estate around the wide stage of the main event space during the competition. Our tent was beside the Tree and Stump Ale Company and across from the tent of Boreas and his Sword and Shield House.

We were wearing Tipsy Pelican aprons, and we had a big Tipsy Pelican Tavern banner beneath our counter. Behind us, several barrels of beer Cassia had enchanted with cold spells earlier in the day were ready to be poured. Charm and I had come over on a rented cart ahead of the others. The old pumpkin man was bringing Cassia and Elsa on his wagon, with more barrels and the rest of the snacks that Charm had prepared.

For the pairing with my pumpkin ale, Charm chose salted turkey strips and spiced, sun-dried cranberries. The portions were small, only meant as snacks to munch on as one drank one's ale, but the flavors accompanied the ale nicely.

I turned my eyes from the crowd and focused on Charm. She had her hands on her waist, and there was a liveliness to her that I hadn't seen in ages. With the apron on and her pink hair tied up in ribbons, she looked like a cute brewmaster's assistant, ready to do business.

She caught me staring. "What is it, Master?"

"Uh, nothing."

"There's no time to be daydreaming, Master. Boreas must be defeated."

"You're right, Charm," I said, patting my cheeks to get into the right frame of mind.

Then a booming voice rang out across the gathering crowd, clearly being amplified by magic. It was the announcer, Avery, who had also hosted the competition the previous year as well. He was a portly man with a thick beard, cheeks that always seemed to blush, and a twinkle in his eye that hinted at his charm.

"Ladies and gentlemen! Our annual Brewmaster's Best Ale Cup is about to start. Please come up and buy your tickets! Each ticket will allow you to purchase a mug of the city's finest ales, brewed by our contestants. Each order of ale will also come with a small snack. Now, please remember, each time a ticket is spent, it counts as a vote toward the brewmaster. The brewmaster with the most tickets by sundown will be this year's champion! Each brewmaster here today is a licensed brewer in the city of Meritas, and they've entered their single best ale for this competition. That's right, ladies and gentlemen! You understand me correctly! You'll be tasting the best brews Meritas has to offer today! So gather around to purchase your tickets! The competition will start as soon as I blow my whistle!"

A crowd quickly formed at the ticketing table staffed by Avery and two clerks.

"He's chipper as always, isn't he?" I said.

Charm nodded. "Mr. Avery is a nice man."

That was a first. Charm rarely gave out compliments. And when she did, I had the habit of thinking twice and making sure they weren't masterfully crafted roundabout insults first. Those were usually directed toward me.

Ten minutes later, the whistle sounded, and each booth was swarmed by lines of people.

"Welcome, sir!" I said. "Please try the Frozen Pumpkin Ale!"

There were sixteen brewers in total. Some were from major brewing companies, while others were from small taverns like mine. It was unlikely that every ale drinker was going to taste all sixteen ales, so several key factors were important to winning the competition.

The first was getting people to line up. Part of the reason I'd chosen a pumpkin-infused ale was because it was unique, and pumpkin was a rare ingredient in beers. My problem with the Honeydew had been that a sizable chunk of people disliked fruity beers and avoided them altogether. Pumpkin was so rarely used in ales that most people didn't have an opinion about it, which made it a safer pick.

The next key factor was the way we named our beer. We chose to call it "frozen" because we cooled our barrels more than normal enchanted beer barrels. This would be difficult for the other small brewers to do throughout the day as they probably could not afford to hire a mage for so long. But with Cassia's help, I'd be able to do it openly and not have to worry about being caught if I cast the enchantment runes myself. The second added benefit of calling it "frozen" was that when the sun truly hit the festival grounds in the afternoon, and temperatures rose to uncomfortable levels, every customer would be looking for a cold drink.

Finally, there was, of course, the way the ale tasted. I needed people to keep coming back to drink mine throughout the day. Repeat customers were what pushed the winner to the top. And more importantly, the return visits solidified the Tipsy Pelican Tavern in their minds so that they would seek us out later. Bran, Amberly, and Dalian had met me at the festival for the first time before becoming regulars at the tavern.

Music sounded from the direction of the stage, and for a moment, I thought the organizers had brought entertainment for the event. But then I saw that it came from Boreas's tent, just beyond the stage. The bastard had hired a musician, a young bard. Tall, handsome, and damn good at his flute. A crowd of onlookers gathered around the musician, drawing attention to Boreas's tent, and many began lining up for his ale.

"That cheating bastard!" I exclaimed. "Are the organizers going to allow this? He's getting a crowd because of the musician, not the merits of his ale! How dare he call himself a brewmaster? This is completely *dishonorable*!"

"There's nothing against it in the rules," Charm said.

"Then the rules should be changed—"

I stopped short as I noticed another group forming ahead, even larger than Boreas's crowd, and they were moving our way. Then I saw the faces of Elsa and Cassia at the center, between the gaps of the crowd. They were on foot, heading this way.

But where is their wagon? I thought.

"Hello, boy. How's the turnout?"

I turned and saw the old pumpkin man. His donkey, a calm animal called Strawberry, was pulled up behind the tent. His wagon was fully loaded with kegs of pumpkin ale.

"What's going on over there?" I said.

"Hmph. You'll see soon enough, you scoundrel."

I turned back. As Elsa and Cassia drew closer, I saw that they were wearing new dresses just like the white one that had been torn during Cassia's fight against Darren Tamblion. Over the dresses, the two young women each wore a Tipsy Pelican Apron. And by the gods, they were lovelier than the royal courtesans I'd rescued from the Mad King. They looked like two angels in matching uniforms. No wonder they were drawing a crowd.

Cassia blushed as they arrived at our tent, probably because my mouth was hanging wide open. She thumbed at the strap of the dress. "I felt a little bad that our agreement didn't go as you planned, due to my injuries, so I thought I'd dress up. It's just for today, though."

"W-Where did you get the dresses?"

"I had them made," Elsa said. "You two ruined my last one, and it was my favorite dress. Now I have an extra just in case you two get into more trouble."

"Amazing," I said.

The new dresses must have cost Elsa a good percentage of her wages, as I did not pay her much. I made a mental note to reimburse her. I knew she'd done it for the contest.

Then I peered over at Charm, feeling a little worried about what her response might be. Her expression was placid as ever, but her fist was outstretched, her thumb pointed to the sky.

"Ahem," someone said. I turned to find a customer holding up a ticket. "A Frozen Pumpkin Ale, please?"

"Yes, of course," Cassia said, quickly pouring him a mug from the barrel on the counter.

Behind this customer was an entire crowd of people. Some of them were on their tiptoes, trying to get a peek at the barmaids. They'd followed Cassia and Elsa to the tent. Even some of the customers in Boreas's line had moved over to ours.

"Good Celeru," I said, "I think we're going to win this thing after all."

"Ah, but one could argue that we're cheating," the old pumpkin man said sagely. "After all, we are attracting customers through the beauty of our staff and not the merits of our ale. It seems a little dishonor—"

"There's nothing against it in the rules!" I snapped. "Now, go unload those barrels from the wagon! We've got a competition to win!"

CHAPTER 28: CONCLUSIONS

By early afternoon, it appeared as if we were nearly even. Boreas had increased his odds by hiring out an entire band of musicians to perform in front of his booth. On our side, several of my regulars had shown up, including Amberly, Bran, Dalian, and Herwin.

"This might be even better than the Honeydew," Dalian said to me as he came back for his fourth mug. His cheeks were already a little rosy.

"It's great, but better? I'm not sure," Amberly said, taking a swig of his own mug, which looked like a teacup in his massive hands.

Each had purchased several tickets, and they'd already spent most of them at my tent.

"They're equally good!" Bran said with a hearty laugh. He downed the rest of his mug with one swoop and raised a ticket for another.

I quickly refilled his mug and thanked all three of the builders for coming.

"We wouldn't miss it for an audience with the elven princess," Bran said, smiling.

They promised to return once they were finished with their drinks and headed off to start an arm-wrestling match. It wasn't an official event of the Summerfest—it was just something they liked to do in the middle of the square. Last time, the match had drawn a larger audience than some of the main events.

Seeing them almost made me wish I weren't a contestant. The Summerfest was a great festival to spend with friends. All the visitors seemed to be truly having a good time and enjoying themselves. People were laughing, chatting, and dancing.

Herwin was several Frozen Pumpkin Ales deep and had worked up the courage to speak to a few young ladies on the square that were hardy ale drinkers themselves. As I was watching him and feeling a little envious, I felt a tap on my shoulder. I turned to find the old pumpkin man standing there. He was holding a mug that was not one of mine.

"Where did you get that?" I said.

"It's the Sword and Shield House's ale, the Dark Purple Lager."

"You traitor!" I exclaimed. I knew this man couldn't be trusted. To think, he spent a ticket on the opponent's ale.

"Calm down, boy," the old pumpkin man said. "I know you've been curious how Boreas's ale fares. Elsa told me about his visit to the tavern. Come on, have a sip. We'll all share this one and only grant him the one ticket."

I frowned, but he was right. I was dying to know what Boreas had brought to the contest this time. I took a swallow then passed it on. Everyone in the tent took a sip, except the pumpkin man, who passed the mug on when it was handed to him. He didn't have any of my ale, either, and I realized he was not a drinker.

"Not bad," Elsa admitted in a slightly frustrated tone.

The beer was good, but it tasted a lot like the Cherry Purple of the previous year, and more importantly, it wasn't better. If anything, the ale seemed like a different take on the same recipe.

"I'm surprised the administrators allowed this recipe," I said. "It seems quite similar to the old one."

Charm looked at me, puzzled. "Why would they not allow it, Master?"

"Boreas said that there's a rule that you can't enter the same..." *Oh, that bastard,* I thought. *He lied to me, didn't he?*

"Has Master been duped by an imbecile less than one-eighth his age?" Charm said in a low voice so that the others would not hear.

I sighed. I had no response to that one.

Charm smiled. Actually smiled. It was a sight to behold.

"Master's ale is superior," Charm said, putting down the mug of Dark Purple Lager. "Charm was right to trust him."

I smiled back at her. "Thanks, Charm."

"His musicians do seem quite popular," Cassia said as she looked across the square.

"It's not over yet, missy," the old pumpkin man said. "We're still neck and neck. Boreas'll be losing half his profits by hiring that troupe."

I nodded down at our stash of tickets. We had an incredible number of them. Even after the festival took its cut, the amount we received would be equal to at least an entire month's worth of revenue for the tavern.

"By gods!" Oakdigger exclaimed. "Is that a circus act that just arrived for Boreas?"

"You've got to be kidding!" I looked over at Boreas's stall. Sure enough, a circus act had arrived, including an acrobat, a juggler, and a flame eater. "Good gods. Is this even an ale competition anymore?"

Something flashed in Elsa's and Cassia's eyes at the same time as they glanced at each other and nodded.

"What was that?"

"We have a secret weapon," Elsa said.

Cassia nodded. "We didn't want to use it unless it was absolutely necessary."

"But now there's no choice," Elsa said.

They turned to Charm, who had begun preparing more turkey and cranberry snacks. She blinked and turned to us. We were all watching her.

"Charm feels suddenly perturbed," Charm said, giving the two women a wary look.

Elsa cracked an evil grin. And Cassia began to twiddle her fingers as if she felt terribly guilty.

"Charm is becoming increasingly perturbed," Charm said.

From behind a barrel, Elsa pulled out a white dress. This one was smaller, matching Charm's stature. Charm looked at the dress then at the women and shook her head. The two women stepped forward, while nodding at the smaller woman.

Charm shook her head again. Elsa and Cassia nodded faster, drawing closer to her like animals ready to pounce on their prey. Charm turned to me. Though her expression had its typical flatness, I could tell she was seeking help.

I looked solemnly into the distance. "Someone once told me that we must win at all costs."

Charm reached out a hand to me like a drowning sailor before she was carried off toward the washrooms on the festival grounds by the two predators. Seven minutes later, a crowd followed them back. The outfit they'd prepared for her was different from their own and resembled a traditional maid's costume, with many flowing ribbons and a big bow in the back.

Charm looked adorable. But I couldn't stop laughing because I knew how ridiculous it was for someone like her to be wearing such a thing. She gave me one threatening look, and my throat clenched, the laughter dying in my chest.

Once again, the tables were turned, and this time, several female patrons were at our tent. Unlike Cassia and Elsa, who seemed to primarily draw young men, Charm drew both men and women equally.

"Kyaaa, you're so adorable! Thank you for the beer—I'll be back!" a lady with heavily jeweled accessories exclaimed.

After she'd walked out of earshot, Charm turned to me. "If the Tipsy Pelican does not win the cup, Charm will make Master suffer the same way Charm is suffering now."

"I don't know exactly how that would work, but it sounds awful," I said.

But it appeared that we were on track to win. And then the unthinkable happened: we ran out of cranberries. It was nearly four o'clock. There were three more hours to the competition. Cassia had gone to the wagon to get another bag of cranberries and found that there were none.

"Charm does not think this is right. Charm remembered making the right amount to match the ale."

"Could we have left a bag back at the tavern?" I said.

"I believe we checked everything as we loaded up," Cassia said.

"Damn," I said. "If we'd known earlier, we could have decreased the number of cranberries per portion and spread things out. But now we've only got enough left for ten more portions. Are you sure we had another bag?"

"Charm is certain."

"Then it must still be at the tavern," I said.

"We could go back to get it," Elsa said. "We should be able to return in time before the end of the competition."

I nodded. "You're right. It's worth a try."

"Charm will go," Charm said.

"You're too big of a draw right now," I said.

Charm frowned, and I could see she was worried that this would cost us the trophy.

"I can go," Cassia said.

"No, I'll go," Elsa said. "I'm getting tired of these boys ogling me, anyway, and I'll know where to look."

I nodded. "Thanks, Elsa. Be back as soon as you can."

"I'll go too," the old pumpkin man said. "Faster with my wagon and Strawberry."

Elsa nodded, and they headed off.

Fifteen minutes later, we'd sold the last of our cranberries. We had to apologize that our cranberries were out. It was impossible to buy more at the festival, as Charm had dried them in the sun and spiced them herself. We could only wait.

The cranberries weren't a major part of the contest, and people were mainly spending their tickets for the beer. But there was still a minor impact on our ticket intake. A surprising number of people really enjoyed the snacks Charm had prepared.

But as the hours passed, it became clear that Elsa wasn't going to make it back in time. From the volume of the crowds, it appeared that we were neck and neck with Boreas. None of the other contenders were anywhere close.

At seven o'clock, the competition drew to a close. All the brewmasters and their teams stepped onto the stage while Avery's clerks counted the tickets. I was sweating as I watched my tickets being counted. Charm and Cassia both held intense gazes. We'd hoped to get a better idea once the tickets were gathered, but my stack looked the same as Boreas's.

The clerks finished counting, and one of them, a young woman with rolled-up sleeves and a can-do attitude, whispered into Avery's ear.

Avery turned to the crowd gathered at the stage and said, with his spell-enhanced voice, "The results are in! Are you readdyyy?"

I was totally not ready.

"Ladies and gentlemen, here are the final results! Coming in third place is the Red Harvest Ale by Ronol Ablehand of the Tree and Stump Ale Company!"

There was a round of applause as the brewmaster of the Red Harvest Ale stepped forward. The same female clerk came up and pinned a blue ribbon to the brewmaster's shirt.

Then the crowd turned back to Avery for the final results.

"And now, the winner of this year's Brewmaster's Best Ale Cup…"

Damn it, I thought. *They aren't even going to announce the second-place winner first?* But it made sense. If Boreas or I won first place, it would be clear who had come in second place.

Avery turned to the brewmasters on the stage. "The best ale in all of Meritas belongs to…"

Silence spread across the crowd. Charm was standing beside me, still wearing her maid's costume and looking nervous and excited at the same time—more emotion than I'd seen on her in the entire previous year combined.

Avery turned and pointed. "Master Arch Gustkin of the Tipsy Pelican Tavern!"

Cassia and I threw up our hands and whooped. We jumped up and down hugging each other.

"Ha ha ha…"

I turned and saw Charm. Her shoulders were shaking. Breath came out of her half-parted mouth in a quick rhythm. She was laughing. A pretty and honest laugh that I will remember for the rest of my life. The crowd was applauding and whooping, and Avery came up and handed me a large golden trophy.

"Well done, Master Arch, and congratulations!" Avery said.

"Thank you," I said, taking the trophy. Then I gave Boreas a wink.

***

Charm carried the trophy and hummed to herself as we made our way back to the tavern. The small smile stuck on her face did not seem to want to recede like the ones before it had. I wondered what had happened to Elsa as I pushed our cart.

Apparently, Cassia was wondering the same thing. "Do you think Mr. Oakdigger's wagon broke down on the way?" she said.

"Possible," I said. "That old rickety thing looked prone to collapse."

But as we neared the tavern, we didn't come across Elsa or the pumpkin man.

"Master, do you smell that?"

I sniffed the air. "Smoke."

"I hope it isn't a serious fire," Cassia said. "It may not be reported quickly enough with so many people at the festival right now."

But as we entered Southbank and neared the tavern, my worst fears began to grow. Then all three of us abandoned the cart and ran. We found the tavern set alight, burning brightly with tall, roaring flames. I saw a body on the ground before the burning tavern.

It was the old pumpkin man. I rushed to him. He was bleeding from his mouth and nostrils. It looked as if he'd taken a hard hit to the head.

"Oakdigger. What happened?"

"He... he took her," the old pumpkin man whispered, the strength gone from his body. "I am sorry, boy. L-Look after them. They are good girls... I had daughters once..."

"Who took her?"

"A m-man... I'm s-orry..."

"Who? Speak!"

But the light in his eyes had dimmed, and all that was left were the dancing shadows of the flames. His life had emptied from his body, and trapped on his face was an expression of fear and uncertainty. There had been nothing to do for him. Even if Charm had been willing to reveal her powers in front of Cassia, no healing magic could revive a brain wound.

I lightly closed the old man's eyes and stood. "Cassia, call the city guard."

"We must go after her, Arch-don!"

"I will, but you need to call the city guard to put out the fire before it spreads to other buildings."

"But—"

"You're the fastest! Go!"

Cassia frowned but turned and left without another word. Then I gave one more glance around to make sure the street was empty, and I turned to Charm.

She lifted her hand, muttering a spell I didn't recognize. A black circle appeared before her raised hand, and the flames began to swirl into it. They weren't being sucked in, but rather, they were drawn to the dark circle like a magnet to steel or a cat to a mouse.

The fire cleared within seconds. I stepped inside and walked briskly throughout the entire tavern. The structure still held, as the walls were partially made of brick and stone, but most of the wooden scaffolding had been burned black. There was broken furniture inside the barroom and glass on the floor, but I found no sign of Elsa.

I'd been afraid that the arsonist had lit the tavern with her inside after he knocked down Oakdigger, but it was empty of people. If the perpetrator had left her there alive, she would have reported it immediately, and the guards would have arrived before we did. But that was not the case, so Oakdigger must have been right. Elsa had been taken.

My mind was racing, darkness releasing within my chest. It didn't make sense. Someone had planned this in advance. The fact he did not strike earlier meant he'd been afraid to. Probably because of Cassia's presence—he didn't want to cross paths with a spirited. But it was unlikely she'd been followed, as it was dangerous to follow an awakened without risking notice.

So how did he know Cassia would be gone? Of course. The Summer-fest competition.

I'd entered the year before and was expected to do so again. All my staff would be there. The arsonist had seen Cassia working at the tavern. It made sense she would be there at the competition too.

That meant he'd expected everyone to be gone. He hadn't intended to kill anyone. The plan had been to burn down the tavern, but the unexpected had happened—Elsa and Oakdigger had returned and seen the perpetrator. Elsa had put up a fight. He'd overpowered her. Knocking over the furniture. Breaking glass.

But why hadn't he killed her if he didn't want witnesses to his crime? Why hadn't he left her for dead like he did to Oakdigger?

That was the only logical solution: kill the witness. Kidnapping didn't make sense.

Unless...

Unless the arsonist, who had expected no one to be in the tavern, was somehow, for some reason, also a person who wanted to kidnap Elsa.

And then the pieces fell together. Because there was only one person who fit that description.

"Mideon!"

CHAPTER 29: BAD MOOD (ARC 4)

I coughed as I stepped out of the smoldering husk of my tavern. The fumes were thick in my nose and lungs. I sucked in deep breaths of the warm summer air and tried to expel it from my chest.

There was a storm brewing within me, one that I hadn't felt in what seemed like a lifetime ago. The storm reminded me of who I really was, though I was not ready to become that man again. My powers were gone, but my rage and my will were not. If I weren't careful, the storm would release, and the quiet life that I'd known for the past year would be shattered.

But someone had destroyed the tavern. *My tavern*. And if that wasn't enough, they'd kidnapped one of my staff.

The first year of running a tavern had been difficult. We did not have an established name, our revenues were meager, and our customers were few and far between. But things had been turning for the better in recent weeks. The barroom was busy on most nights. Our patrons were kind and loyal. And today, I had won the Summerfest Brewmaster's Best Ale Cup.

Things were finally going well. And now my tavern lay in ruin.

I breathed deeply as the scenes inside the burnt walls ran through my mind. My chairs and engraved tables were charred beyond repair. The long block of mahogany that made my bar's countertop had been turned black and brittle. The ceiling above the dining room table in the main hall had collapsed. The fire had even reached the storage room, burning several of my barrels and boiling my beer.

I began to laugh. I couldn't help but see the humor of the situation. My voice rang out into the night. My chest convulsed with air and sound. "They have no idea... they have no idea of what's coming."

"Master..." Charm said with her typical expression, although there was a hint of worry in her voice.

I wiped my eyes and looked over at her. "Have you found her?"

Charm hesitated then muttered a spell. One hand clutched the dress that Elsa had given her. The other held a glowing sphere. I'd seen her use the spell before, but I didn't recognize the incantation, nor did I understand how the spell worked.

"Charm has her location," Charm said.

"Let's go," I said.

We ran, speeding through the empty streets like a pair of dark wolves. If people had turned their eyes in our direction, they would have seen only shadows. I felt my gateless body strain as my mind pushed to keep up with Charm. Though she didn't have the power of awakened gates either, she seemed only minutely affected by the hindrance.

She didn't slow as we reached the end of another street. That meant that whoever we were following was also moving at a fast pace. I glanced over at Charm and found a flat, impassive expression on her face. Even exerting our bodies at this level, she didn't break a sweat or let a wrinkle crease her brow.

But despite not having the Gate of Breath open, I was able to maintain my speed. Two hundred years of experience and training didn't count for nothing. The muscle memory was still there, as was the connection between my mind and my body.

We turned a corner. "How much farther?" I asked, feeling my body nearing its limits.

"Three blocks. When we arrive, Charm will dispose of the arsonist."

"No," I said. "He's mine."

"Master is not in a state to fight. The arsonist may be dangerous."

"Secure Elsa. That's all you need to worry about."

We ran down two more blocks, made a turn, and sped down another. A moment later, I saw a figure in the distant darkness—a large, hooded shape moving fast, *incredibly fast*, for someone with so much mass. It was almost unnatural.

Then it clicked. No wonder it had taken us so long to catch up. The arsonist had opened the First Gate.

Slumped over his shoulder was Elsa. Her body was limp. I hoped that she was only unconscious.

As we closed in, he turned his head and looked at us. I would have preferred to launch a surprise attack, but my options were limited, as they tended to be lately.

Instead of picking up speed, he slid to a stop in the alley and turned to face us. We matched his movements, coming to a stop several paces across from him.

His eyes and nose were covered by his hood, but I could see his smile and the sharp yellow teeth behind it. Elsa's eyes were closed, but her color looked okay.

"He told me only to start the fire," the man said. "But if you're here, it means I get to kill you. No witnesses."

I leaped forward, throwing a punch at his face. He deflected quickly, blocking it with his right forearm. I came at him with a second fist. He couldn't respond easily—that arm and shoulder was carrying Elsa. He jumped backward, throwing her sideways, toward the ground, to free his left arm. I followed with a third punch. He blocked that one as well and responded with his own now that his hands were free.

I caught his fist with crossed arms. It was a mighty blow, a real sledgehammer. I would have broken both my arms if I hadn't had the know-how to deflect the force of such a blow. I caught it like a thrown ball and slowed it, displacing its power across my whole body. It threw me back a dozen paces, and I fell to a knee and slid to a stop.

I let out a breath. Nothing was broken, but the encounter had left me winded.

He barked a laugh. "Do you see my power?"

"Do you see your hostage?"

"Huh?" He looked around, but Elsa was not where he'd thrown her.

While I was attacking, Charm had swooped in and caught Elsa, and now the placid, smaller young woman was holding Elsa in her arms like a freshly baked pie. It was a strange sight to behold.

"She's alive but unconscious, Master," Charm said neutrally.

The arsonist sucked in a sharp breath. "Wench!" He moved toward Charm, but I jumped in front of him and kicked him in the hip. The blow pushed him backward, but he didn't fall.

"Go," I said to Charm.

"Master should take Elsa. Charm will fight."

"No, I already told you. I will handle this. He burned down *my* tavern. He's mine."

"Master does not have any gates open, while his opponent has one. Master is physically overmatched."

"I'll be fine. I beat that radiant, didn't I?" I said, without taking my eyes off of the arsonist.

"Through trickery and self-injury," Charm said. "The risks are too high."

"Cassia will be expecting us," I said, growing impatient. "Take Elsa and leave."

Charm began setting Elsa down. "Charm will—"

"You will leave!"

"But Master should not—"

"I have commanded you!" The words came out of me before I could hold my tongue. I hadn't meant to say them.

When I turned to look, the alley was already empty. It was the second time I'd broken my promise. The shadows rose within me, but I knew I had someone to release them upon.

The hooded giant began to laugh. "That was dumb of you. That one seemed dangerous. But now it's just you and me."

The man pulled back his hood, and I recognized his face instantly. It was the bear man who had made the mistake of punching Galston.

"I-It's you... Gerlanda!"

"My name is not Gerlanda!" he shrieked. "I don't know who told you that name, but it is not mine. My real name is—"

"Yeah, yeah, whatever. Did Mideon order you to burn my tavern?"

Gerlanda frowned at being interrupted, but then he broke into a grin. "He did. Then I saw the girl. Figured it'd be a good souvenir for the boss."

I nodded. "You killed the pumpkin man."

"Who? Oh, you mean that old man with the wagon? I only gave him a light tap," Gerlanda said with a smirk. "I guess I just don't know my strength."

I shrugged. "Well, it's not my problem. He's not part of my tavern."

"How about that girl?" Gerlanda said, his grin growing uglier. "Let me tell you, after Mideon's done with her, I'm going to ask for a turn. Then I'll hand her off to my buddies."

"Hmm… yes, I would have to say *that* is my problem. She's one of my staff, you see, and for a kidnapping, I'd typically just break a couple of legs." I crouched slowly and tightened my fist. "But I'm sorry to say that you've caught me in a *bad mood*."

Gerlanda laughed. "Who do you think you are?"

"Haven't you figured it out?"

Gerlanda frowned as if unsure he had missed something.

I gave him a deadened look. "I'm the one who's going to kill you."

CHAPTER 30: THE BEAR MAN AND THE TAVERN KEEPER, PART TWO

The bear man paused, holding a breath, and I saw it in his eyes. Fear. There had been no bravado in my words, only certainty. "I'm the one who's going to kill you," I'd stated, as if it had been decided the moment our trajectories crossed. I made my statement without emotion. My words were as sterile as the simplest mathematical equation, and like *one and one makes two*, they held an unbreakable truth.

A flash of terror replaced the bear man's self-confidence from a moment earlier. He was experiencing the epiphany of an apex predator coming in contact with a human hunter for the first time. He tried to brush aside the fear with a snarl, launching forward. It was foolishness. He came with plenty of speed but not enough finesse and I dodged his first attack. I was reminded of my childhood, fighting against larger boys. In those days, I'd had only my natural body and my wits to fend off superior strength. That was true of this fight, too, but compared to back then, things were also very different. Two hundred years of battle experience different.

His second attack came as a roundhouse kick. A slow move, typically, but with the Gate of Breath open, it came fast and hard. However, I'd seen the intention in his body before he even lifted his leg. I stepped out of range but not more than necessary. His foot passed my face, missing it by a hair's breadth.

If he'd been a truly skilled fighter, I would have been at a disadvantage. But the bear man's movements were sloppy and wasteful. High Templar Darren Tamblion's battle prowess had been a real threat, but the man before me was nothing more than an over-muscled brute.

I ended it quickly. He came at me with several swings, and upon his third punch, I responded with my own, ducking beneath his and shooting my hand forward. Gerlanda's enraged roar was cut short as I connected with his body, his voice catching in his throat. He looked down, and his eyes went wide at the sight of my hand puncturing his chest.

Blood spilled from his mouth. He glared at me, confused. "I opened the Gate of Breath!" he spluttered. "I was going to defeat Galston the Gallant one day..."

"Ah, apologies," I said, drawing out my hand and taking a piece of him with me.

He fell to his knees, his eye level dropping to my own. Face slack. Eyes draining of life.

I looked down at the steaming-hot heart in my hand. "I guess I just don't know my own strength."

He collapsed to the ground without uttering another word.

I dropped the heart and whispered, "Rule of Ruin Forty-Two, Contracting Cone."

A glob of purple light surrounded Gerlanda and began to condense, collecting together his body and the bloody dirt around it. The sounds of crunching and breaking would have turned any other man's stomach, but I was the Stormblood, and once I set to a task, I did it without hesitation or indecision.

My aura ran out before I could get his body to the size I wanted. Back in the day, I could condense a man to the size of a pea. But my halos ran out, and the sphere was the size of a child's ball, made of dark purple and specks of glimmering silver. It dropped to the ground as the spell vanished.

I kicked the condensed ball into an open storm drain and walked back down the alley. The arsonist of my tavern's burning had been dealt with, but there were still other perpetrators who would be held responsible.

As I turned the corner, I suddenly felt something move. I looked up in the direction of where I'd detected the motion, on the roof of the three-story building directly above me. Although the alley was dark, from that vantage point, the viewer would have seen my fight with Gerlanda.

I listened for more movement, but I heard nothing more. *Did they see me cast my spell?* They could not have been there while Charm was still with me. She would have sensed them immediately.

Gerlanda had been growling and yelling. Someone must have heard and come looking. I stayed still, pressing my back against the wall, lying low in the shadows. The only sound was that of the festival several city blocks away.

I looked back at where I'd cast my spell. I doubted anyone could have discerned my face from that distance. But if I were wrong, I could have a serious problem on my hands. Beyond seeing my spellcasting, the viewer would have witnessed a murder.

I made a run for it, darting through the shadows of the alley, making sure to keep myself hidden in the darkness. The sun was well past the horizon, and the sky was a dark shade of purple. The tavern was several blocks away, but I didn't take a direct route. I zigzagged and made circles to ensure that I wasn't followed. I periodically stopped to listen, but I heard nothing.

Finally, I stopped by a canal and rinsed my hands of Gerlanda's blood, taking the time to think things over. I was quite certain I hadn't been followed by any layman. Only a competent mage could have masked their presence from me, and the chances that such a mage accidentally came upon my fight with Gerlanda right after Charm left were very low. But I could not be sure I hadn't been seen by some passerby.

Did a cat on the rooftops make the sound?

No. It had been a person's presence. My intuitions did not lie. I could only hope that they hadn't been looking in our direction, or at the very least, hadn't seen my face.

I walked quickly back to the tavern. My appearance was undoubtedly weary and ragged, as I'd spent considerable energy in the chase and the fight. But that would be consistent with the story. How else was a young tavern keeper supposed to look after frantically searching for his missing barmaid?

Several guards surrounded the smoking tavern as I strolled up. Cassia and Elsa were nowhere to be seen, but Charm was standing in the front, wearing the maid's costume that looked a little strange under the circumstances. I assumed she had told Cassia and the guards that we had split up to search for Elsa.

"Where are the girls?" I said to Charm.

"Charm asked Miss Cassia to take Miss Elsa to an inn for the night." Charm glanced down at my left hand and made an imperceptible twitch of her eyebrow.

I followed her gaze and noticed that there was a light streak of red on my arm that I had missed. I slowly rolled down the sleeve while making sure none of the guards were watching.

A man I recognized as Kainlin, Southbank's ward captain, came around the back corner of the tavern, his head turned upward as he inspected the damage. He was tall with a grim face and a short, trimmed mustache. His manner was all military and command, a veteran soldier. He'd been in the Meritan army before he took command of Southbank's ward guard, I'd heard. Beside him was another city guard in plate armor, wearing a lieutenant's insignia. She was much younger, perhaps Cassia's age, with dark-green hair pulled back in a ponytail. Her face held a slightly distressed expression.

"What did you tell them?" I said to Charm as I watched the soldiers.

"Charm explained to the captain that Master and Charm had split up to search for Miss Elsa. Charm found Miss Elsa and took her back."

As I'd expected. I wanted to ask how she'd explained the disappearance of the fire to Cassia, but Captain Kainlin and his lieutenant spotted us and made their way over.

"Are you the owner?" Kainlin said.

"I am."

"Do you know that we haven't had a murder in the ward of Southbank in over a decade?" Kainlin said with contempt. "Only fine citizenry here. Then your tavern opens up, and Kerrytown starts seeing lowlifes running amok. Now we have arson and death on our hands."

I blinked. "Are you suggesting this is somehow my fault?"

"Clearly, one of your drunken ruffians burned down your tavern and murdered another drunk in the process."

"My patrons wouldn't do something like this," I said. "And that man was not a drunk or one of my patrons. He was a pumpkin seller."

Kainlin laughed. "Not a drunk? I've known Gediah Oakdigger for twenty years. He was a soldier in the duke's army before he was discharged for drunken behavior. I know about his pumpkin business. He tried to open shop here in Southbank, but I saw to it that that bumbling fool was kept out of this fine ward. We don't like gutter people around here."

I frowned. "He didn't drink a drop of my brew, even when o-ffered. If he was a drunk before, he must have given it up."

"Ridiculous," Kainlin scoffed. "He couldn't live without the drink. I knew that piece of garbage would end up dead on the street one day, just like I knew your tavern wouldn't last long once you moved in."

I shrugged. I didn't feel like arguing. "What's your next course of action?"

"Well, we can't have an arsonist on the loose, can we? Which of your patrons had grievances against you?"

"None."

"None? You run a tavern. Even a lawless, run-down place like yours would have unhappy customers."

"Well, I suppose you're right. There was this one guy..."

"Yes?"

"He had a thing for Elsa, the young woman that was taken."

Kainlin motioned to his lieutenant, who pulled out a parchment pad and began taking notes. "Go on."

"He came several times. Threatened to destroy the tavern. Tried to forcibly take Elsa with him with several men one time."

"There we go," Kainlin said, smiling. "That sounds like our man. What was his name?"

"Mideon Greengrass."

His lieutenant began writing, but Kainlin snatched the parchment from her hand. He turned to me, with a deep scowl on his face. "You'd better watch your tongue."

"I have multiple witnesses who can attest to Mideon threatening the tavern and Elsa," I said.

"That is *Lord* Greengrass that you are talking about," the captain said, stepping closer.

The young lieutenant at his side inched backward, clearly uncomfortable.

"Oh," I said. "Guess his dad is your direct boss, huh? Well... this is awkward."

"Be careful of who you accuse without evidence," Kainlin said, stepping even closer. "Maybe this Elsa started the fire herself and tried to make a run for it. Maybe *you* were the one preying on her."

"Is this guy an idiot?" I said, turning to his lieutenant.

"What did you just say?"

I ignored him, continuing my dialogue with the young woman. "Is he really suggesting one of my staff started the fire, murdered her friend, hit herself over the head, then somehow flew to an alley while unconscious?"

The veins on Kainlin's neck bulged as he glared at me. But then he smiled thinly. "I heard your business was poor. I guess this will be the last we'll be seeing of you. Maybe someone will buy this place up and build a proper establishment. I'm closing this investigation since the owner is uncooperative."

He turned and walked away. His lieutenant frowned as she watched him leave. She bowed apologetically to Charm and me then quickly followed after him. I sighed.

"Master," Charm said after they'd left.

"Yeah?"

"That was handled very stupidly."

"Thanks."

A pair of medics placed Oakdigger's covered body on a stretcher and carried him to a wagon.

"Where will Mr. Oakdigger be taken?" Charm asked the pair.

"The city morgue," the one laying the cloth said without looking up.

"What will happen to him there?"

"The body will be held for seven days. If no one claims him, he'll be cremated and placed in the city grave."

"You mean an unmarked grave," I said. "He was a soldier, wasn't he? Doesn't he have a place in the military cemetery?"

This caught the medic by surprise, and he looked to the other one for an answer.

The second medic shook his head. "According to Captain Kainlin, he was dishonorably discharged. We will double-check the records of course."

We said nothing more, and the medics carried Oakdigger away. I walked through the tavern to take better stock of the damage. I didn't like what I found. In the storage room, the few barrels of beer closest to the rune crystals were untouched by the fire. The rune crystals kept the cold spell running and was the coldest part of the room. The rest of the barrels had boiled or burned and been ruined.

The stairway to the second floor was unsafe for stepping, so I didn't check upstairs, but I could only assume things were pretty bad up there because fire tended to climb. The main hall was wrecked, as was the bar room. The stone walls held, but the wooden pillars and beams were black and brittle.

There was one saving grace, however, and it was likely the reason I didn't fall into complete despair. The brewery and all its equipment—which I had purposely chosen to keep downstairs in the basement when we bought the inn—appeared to be entirely untouched by the destruction. If the fire had reached down there, I would have likely given up the tavern business on the spot. But when I headed down the stairs, I found my kettles and pipes and chillers and fermenters shining like treasures in a fairy tale's dragon lair.

CHAPTER 31: WOULDN'T WANT TO INTRUDE

Charm said nothing as she led me to the inn that she and Cassia had chosen. I didn't know what to say as I followed behind her, watching her two pigtails sway in the night breeze. I assumed she was upset with me.

"Master killed him, then?" she said suddenly as we entered the ward of Keeper's Garden.

I nodded. She sighed and didn't say anything else. I thought she'd been worried I'd lose, but she seemed more upset that I hadn't. *What was that about?*

"Hey, Charm, about earlier... I'm sorry that I ordered you—"

"Charm has already forgotten."

"But—"

"Would Master prefer that Charm remember?"

"Uh... no. Well..."

"Then let the matter rest, Master."

"Okay." I sighed.

"What will Master do next?"

"Well, I guess we'll have to rebuild the tavern. We'll have some decent revenue tomorrow from the Summerfest sales. That combined with what we have in our lockbox should be just enough to cover the repairs. But it'll be a tight few weeks until we can get up and running and start serving again."

"Our coffers were empty, Master."

I stopped walking. "What?"

"The large man must have stolen our savings. Master searched him, didn't he?" Charm turned and gave me a raised eyebrow.

"S-Searched him?" I said dumbly.

"Surely Master did not dispose of the arsonist before making sure nothing was taken from his tavern."

"Oh... crap."

Charm didn't say anything, but I could tell what she was thinking. *If Master had let Charm handle the matter, Charm would not have made the mistake of destroying the body along with all the profits that we saved over the past year. Charm would have done her duty without fault.*

"I know, I know," I said.

We walked several blocks in silence. The streets were mostly empty, and in the distance, the sounds of merriment could be heard coming from the festival.

"How did Cassia react when you showed up with Elsa?" I was a little worried that Cassia would notice how easily Charm carried her.

"Charm would not make such foolish mistakes," she said, turning to look at me as if she had read my thoughts. "Charm made a show of bravely struggling to carry Miss Elsa back to the tavern."

"Right…"

"Charm explained that Charm had found Miss Elsa abandoned in the alley all alone. Charm did not reveal that she saw the arsonist."

Charm came to a stop in front of a small inn burrowed between a coffee shop and a general store. The inn wasn't poor or luxurious. It was right down the middle of the range and probably still far more than what we could afford. We'd have to find a cheaper place to stay tomorrow. We'd also have to figure out plenty more things since I'd kicked all our savings down the drain along with Gerlanda.

The clerk at the front desk was a half-asleep teenage boy, likely the son of the innkeeper. "She said you'd be coming," he said groggily when we asked for Cassia. "Fifth room from the stairs."

Cassia was sitting in the room, staring at the floor when we entered. Elsa was beside her in the bed.

Cassia looked up. "She woke and went back to sleep. The fumes got to her, but she's okay now."

Elsa looked all right asleep in the bed. Her clothes had been changed, and her skin was clean. Cassia must have wiped her down with a wet towel. Charm wandered to Elsa's side and put her hand on the sleeping woman's forehead.

"It's so sad—what happened to Mr. Oakdigger," Cassia said. "I feel so bad for his family. Have the guards located them?"

"I don't think he's got any family," I said. "He said he used to have daughters. If they're still alive, they must be estranged."

"But surely he has someone," Cassia said hopefully. "Otherwise, who will claim the body?"

I shrugged. "Who knows? According to the ward captain, the old man was kicked out of the city guard for being a drunk. Maybe he got kicked out of his family too."

"Captain Kainlin is a very rude man," Charm said. "Charm takes his words with grains of salt."

Cassia looked down. After a moment, she turned to me. "How is the tavern, Arch-don?"

I took a seat at the small table against the wall and sighed. "It's pretty toasty. Salvageable, but repairs will be pricey."

"The arsonist stole all our savings too," Charm said matter-of-factly.

I avoided eye contact with her.

"How could someone do this?" Cassia said quietly. "I... I should have gone with her."

"It is not Miss Cassia's responsibility," Charm said, giving me a look. "Charm is just thankful that Miss Elsa is okay."

Cassia nodded, but her eyes told me she put the blame on herself.

I sighed. "Well... it's late. We'd better get some sleep."

I looked around. There were the three ladies and me in the room. And one large bed.

Three ladies. And me. My first thought was very, very stupid, and I was glad I came to my senses after only a brief hesitation.

"Uh... well, guess I'd better go get a room," I said.

"Oh, um... the innkeeper said all the rooms were booked," Cassia said. "This is the last one, in fact."

One large bed. Three ladies. Me. The very stupid thought returned. It stayed a moment longer this time, but once again, I was able to come to my senses.

"Oh. Uh... well, I'll find another inn nearby, then."

"She said they're all booked because of the festival," Cassia said. "This room was booked, too, but the guest didn't show up the second night. The innkeeper was very kind to give it to us. I don't think she was supposed to since it was already paid for."

"So there's only one room..."

Cassia nodded. The very stupid thought didn't go away this time. I just stood there, blinking. Charm gave me a flat-eyed brow twitch.

Then Cassia said, "Don't worry. The extra bed they're bringing from their other inn in Oakden Ward should arrive at any moment."

"Oh, right, of course. An extra bed. Uh... well, I mean... still, I should find somewhere else to stay. I wouldn't want to intrude."

"But—" Cassia began.

"Okay, you've convinced me."

CHAPTER 32: JUST VERY HEALTHY

The innkeeper brought a rollaway cot and gave me a peering look when she spotted who it was for. "Your brother?" she said to no one in particular, although none of the three ladies looked related to me or to each other.

Cassia was of middling height, blond, and blue-eyed. Quite clearly a northerner. Elsa, who was still asleep in the bed, was taller than most of the men in Meritas and had high cheekbones, violet eyes, and a tan complexion. Charm was the smallest in stature and the most girlish in appearance, though her manner would make you think otherwise.

Charm ended up replying to the innkeeper in her typical monotone fashion, which was the worst possible scenario. "There is no blood relation. He is my master."

"Your master?" The innkeeper leaned in, eyes widening.

"Ah," Cassia chimed in, realizing the dire situation or perhaps seeing the expression on my face. "He's our employer, the tavern owner."

"Nothing to be worried about, ma'am," said a third voice. "He'll face the consequences if he climbs into the wrong bed."

We all turned and saw that Elsa was awake and sitting in her bed. Although she still looked pale, there was some color in her cheeks, and the rest of her features were as jaw-droppingly beautiful as ever. I was caught off guard enough that I nearly didn't catch the self-referential humor in her words.

The innkeeper gave me one last suspicious glance and left. Once she was gone, Elsa told us what she remembered from before she'd been taken, and Charm explained our altered version of events, from Oakdigger's death to finding Elsa.

"He was very large and moved very fast," Elsa said. "I think I tried to fight him off, but the last thing I remember is falling to the ground. I... I had no idea about Mr. Oakdigger outside..." She trailed off into silence, rubbing her hands together uncomfortably with a hard expression on her face. I could tell what she was thinking. It was the same thing Cassia had been thinking. She was holding herself responsible for the old pumpkin man's death.

"You can't fault yourself for evil's actions. Evil is as boundless as the sea, and its blame will drown your spirits in its darkness."

They all turned to look at me, and I blinked, realizing I had spoken the words.

"That was very philosophical, Heru," Elsa said. "I think I understand..."

"Uh... just something I heard once," I said quickly.

Cassia frowned, looking down and shaking her head subtly to herself. I guessed she didn't agree with me. Charm's expression was unreadable.

We didn't say much more for the rest of the night, and none of us had any appetite for dinner. We were tired, and we knew the next day would be a hard one, so we went straight to bed. But I didn't sleep. I lay awake, listening to the rustling of covers and the breathing and the quiet feminine murmurs that came from the bed only a few feet from my own.

When the moonlight peaked, I sat up and looked over at them. The three young women were cuddled close together. Charm was in the middle, though she didn't look entirely comfortable, with both Elsa's and Cassia's arms wrapped tightly around her.

Charm, you have no idea how lucky you are, I thought. *Men would sell their souls to be in the position you're in now.*

I sighed and stood quietly and slipped out the door. Outside the inn, the summer night air was warm against my cheeks. In the distance, the festival raged on with laughter and song. I turned in its direction and began walking.

On my seventh step, I felt a presence on the roof behind me. My first instinct was that it was the same person who had seen me in the alley with Gerlanda. But when I turned, I saw Charm sitting cross-legged on the inn's roof tiling. The window to our room was open beside her. She peered down at me like a haughty god.

"What?" I said. "Did I wake you?"

"Charm could not sleep. She was afraid of a pervert attacking in the night."

"I'm not a pervert!" I exclaimed. "I'm just very healthy!"

"Charm thinks that is exactly what a pervert would say."

"And an innocent man would readily admit to being a pervert?"

"An innocent man would not readily agree to sleep in the same room as several young maidens."

"*Several* young maidens? I counted only two."

I ducked as a piece of tile flew an inch past my head and exploded behind me. I'd barely caught her throwing it. "Watch it! You're going to wake everyone up!"

"Where is Master going?"

"I couldn't sleep. Going for a walk."

Charm frowned. "If Master is going to get involved with things he shouldn't be involved with, then he should make a decision about who he is."

"What do you mean?"

"Is Master a somewhat skilled brewmaster and very unskilled tavern keeper, or is he a hero of legend?"

"*Somewhat?* Wait a minute—there were two insults in that question!"

"Charm is serious, Master. If Master continues to act beyond the role of a tavern keeper, he will attract the danger that comes with being a hero."

"I'm not being a hero," I snapped. "They burned down my tavern. Even a tavern keeper has to protect his business."

"Would an ordinary tavern keeper kill arsonists and get revenge on the nobles that wronged him?"

I thought about it. They probably wouldn't. They would pack up and move on. Open up in a different ward, where they might find a local government who would treat them nicer.

Charm arched a brow at me when I didn't respond. "Did Master not close his gates so that he could experience the simple life?"

"Yeah."

"This is that life. But doing what Master is doing now is cheating."

"So, I'm a cheater. What of it?"

"Power draws power. Master cannot be the Stormblood, who leaves armies in ruin with the sweep of the hand and also live as an everyday small business owner."

"Nobody has to know."

"They will know," Charm said with more emotion in her voice. "Power cannot be hidden. Especially if it is used."

I frowned.

"Master must make a decision. Does he want to keep his tavern with his beautiful barmaids and remain a pervert, or does he wish to return to his old life of glory and destruction?"

"You're giving me a choice? That's unusual. Usually, you're demanding that I open my gates again... wait a minute—did you say 'remain a pervert'?!"

Charm absentmindedly stroked the silken pink hair at her shoulder. She rubbed the strands between her fingers. "Charm finds that she is getting used to this life. It is not as bad as she thought it would be." She tossed the hair backward and returned her eyes to me. "But in the end, it is Master's decision. If Master chose to return, Charm would not be upset. But Charm does not think he will return. Charm thinks Master will continue to walk the narrow path between his old and new lives until one day he will be forced to make a decision."

"If that's what you believe, then why even come and tell me all this?"

Charm looked away, almost sadly. She muttered something that I couldn't quite make out. It sounded like "Itiut."

I sighed, waiting to see if she'd say anything else, but she didn't.

"Go back to bed," I said, turning to leave. "I'll be back before dawn."

I didn't look to see what she did, but I didn't hear any movement behind me as I walked.

CHAPTER 33: MEMORIES OF THE SEA

Despite the height of the moon, the festival was nowhere near finished. Crowds packed the great square of Lumitra Ward, standing, sitting, coalesced together, with mugs of ale in their hands and laughter in their chests. On the center stage, a band of musicians played a loud quick-noted jingle, while men and women danced with sweat-stuck clothes. Shopkeepers worked double fast as they sold their wares and served their customers. Even the children were still awake, running around with masks on their faces, chasing each other with recently bought wooden swords and dolls.

It was like walking into a party I hadn't been invited to. That was not true of course—I'd been invited. Better yet, I'd won a major competition. And if my tavern hadn't been burned down, I'd be reaping the rewards with a stall at the center of celebrations and a smile on my face bigger than anyone else's.

Instead, I found myself walking in a quiet rhythm. I moved through the crowds in a prowl, not fast but not slow either. My pace matched the movements of those around me, and I slipped through without catching the attention of those I passed.

I didn't intend to use Water Step, but once I noticed myself in its rhythm, I didn't stop. I wasn't there for joyous reveling. I had business to attend to, and it was better that I was not seen or noticed.

I moved away from the entertainment stage and the food-and-beverage stalls, heading toward the night market. The path was less crowded here, filled with shoppers looking to buy trinkets and clothes and handcrafts. This area of Summerfest was more popular during the day, and many of its stalls had already closed for the night.

I only had two silver shimmers on me. That was the amount I typically kept in my coin wallet. Not a small sum but not large either. Perhaps only a bit more than what the typical tavern keeper had in his purse. It was all the currency I now owned.

With my gates open, I'd never had to think about wealth. My body hadn't suffered from the ailments or necessities of food, shelter, or temperature. I could spend months alone in the wilderness without sustenance of any kind. But if the same were to happen today—if for some reason I needed to escape at a moment's notice—I'd need to purchase food, lodging, clothing, supplies, weapons, and whatever else the situation required. The needs were endless, and most of them required coin. It was a new thing that my life depended on for survival.

I turned on my heel as I saw the shop I was looking for. It was situated between a candy stall and a dressmaker, but unlike them, it didn't have a tent. The place was simple and packed with children. The large wooden board propped up behind the shopkeeper was covered with masks. There were fox masks and deer masks and cat masks and rabbit masks.

Some of the children were fighting over the last rabbit mask.

"I saw it first!" said a little boy.

"I touched it first!" said another boy.

"I paid for it first!" said a little girl, who jammed a handful of minor coins into the shopkeeper's hands.

The faces on the two boys dropped as they realized they'd been outwitted.

The shopkeeper scratched his head and reluctantly pocketed the coins. "I'll have more rabbit masks in stock next week," he said to the children. "I didn't think the rabbit masks would be so popular."

"But the summer festival will be over next week!" said one of the boys.

The shopkeeper smiled good-naturedly. "You can find me at the Lumitra Market on weekdays or at the Keeper's Garden Market every other weekend."

The boys pouted while the little girl donned her rabbit mask and hopped around them with her hands pressed together. I scanned the wall of masks for one that would be suitable for my purposes. Most were too colorful and fun, and I needed something quite the opposite. My eyes settled on a beast I didn't recognize.

"Young sir, does something catch your eye?"

It took me a second to realize he was addressing me. "Which animal is that?" I pointed up at a dark-colored mask with thin punctured slits for eyes.

"Ah... that is the Greenfin," the man said, his voice turning a little deeper, perhaps even dark.

"Greenfin... sounds familiar," I said. "It is a fish?"

"You could call it a fish, but most would not. It is one of the Five Sacred Ancients."

I frowned. "There are only Four Sacred Ancients."

The man smiled. "Now there are four. But there once were many more. Some say as many as twelve before the dawn of man. The Greenfin is the fifth."

The Sacred Ancients were creatures of old that could use magic as a mage would, and their gates were open like an awakened. Elder Dragons were the oldest of the Sacred Ancients, or so I'd been told.

I scratched my head. *Greenfin... where have I heard that before?*

Two hundred twenty years of memories were a lot to get through, even for a nineteen-year-old brain, but the memory was somewhere in there. *It was a hot and wet place...*

Then it came to me in a flash. I was on a dozen-man fishing vessel that had picked me up after I'd been left stranded on a tropical islet in the Paradise Isles. They hunted the rare Maunduin fish, a highly prized delicacy that could only be found in the waters of the Isles. The fishermen spent the season catching fish and selling them to ports from Belliganna to Vendingrad.

The quartermaster was a talker with all sorts of wild stories. But the ship's captain was a stern man who never had more than three words to say in a sentence. He was tall and strongly built, and his manner was gruff. He commanded his ship with discipline and rigidity.

One night, after the rest of the crew had gone to sleep, the captain and I found each other on the stern deck, watching the stars. That night, he told me about his family back home and how they were waiting for him to return—his young beautiful wife and their daughter and the second child, who would have been born by that point but whom he had not yet met. He told me about the fishing nets his wife had woven and how they rarely broke. She had fine nimble hands and was an expert craftswoman. Many men, even the local mayor's son, had asked for her hand in marriage, but she had declined them all.

When the captain finally had gotten the courage to ask her to marry him, the first thing she said was "What took you so long?"

He chuckled at that. It was the first time I'd heard him laugh since he'd picked me up from the beach two weeks prior. Then he told me why he couldn't sleep and the reason he was standing on the deck with me, watching the stars.

When he was a young man of sixteen years, he'd left his village to become a far-sea fisherman. His father was a blacksmith and had wanted him to take up the family business, but the young man had hopes of seeing the world and traveling the seas. The merchant ships wouldn't take him, but he befriended a dockworker who was close with a first mate on one of the fishing ships that pulled into port once every two weeks before they continued their journey to Belliganna, the great city that would pay a premium for their rune-cold hulls of freshly caught tropical fish.

The young man spent his first year scrubbing the decks, loading and unloading cargo, and tending to the vessel. In the second year, they taught him to use the nets. In the third year, they taught him to throw a harpoon. By the fourth year, he'd mastered the nets, and his harpoon could hit a Maunduin three hundred paces away.

In the fifth year, the nightmare happened. It was the final night of their excursion that season. They were returning home after two months of catching their biggest haul of the year. The sun had already set, yet in the distance, one of the fishermen spotted a glowing orange light. No one had seen anything like it before.

Some of the crew wanted to go take a look, while others wished to avoid the strange light and continue the voyage home. The young man sided with those that wanted to see where the light originated. He was only twenty-one by then, and his five years on the fishing ship had yet to fill his desire for adventure. Votes were taken among the crew, and the newest member on the ship, the young man, tipped the scales in favor of investigating the golden light.

The fisherman roped the sails and turned the rudder, bringing the ship onto the glowing water. The men peered over the railings and saw what appeared to be like hundreds of flickering lanterns beneath the surface of the sea. Now some of the men wanted to swim beneath the water to get a better look. Once again, the young man was one of them. They decided to tie a rope around one of the men, who would dive down and lay his eyes directly on the origin of the shining light.

In the midst of an argument over who was the best diver on the ship, the water turned. The young man noticed it first. Something was pulling the water, drawing the ship away from the golden light.

He ran to the railing, and in the distant water, he saw the impossible: a massive, twisting whirlpool. The rest of the men saw it too. They couldn't believe their eyes. But there was no time for discussion. The men got into their sailing positions, and they pulled the sail, turning the ship away from the danger. Some of the men called out the obvious as they pulled the lines, saying that whirlpools didn't exist in that part of the sea. But what they'd seen with their own eyes had already proven otherwise.

The winds picked up, pushing them back just as the seas did. A massive black pit formed in the center of the swirling waters, and despite the fishermen's best efforts, the ship circled toward it. Then the young man saw something massive move in the water. An unearthly body, several times larger than the great whales of the Primordial Sea, rose above the surface in the distance before diving back under into the whirlpool's currents. Its skin was made of scales the size of ships, and its diamond-shaped head held four dark-green fins and a single gleaming eye. The monster moved through the whirlpool, seemingly untouched by the pressure of the water, rising out and diving back in with its great serpentlike body.

The fishermen watched the monster in shock and panic. The currents of the whirlpool grew stronger, and there was no escape.

Closer and closer, they swirled toward the pit of the whirlpool, the ship on the verge of being swallowed into its center.

A thought came to the young man. He didn't know why he was so certain of its truth, but the moment he saw the monster, he knew the unnatural whirlpool was its creation. He rushed below the decks and grabbed the biggest harpoon available. Then he climbed to the bow of the ship, placed one leg on the edge, and raised the harpoon high above his head.

There would be no time for a second throw. He had only one chance. He waited for the monster to burst above the currents once more, its great head revealed as it trailed seawater several hundred paces away. It was farther away than anything he'd hit before. But the young man did not feel fear or uncertainty. His mind was clear, and his body was full of strength and vitality. There was one thing left in the world that he could do, so he would do it well. He aimed for where the monster would be, not where it was. He arched his shoulder, twisted his torso, and pushed out his arm in a single hurl. The iron harpoon shot forward, soaring through the dark skies in a shining silver arc that ended in the black pupil of the monster's eye.

An earth-shattering scream rang out across the sea, and the Greenfin fell backward in a titanic splash of seawater. The whirlpool that had been picking up speed slowed, running out of energy, leaving the fishing ship spinning to a halt on flattening water. The golden light from beneath the sea could still be seen not far from the ship, but the men had lost their appetites for adventure and investigation. They brought their sails to full and made their escape.

A few years later, the captain's mantle was passed on to the young man, and a few years after that, he would summon the courage to ask a young craftswoman for her hand in marriage. The captain never came across a mysterious golden light in the seas again. He never found out why the Greenfin had summoned the whirlpool. But whenever he left his family and set out to sea, he would wonder if their paths would cross again.

I tried recalling the captain's name, but it didn't come to me. Well over a century had passed since the story of the sea monster had been told to me.

CHAPTER 34: AN UGLY MASK

"**S**ir?" said a voice that was followed by a polite cough. "Would you like to make a purchase?"

I found myself holding the Greenfin mask, surrounded by children who had quieted and were staring at me with piqued curiosity. There must have been a strange expression on my face. I blinked, pushing away the long-lost memory.

"Uh..."

"Or do you need another minute to think it over?" the shopkeeper said.

I hadn't thought about my time on the fishermen's ship for decades. It was strange how I'd never heard of the Greenfin again. I looked down at the dark-green mask. It had one big bulging eye in the center and four wooden fins carved out on the sides. Thin slits that looked like gills gave the eyes space to see through. It was a terrible thing to look at.

"It's ugly," said one of the boys, who was clearly not blind.

"Ugly mask," repeated the girl with the rabbit mask.

"Scary," said the other boy.

"Very scary," repeated the girl.

"Ugly and scary, huh?" I said, smiling. "I'll take it."

The kids all backed away, clutching their rabbit and fox masks, as if shocked by my choice. I nodded gravely. Perhaps they understood the importance of the decision. Only the foolish chose their symbols without thought.

The Mad King's Red Lion reminded his enemies of his power and ruthlessness. King Kindelore's Blue Bear stood for strength and honor. The mercenary troop, the Mad Dogs, whose banner was the same as their name, was a reminder to all of their deadly and crazed fighting methods.

I wasn't sure what exactly the Greenfin was supposed to represent, but I supposed it would serve its purpose that night. I hoped it would instill the same fright that the children had felt in all who saw me wear it. The children parted and moved out of my way as I paid for the mask and tied it above the top of my head. I wasn't quite ready to wear it over my face just yet.

The mask cost ten coppers. Not cheap, not expensive. However, for ten copper burnishes, you could have ten prize-winning mugs of Frozen Pumpkin Ale at my tavern—back when I had a tavern.

The thought turned my mood dark, and I wanted to be off on my business immediately. But there was still one more thing to purchase. I needed a cape. I knew only fools and nobles wore capes, but I needed a bit of flash for my task. Most of the fabric stalls had already closed, however, so it took some time to search for what I needed.

After making several circles through the festival square, I found a fine dark-green cloak to match my mask. It had a hood and golden twine that tied over the shoulders, and the fabric's stunning sheen made it look a whole lot more expensive than what I'd paid for it—which was the rest of my money, an amount that was a lot to me but nothing more than pocket change to the men I would be visiting. Luckily, as long as they didn't touch my cloak, it was unlikely they would be able to decipher its true value.

I left the festival grounds and made my way back toward Southbank. There were three neighborhoods in Southbank. Kerrytown was where the tavern was located. It was a small commercial hub, packed with restaurants and shops. Berrylane was a mostly residential area, made up of townhouses and inns.

Then there was Amberstale, where the banks and businesses and guards' tower were located. It was also where the superintendent of the ward and his son made their residence. They had a large estate. The mansion inside was a milk-white structure of three floors, located only a block down from the guards' tower. The house was newer than most and finely built. I'd passed by it on many occasions.

The ward of Southbank was not the wealthiest in Meritas, but it was a close fourth and rising. Middle-class families and aspiring merchants had been making the move to Southbank. Taxes were paid on time and collected easily. As in any ward, a small percentage of the tax revenues went to the office of the superintendent, who managed the ward, and the rest went to the Duke of Meritas.

The wealthier the ward, the wealthier the superintendent. I had never met the man, but I'd heard rumors about the superintendent of Southbank over the past year. He was the youngest of the Greengrass family. His oldest brother was a baron with lands far west of Meritas. The baron had inherited all of the family's land, and little was expected of the youngest son. But the younger Greengrass brother had managed to secure relations and an official role in the city.

I had no problems with the superintendent, and by most accounts, he was an honorable man. But the same could not be said of his son. As I reached the edge of the market, where the crowds thinned to the darkness of empty alleys, I lowered the Greenfin over my face and tied the hooded cape around my shoulders.

CHAPTER 35: A ROLE TO PLAY

I touched my hand against the outer wall of the mansion estate. After checking to make sure no one was watching, I scaled the wall, caught the ledge, and raised myself over the top. I came to a quiet landing on the other side, kneeling in a finely cut grass lawn.

The grounds were large, and the house was another hundred paces away. The large balconied and tall-windowed room on the third floor was no doubt the superintendent's quarters. I looked around to see if I could guess which was Mideon's, but it likely didn't matter much, anyway. The night was not that late, and I figured he'd still be at the festival. I crouched in the shadows, awaiting his arrival while staying out of sight of the five guards who patrolled the house.

As I waited, I began to wonder if he would come home at all. I spent the time getting to know the layout of the house better. I learned that there were six bedrooms, not including the servants' quarters on the first floor. The guards didn't sleep in the house but in rotating shifts at the barracks in the guards tower down the road.

After two hours, there was no sign of Mideon. Perhaps he'd decided to spend the night at a brothel.

Another hour passed before I heard a loud, obnoxious group coming toward the front gates. I recognized Mideon's voice. He was with his cronies.

"That one was cute today," Mideon said in a drunken drawl. "She was acting all hesitant at first, but then she finally gave up the goods."

"That's right!" said one of his friends. "She should be grateful to be working in the business bureau. Not everyone's got a nice job like that these days."

"Tomorrow, we'll go pay a visit to Lieutenant Leise!" came Mideon's voice again. "If she doesn't show me what's under her armor, I'll have her assigned to guarding carrots in my garden!"

There was a burst of loud male laughter. Then the men said their goodbyes and made promises to meet again the next day.

Mideon entered through the gates and moved quietly across the grounds. He didn't seem surprised that no guards opened the door for him as he entered. Perhaps he was too drunk to pay attention to it, or perhaps he preferred it that way so he wouldn't wake his father at this late hour.

I'd gotten a little bored while waiting for Mideon to arrive, so I'd put the five patrol guards to sleep with five quick taps to the back of five necks. There was a nerve there that would render a person unconscious if properly struck. Not much strength was needed, but precision and technique were tantamount. Needless to say, I had it perfected.

My plan was to visit Greengrass Senior and have a little chat with him first if Mideon didn't make it home before the sun rose. Then I'd go visit whichever brothel he was holed up in and pay my respects there. But luckily, Greengrass Junior arrived while there was still plenty of darkness left in the sky.

I climbed up to the balcony of his room on the second floor just as he entered through the hall door inside. The sliding wooden doors of the balcony were open a crack, sending in a warm summer breeze that billowed the curtains. I'd unlocked and opened them earlier.

I slipped into the room, sticking to the dark shadows against the walls, and lowered myself into a seat beside the exit on the other side. Mideon didn't notice me as he undressed. I was getting tired of waiting, so I said, "Hello."

He snapped his head at me and let out an ear-piercing scream as he saw me, falling, scrambling back against the floor. The guards were already taken care of, but I'd left the servant staff untouched. It would complicate things if a maid showed up.

I sighed, left my seat, and moved to him. I saw that he was going to scream again, and I leaped forward and caught his mouth in my hand then lifted him up by the head and slammed his back against the wall.

"Do you know who I am?" I said in a deep voice befitting a scary masked man hidden in the shadows.

He wiggled his head, his breath held back by my hand, his wide eyes focused on the Greenfin mask that covered my face.

"Good. I like it when people haven't heard of me. It means that my secret has been kept. It's something you'll be doing, too, if I decide to let you live."

A muffled whimper came from his throat.

"Next question," I said. "Do you know why I'm here?"

He looked at me with confusion and horror. It was apparent that despite all his bluster, he wasn't much of a man for violence.

But I had a role to play, so I continued. "I don't like it when my men are killed. Neither does my employer."

A guilty man would have shown more fear, but his eyes were filled with confusion. I pressed on. "You're going to tell me why you killed him. Then you'll tell me how you discovered his identity. I am going to release my hand, and if anything comes out of your mouth other than what I have asked, I am going to hurt you. Badly."

I released my hand, and the first thing the idiot did was scream for guards. I slapped my hand over his mouth again and hoped the servants downstairs hadn't heard. Even if they had, I wondered if they would come running to the aid of a man like Mideon. We waited. No one came, and the terror in his eyes grew.

"You're thinking, *Where are the guards? Why is the house so silent?* Have you figured out the reason? It's because they are incapacitated. My people are in your courtyard, keeping watch. Don't worry—your guards are quite all right, though they might experience a stiff neck in the morning. You see, I'm a fair man. Your guards have done nothing to displease me, so they will walk away unscathed. You, Mideon Greengrass, however, have done me much wrong."

I leaned in closer, my Greenfin mask only inches from his face. "We are going to attempt this one more time. I'm going to release my hand, and you are going to tell me what you know. But before you answer my question, there is one that *I* must answer for you. I threatened you a moment earlier, promising you excruciating pain if you did not obey me. You did not obey me. So now you must be wondering if I'm a man of my word."

Mideon shook his head, with fear in his eyes. Pleading.

I took a fistful of the lordling grapes between his legs and tightened my grip until they were ready to burst. He let out a muffled scream far louder than the ones before. Tears welled up in his eyes.

"Now, let's try this again," I said. "You're going to tell me why you killed my man and how you discovered his true identity." I released my hand over his mouth.

"Please, sir," Mideon said, gasping. "I don't know what you're talking about. I-I beg you—I don't know."

It seemed he hadn't intended Oakdigger's death, for he still hadn't connected it with my appearance. So Gerlanda had kidnapped Elsa and murdered the pumpkin man of his own accord. But I was certain Mideon had ordered Gerlanda to set the fire.

In any case, I had to continue my act. I covered his mouth again and tightened the grip of my other hand until something crunched. Mideon wailed in agony.

"Lord Mideon," I said politely. "I've already warned you not to lie to me. Since you're so fond of fire, I'll burn your house to the ground with your family within it if you do not give me my answer. So let's stop this foolishness. Whoever you are working for, I promise you, they are not a worse man than I."

"F-Fire? H-How d-do you…?"

"I know everything—everything except for why you killed my man. I assume the fire was to hide his murder. A poor job there. You should have burned him inside. That still would not have hidden your crime, but it would have been slightly more believable."

"Who… what man? Y-You mean the market seller? The old man?"

I punched him in the stomach. He bowed over, coughing. I leaned into his ear. "Yes! Who else do you think I've been talking about? Are you suggesting there are other men you've killed, and you can't keep track of them all?"

"No! No, there are no—" Mideon coughed a glob of red spit. "There are no others! I didn't kill him! I only told my man to set the fire! There wasn't supposed to be a murder!"

"Don't lie to me!" I brought him back up with my hand on his shirt collar and got into his face. "You ordered his death!"

"No! I just ordered him to burn the tavern! I swear! No one was supposed to die!"

"That's not what your man said," I said coolly.

Mideon's face dropped. "What? Where is Burtrund?"

Apparently, Gerlanda's real name was Burtrund.

"He's already paid the price for killing my man."

"Oh-Oh, Celeru..." His legs shook as he cupped his crotch as if everything inside of him would escape if he didn't hold on tight.

"But before he paid," I continued, "he told me you ordered him to murder my man."

"No! You must believe me. I only told him to make sure there were no witnesses. I didn't think he'd kill anyone! I swear! I'm not a murderer!"

"So, your claim of innocence is that you *only* set fires to businesses and associate yourself with murderers. You're not a very good liar, Mideon Greengrass."

"It was my first time... I-I have a personal issue with that tavern... but I didn't want anyone to die!"

"What issue?"

Mideon looked unsure of how to explain the situation. "They insulted my honor and swindled me out of money."

Well, that was close to the truth but certainly a personal spin on the situation. But not far off enough to call it a lie. It was a good sign, showing that he was taking my authority seriously.

"So, you expect me to believe you set a tavern on fire and *accidentally* killed one of the most prized and talented men my employer has ever had?"

"Y-Your employer?"

I paused, pretending to be swayed. "You know nothing of Oakdigger's mission?"

"N-No... of course not. It was an accident."

"I would not call arson and a murder an accident, little lordling," I spat. "I would call that a crime. But it appears that your intention was not to intervene with our affairs."

"No, I wouldn't dare—" He paused to let out a pained rasp, clutching his privates tighter. "I-I wouldn't. Please sir, let me go. I will not stand in your way."

"Hmm…" I said as if considering what to do with him.

"My father will repay you any cost you might have incurred."

"Oh? Is that right, Superintendent?" I said, turning my head.

Mideon frowned at me then looked in the direction I had turned. I was facing the cabinet. I opened it, revealing Greengrass Senior, tied up and gagged. He was awake, though, and he'd heard everything.

"Father!"

There was a mix of anger and fear in the older man's eyes, though he could not say much with the cloth gag in his mouth.

"Consider yourself lucky, Superintendent," I said. "It appears your son is a fool and a criminal, but he is not as guilty as I had thought. Now, as for what to do with you two…"

Mideon shook and I smelled something coming from his trousers.

"Typically, I'd require blood for the death of my man. And of course, your family's station in this city would be removed and your estates and properties dismembered. But I suppose your friend Burtund has already paid for the crime. You will not miss him, will you, little Greengrass?"

"No... of course not. There's no room for murderers in my company."

That was rich, coming from the arsonist. "And his friends? They won't seek retribution, will they?"

"No, of course not. I'll make certain of it."

"Good. And what will you do for my man that you murdered?"

"Uh..."

A muffled noise came from the tied-and-bound older Greengrass.

"That's a good idea, Superintendent," I said as if I understood what he was saying. "But let's hear what your son thinks."

"Umm... I will ensure that his body is returned to you."

"Mmm... that would reveal his true identity. Surely there's something you could do for him? He was once a soldier, you know."

"Erm... he will get the highest military burial! With full honors... and a place in the royal cemetery. We shall cover all costs personally!"

I nodded. "I suppose that will suffice. And his family? What will they get for the early death of their dear father?" I wasn't sure if Oakdigger's daughters were living or dead.

"They'll be paid of course. A full captain's retirement pension."

"Does that suit you, Superintendent?" I asked.

Mideon's father bobbed his head enthusiastically.

"Ah, you know," I said, coming up with an idea of my own. "Perhaps your Captain Kainlin of the ward guard can speak at the funeral. My man Oakdigger mentioned him before. I believe they were in the duke's army together. Perhaps Kainlin could speak some words of Oakdigger's heroism in the old days."

"It will be the most heroic speech ever given!" Mideon said.

"Y-Yes, good, good," I said, glad that my mask hid my face.

There was one other thing I wanted, but Charm's words stuck with me, and I didn't want to give any hint that I was related to the Tipsy Pelican Tavern, despite the fact that at that moment, I could have asked for the heavens from them. I was in dire need of funds for repairs, but I had already hinted that I worked for the Duke of Meritas by suggesting that I would have the Greengrass family removed from their stations. There was no one who could do such a thing besides the duke. But that also meant a man in my situation would not ask for coin.

So it was safer to say nothing about it and let them believe they had accidentally stepped on the foot of someone with far greater power, involved in far more dangerous affairs.

"Very well, then," I said. "I hope there won't be any more interference in this ward. There are forces at play in this city beyond what you can imagine, and I won't have you fouling it up with your mistakes."

Mideon bobbed his head like a good humble sycophant.

"You will, of course, not speak about my visit to anyone," I continued. "And if I find out you have been involved with another arson, murder, or anything else not by the book, I will return. And let me make yet another promise. If I visit you a second time, there will not be a third, for there will be nothing left to visit."

"I-I understand," Mideon said, while clutching the spot between his pants. "There will be no more disturbances."

"In that case, it has been a pleasure, gentleman." I left the room through the balcony doors and leaped onto the railing. I swept an arm, hailing to my imaginary men, who were supposed to be on the lookout. "Move out!"

With my cape billowing in the wind, I jumped into the air with what I hoped looked like majestic grace. It was the last flourish to my false persona and a risky move. Jumping from the third story was easy with the Gate of Breath open. Without it, I would need to perfect my landing, dropping into a roll to spread out the impact.

I didn't. I landed wrongly on my heel and limped away into the darkness, mumbling curses, before the Greengrasses could spot me.

CHAPTER 36: WHOLE

"**A**rch-don... is this really the right time to be serving beer?" Cassia said when she saw me roll up with my cart and kegs.

"Of course, it is," I said lazily. "Old Oakdigger would want his pumpkins here."

I'd been operating out of the cart for more than two weeks. Since the fire, we had set up a small station on the tavern's front steps and did the best we could with what we had. The brewery in the basement had been untouched, and we still had some undestroyed beer left, so we were able to keep serving outdoors on makeshift tables and chairs.

Most of my patrons showed up each night to support us, and many people stopped by after hearing about our win at the Summerfest. However, the newcomers didn't stick around long. A burned-down tavern with the smell of scorched wood wasn't the best ambience for a drink.

Strangely, my top three regulars were nowhere to be found. The builders, Bran, Amberly, and Dalian, had been missing for two weeks. Even Herwin didn't know what had happened to them. In the last few days, during bouts of particularly dark moods, I wondered if they'd found a better tavern to spend their time in. But mostly, I just missed their easy laughter and good humor.

Cassia stood beside me and peered over the royal cemetery. "There are quite a lot of people gathered, aren't there?"

That was an understatement. Nearly the entire city guard of Southbank and a good portion of the Keeper's Garden's guard had gathered. Many shopkeepers from the old pumpkin man's market were there as well as others I did not recognize.

In addition to the audience, the superintendent was there along with an entire marching band, a high priest from the White Church, dove bearers, and rows of flower bouquets. At the very front, beside the podium, was an open casket. Oakdigger lay inside, wearing a white tunic, with a light blush on his cheeks and flowers woven in his hair, looking a million times better than he ever did alive.

Captain Kainlin stepped up in front of a podium before the casket to give a speech, and I poured myself a hearty mug of ale. I peered around for his green-haired lieutenant, but I didn't see her. Cassia gave me a disapproving look as I took my first gulp of ale, but she kept her thoughts to herself.

I raised my mug at her in return. "This is going to be a great show. Trust me."

Kainlin looked like he'd just swallowed a ferret. He exchanged an angry glance with the superintendent as if they'd been fighting just moments earlier. The superintendent returned a look that promised death. Kainlin gritted his teeth and began his speech.

"On this sorrowful day… we gather in remembrance of a g-great man." He read from a scroll with a rigid expression that suggested it was taking every fiber of his being to get through the speech.

I wasn't sure who they'd gotten to write the thing, but Captain Kainlin described vague details about Oakdigger's service in the military. The words *great* and *virtuous* and *noble* were used many times. Captain Kainlin's right eye spasmed as he read, while Superintendent Greengrass kept looking over his shoulder as if he were expecting to see a ghost.

I sat in the back and sipped on my ale. Nobody seemed interested in a pour, which was fine. I'd mainly brought the cart for my own pleasure that day. After the speech was given and the horns blown and the prayers prayed, three young women approached me at the cart.

"Are you Master Arch?" said the oldest one, who was holding the hand of a little boy perhaps four or five years old.

"Yes."

"We are Oakdigger's daughters. I'm Anna. This is Lorie and Karolin," she said, gesturing to her sisters.

They looked to be in their early to late twenties and were well-dressed and well-mannered. The oldest-looking one, Anna, was tall and surprisingly beautiful—surprising because it seemed unbelievable that the old coot Oakdigger had a hand in spawning such a lovely lady.

"We heard he was with you not long before his death," Anna continued.

"Ah... yes, he was helping me with my ale for a Summerfest competition. I'm very sorry for your loss."

The youngest-looking one, Lorie, nodded. She seemed the most upset. Her eyes were red, likely from crying. "The man who killed him is still out there. How could they not catch him?"

I scratched my neck. By rolling Gerlanda up into a ball, I'd taken away any closure for Oakdigger's daughters. The authorities would never find the killer.

"Was Oakdigger drinking when he was with you?" said Karolin, the middle sister, before I could form a proper response to her sister's question. "You run a tavern, don't you?" I couldn't help but notice the masked anger in her voice.

"Oh, uh... no, he didn't drink. He did help me, though," I said, trying to come up with something positive to say. "I'd begun brewing a pumpkin ale, and I sourced my pumpkins from him. He did a very good job. We won first place in the contest."

"You must be very upset about losing your tavern," Karolin said.

"Ah yes... well, we'll be back up and running soon enough." The words were beginning to feel like a lie. I'd been saying them for two weeks straight. I pushed on. "You are, of course, all welcome to come visit once we're open. I'm sure Elsa and Cassia would like to meet you as well."

"Who are they?"

"They're my staff. They help me out at the tavern."

"They were close with him?"

"Well... I don't know about close. They were friendly. We often bought pumpkins from him, and we were together at the Summer-fest."

Karolin apparently didn't like that answer because she turned and walked away without another word.

"Did I say something wrong?" I said to the remaining two sisters.

"No," Anna said. "It's... complicated."

"I'll go talk to her," Lorie said to Anna. "It was nice meeting you, Master Arch." She gave a quick little bow and walked away.

"Yes, you too." I looked back up at Anna and smiled awkwardly.

I didn't understand what that was about, and I certainly didn't want to get involved. This was none of my business. But Anna clearly mistook my smile as a desire to understand the situation, because she began to explain everything.

"We stopped contact with our father many years ago. He was a drunkard on the streets. He would come to us whenever he needed money. He'd curse us if we didn't have enough to give him. One day, we told him to stop coming to us. He said many horrible things that day, but we didn't see him again until many years later. When he came back, he said he'd given up the drinking and begun farming on a small patch of land outside the city. He began selling pumpkins at the market. But none of us wanted to see him again. We told him to leave."

Anna looked down and brushed back the hair of the little boy who was clutching her dress behind her leg. "We didn't hear from him after that, and it's hard to see that he's been getting on happily without us even though we were the ones that cut him out of our lives."

I looked away. It really wasn't any of my business, but I couldn't help but say something. Most people I'd come across were cowards in their last moments, and Oakdigger wasn't.

"He mentioned you three," I said. "I was there with him. You were in his thoughts at the end."

Anna blinked. For a second, her eyes turned glossy. But then it was gone, and the expression was replaced with a calm smile. "Thank you for telling me."

The boy at her side clutched more tightly to her leg as he saw her reaction. She looked down at him. "Would you like to say hello, Deni?"

Deni shook his head and kept on staring at me uncertainly.

"Whose child is he?" I said.

Anna smiled at me. "He's mine."

"Oh," I said, not sure what else to say.

A moment passed, then Anna said, "The superintendent said that my father had achieved the rank of captain and that as his family, we were entitled to his pension. I don't know why he never tried to claim that money before..."

I kept my mouth shut and in a plain smile.

"Well, thank you," Anna said finally. "Perhaps I'll see you at your tavern once it's open."

"Please do. We'll be back up and running soon enough."

Damn. Those words again. The more I said them, the less I believed them.

Anna gave me a polite nod and led her son away, leaving me alone at the cart. I picked up my mug, downed the rest of it, and found Cassia beside me when I placed it back down. She had a big golden smile on her face, and it irked me.

"What?"

"You were so kind to them. I was right about you. You are a good person, Arch-don."

"Of course, I was nice to them. Didn't you hear? I might have gained us three new customers. And these ones happen to female. Do you know how hard it is to get ladies to come to a tavern filled with sweaty men? Let me answer that for you: it's harder than a dragon scale. An even mix of men and women is key to any good tavern."

"Hmph. I don't believe you. I think you did it from the goodness of your heart."

"Whatever." I was in no mood to argue. "Where's Elsa and Charm? We should be heading back soon. Got a burnt block of firewood to run."

Cassia frowned a little. "They're at the front, paying their respects... will we be able to repair the tavern, Arch-don?"

"Oh, sure, shouldn't be a problem," I said cheerfully. "I've already checked and double-checked our finances. The materials will only cost us every copper we have—and yes, that's including what we've earned from the Summerfest competition. We're barely staying afloat by serving drinks on the street, but it's only a matter of time before the neighbors start complaining."

I hadn't come into much contact with the other business owners in Kerrytown, but they'd actually turned out to be a good bunch of people. Most had come to me at some point over the last two weeks to give their condolences. The burning down of one's establishment was the deepest and darkest nightmare of any business owner. The only one who was less than gracious was the owner of the Grand Taphouse, a man called Geraldo, who had started to lodge complaints with the business bureau as well as just coming over to gloat at the destruction of a rival.

But aside from Geraldo, even the other business owners could only turn a blind eye for so long. Our burnt husk of a tavern, along with the loud outdoor operation that replaced it, wasn't something any establishment would want on their street.

Cassia's worried look was deepening.

"The good news," I continued in my cheerful tone, "is that the labor cost is through the roof, especially since said roof needs a complete overhaul. It'll take at least a couple of weeks to rebuild and a dozen men to do the job. And best of all, it'll cost the same as the materials, which we can barely pay for. But you know what? *We'll be back up and running soon enough.*"

I gritted my teeth. Those words had become my mantra. I would damn myself to make them true.

"Arch-don," Cassia said with a deep wrinkle in her brow. "That's terrible…"

She was right. We actually had more people coming by than ever before. After the Summerfest win, we had numerous new guests interested in trying our ales. I kept telling them to be sure to come again next month for the reopening. But I really had no idea how long it would take to gather the funds to rebuild the tavern. Or if it was even possible.

A couple of funeral goers came up for a beer now that the event was ending. They looked like they worked for the superintendent. I took their money and gave them full mugs. Then I poured myself another as well. The two men were in the middle of a conversation, speaking in hushed tones.

"I heard the duke's man threw Mideon off the balcony, and he landed on his stones..."

"Makes sense," said the second guy. "That's why he hasn't been seen lately and why the superintendent looks so spooked." He shivered. "I hope I never get a visit from the Greenfin..."

So the word had already spread, though it didn't sound entirely accurate—I hadn't thrown Mideon off the balcony. But they were right about his stones. The rumors weren't ideal, but I doubted anything would come back to me. I had played my part perfectly.

The men took their beers and walked off. I called out to them, making sure that they would bring back the mugs when they were done.

"We'll figure out something," Cassia was saying half to herself. "I don't have much money, but I'll give you everything I have."

"Eh... don't worry about it," I said. The last thing I wanted was charity from the clergy of the White Church. "How's your business coming along? Things okay over at the church?"

Cassia nodded. "A new bishop has been installed, and Tamblion has been sent to Yestereaster for questioning by the archbishop. It was a major oversight for such a man to have been appointed."

"I'm surprised Kathy would pick such a man. She isn't the type to overlook a thing like that."

"K-K-Kathy?" Cassia practically turned white.

"Uh... yeah, your archbishop?"

"Arch-don is on a first-name—*nickname*—basis with Archbishop Katharis?"

"Course I am. That brat owes me big time."

"Brat?" Cassia said, this time with less surprise and more displeasure. "You called Lord Strongarm a brat, and he is indeed much younger than you. But Archbishop Katharis is more than twice your age, is she not?"

"Not physically," I said with a grin. "I'm nineteen. She's only seventeen."

"Master believes everyone is younger than him. Even those who are not," said an ominous and deadly voice from behind us that sent shivers down my spine.

We turned and found Charm standing behind the cart. Cassia looked a little worried that Charm had overheard our conversation. I'd nearly forgotten that Cassia didn't realize Charm knew of my true identity. That was probably for the best.

"The most important thing is emotional age," I said.

Charm arched an eyebrow.

"What, you have something to say about that?" I snapped.

"Of course not, Master. One does not need to lend their voice to the obvious."

"What does that mean?" I was feeling a little tipsy. *Damn body can't even handle a couple mugs of ale.*

Just then, the marching band began to play, the gathered soldiers saluted in one motion, and Oakdigger's casket was lowered into the earth.

I raised my mug in a salute to the old man. "They were good pumpkins," I muttered. "We made a fine ale."

As the funeral came to an end and the crowds dispersed, Elsa found us, with tears still in her eyes. It was obvious that she had been crying the entire time, undoubtedly still feeling guilty about the whole thing. None of us had any words of comfort to say to her that hadn't already been said. Cassia gave her a hug, and Charm held her hand as we headed back to the tavern.

As we walked, I tried to come up with a plan for the coming weeks. I figured we could pull off maybe one or two more nights before I got complaints from the neighbors. Geraldo was already complaining to anyone who would listen, even though the Grand Taphouse was the farthest from the Tipsy Pelican Tavern on the block. I almost wanted to send the Greenfin to pay him a visit. Of course, that wasn't an option. A move like that would divert all attention of the mysterious Greenfin to the Tipsy Pelican Tavern by making people wonder why the duke's man would interfere in yet another tavern's affairs in the same location.

But I couldn't keep operating on the street even if Geraldo hadn't been complaining. The patience of my neighbors was wearing thin. I'd probably have to find somewhere cheap to rent in the meantime. It would be in another ward. Probably not a place as bad as Yumentown or Addenwood Row, but it would need to be very inexpensive for me to save enough profits to repair the tavern.

I'd lose a lot of my regulars if I did move. My patrons liked Southbank, and they lived nearby. Most wouldn't be able to travel far to find me each night. Sure, they'd come when they could, but that wasn't the same. I'd have to find new patrons. Make new connections in the alternate ward. Build up again from scratch. It could be a year before I'd be able to come back to Southbank, even longer if things didn't go well. And if I suffered several weeks without customers, like I had before...

My feet came to a stop. Without noticing, each of us lost in thought, we had made our way back to the Tipsy Pelican Tavern. The entire street was empty except for three men.

They stood in front of the tavern. They wore dusty clothes and had big, calloused hands. But most distinctively, they were large men, even the smallest among them. And the largest was built like a mountain. Each man had a wide grin on his face.

"Hello there," I said, happy to see their friendly faces again. "Long time, no see. I was wondering where you three ran off to. As you can see, things have changed over the past couple of weeks. We're setting up for an outdoor affair tonight, but we can't get too loud, or else it'll upset the neighbors. But don't worry—we'll be back up and running soon en—"

I choked, and I couldn't say the words. I just couldn't. I could lie about the tavern's future to strangers and perhaps even to myself, but not to these men who had taken seats at my tables most nights of each week.

"Actually," I said, pulling myself together. "Actually, we probably won't be back for a while... but we'll keep serving somewhere."

"Ah, that's too bad, but I can see why," Dalian said. "That, right there, is a two-week job for a dozen men."

"Hmm..." Amberly said in a deep baritone that resonated from his massive chest as he looked over the burnt walls. "It could be possible to do it with less."

"True," Dalian said, nodding sagely. "I suppose you could do it with as few as three men. But they'd need to be the best carpenters in the whole city."

"The very best," Amberly said. "And they'd need to have time off from their schedules to work on the job."

"Also true," Dalian said. "They'd need to have worked double shifts for two weeks straight to get that kind of time off on such short notice. Men like that are in high demand, you know."

I blinked, realizing their meaning. Elsa was grinning wildly. Cassia had tears welling in her eyes. Even Charm was smiling.

"I-I couldn't ask you to..." I began. "I don't have enough to pay you."

Bran, who had been silent with a pleasant expression on his face the whole time, laid his giant hand on my shoulder. It felt like a falling boulder, but his words lifted a far greater weight.

"We'll have it done in a fortnight, Master Arch. You can count on us."

"But..."

"You've bought us more than enough rounds over the past year to cover a little fix up," Dalian said.

"Consider this one on the house from the three of us," Amberly said.

Elsa launched forward and gave each of them a kiss on the cheek. Cassia was next, hugging them. Charm went up to each and gave a low bow.

It was not "a little fix up." It was going to be hard work for three men. Very hard work if they were going to do it within two weeks, especially if they were already tired from working double shifts with little sleep.

But here they were, at my doorstep, offering to help in my time of desperation. And a strange feeling welled up inside of me. It was a sensation I'd never felt in my two hundred twenty-one years of life.

I had been the strongest man in the world. The one person everyone else depended on when they were in need, when they had no one else to turn to. But I had never been in their shoes. I had never been on the other side. And even when the tavern burned down, I did not turn to anyone for support. But upon hearing the words of these three men, I realized I needed their help.

My need was not for the tavern to be rebuilt so that I could continue perfecting my brew craft, serving my regulars, and growing my little business. It was a deeper need, something far more important, something that I had perhaps been in search of for a very long time. I hadn't known I needed it, and perhaps these men didn't either, but still, they had come to my rescue.

I still cannot quite tell you what it was that stirred this strange new sensation within me because I don't fully understand it yet. But what I can tell you is that it felt warmer than an early morning in summer and brighter than a firefly in twilight.

It made me feel weightless and whole.

EPILOGUE: FIFTEEN YEARS EARLIER

Aedor counted two hundred forty-one awakened mages. With his Gate of Perception open, it was an easy task, despite the distance across the snow. Each of the mages wore black robes that contrasted against the white of the snow and the spiraling dark tower that reached into the sky behind their forces. Among the mages, Aedor counted three who had also opened the Fifth Gate, the Gate of Perception.

Aedor smiled faintly. This army of awakened souls was a threat to any country, and each of the perceivers was as destructive as a hurricane. But he knew that what lay in the spire beyond their forces was far worse.

"They're the ones that summoned him," Aedor said to the young man standing beside him.

The man, who was in fact not young at all, didn't say anything in return, but Aedor continued as if a question had been asked.

"After the summoning, Izirath renounced the allegiance of the Dark Robes. The fools thought the Demon Lord would do as they wished after reviving him, but the Demon Lord did not. Izirath disappeared. Then, some thirty years later, the king of Karrdentia beheads a farmer woman for blasphemy against the crown. Next thing you know, the kingdom of half a million has been wiped off the map, and a spire as tall as an eagle's reach stands in its place."

"The demon lord had taken a wife and lived in peace?" Aedor's companion asked. He was of average height. Two battle-axes of black steel, one small and one large, were mounted on his back.

Aedor nodded. "According to the villagers I spoke to, they'd been with each other for several years. Some commoners in the surrounding lands even praise the Demon Lord for getting his revenge against the king for her execution. Now the Dark Robes have returned, hoping their lord will continue his destr—oh." Aedor turned his head toward the army of dark mages. "They've begun."

Multicolored halos were expanding among the Dark Robes across the snowy plains.

"All of them," Aedor said with a quiver in his voice that he failed to hide. "They must have finally noticed the number of your opened gates."

Each of the two hundred forty-one mages had begun casting, some forming spheres and spears of destruction, others chanting buffs.

"Dragon's breath, some of them are really strong!" Aedor raised his hand above his head, palm out. "Aegis of Aedor."

A dome of golden light descended over him. It was his only original spell, but he was proud of it. Even his master had yet to break it. Aedor turned and looked to his side. He blinked. His master stood outside his dome and hadn't moved. "Master, are you certain you are not in need of *any* defensive measures?"

The young man didn't reply, and before Aedor could say anything else, the wave of destruction descended upon them. The destructive energies exploded against his shield, turning his surroundings into flashes of blinding light and thundering annihilation. The spells were even more powerful than Aedor had expected. If he hadn't put up the shield, he would have been completely pulverized.

He looked at where his master had stood. A thick cloud of smoke and dust surrounded him, obstructing his view. But Aedor's eyes were of the Fifth Gate, so he saw the world clear as spring water. His master was entirely unharmed. His manner was that of someone who might have just exited the warm pools of a hot spring.

Then Aedor saw his master's lips move, and he heard words that were barely more than a whisper. These were words of magic, spoken with practiced quiet so that the enemy would not know what was coming. But Aedor's ears were of the Fifth Gate, and he tuned them to his master's words, hearing each syllable like the striking of a bell.

"Rule of Ruin Sixty-One, Pointed Pillar."

A beam of light exploded from the plume of smoke, blowing it clear, shooting across the snow. Aedor's master twirled his pointed index finger in the air. His motion made a squiggly line as if he were writing a signature. The beam held on to his finger and followed all the way across the expanse of snow, tracing loops through the army of Dark Robes.

It was over in seconds. Two hundred and forty-one awakened mages had become several thousand pieces of sliced limbs and appendages. There were no survivors.

Aedor found his breath caught in his throat, and he slowly released it as he took in what he'd just witnessed. The Dark Robes were a secret order of powerful dark mages that had existed for centuries—no, *millennia*. And Aedor had just watched their complete decimation in the span of moments.

He turned his eyes to his master. Once again, he felt awe, respect, and as always, envy. He ached to learn the Rules of Greater Ruin, but his master hadn't taught them to him. That was partly because his master didn't believe Aedor was ready for such power. But Aedor knew it was also because of the spells' difficulty, although when his master cast Pointed Pillar, it looked as if he were choosing courses on a menu.

His master looked up at the tall purple spire, and Aedor followed his gaze. Only now did he notice the power coming from it. Aedor felt a pang of shame for not catching it sooner. This was followed by the relief that his master did not appear to notice his mistake. His master would have chided him once again for "missing the essence of the matter." Aedor hated hearing those words. Though he knew his master was older and wiser, he could not help but feel that they were the same age because of his appearance.

But as Aedor let his perception touch upon the spire's leaking aura, he realized the full deficit of his mistake. Though the dark powers originating from the spire were veiled and subtle, they were leaps and bounds greater than the army of Dark Robes. Any normal mage would not be able to sense such things, but the Fifth Gate—the Gate of Perception—allowed Aedor to sense all things.

The more he perceived the spire's power, the colder his heart became. The rumors were true. The Demon Lord's power was colossal.

Aedor had never felt anything like it before. His master's powers had frightened him when he first sensed them, and just moments earlier, he had been in complete awe of him. But this... this was something entirely different. The halos bleeding from the spire were not only superior to his master's, but they were also more terrifying in their substance.

The Demon Lord's magic was black and sickly and sticky. It felt diseased, as if even perceiving it could corrode a man's soul. Aedor took an involuntary step backward.

"The spire is held together by the Demon Lord's magic," his master said as if he was only noting a detail in architecture.

Aedor looked at his master. *How can he be so calm?* Surely, he, too, could feel the power coming from the spire.

His master stepped forward in the snow, walking toward the spire. Aedor wanted to tell him to wait, but he couldn't get his mouth working. It opened, but no breath or sound escaped.

"Aedor," his master muttered. He was already many paces away, but he knew Aedor could hear him.

"M-Master?"

"I might not make it out of this one." The set of black battle-axes clinked on the young man's back as he walked. "But if the spire falls, it will mean I've won. I've decided... I'm going to take a break for a time. Come find me afterward."

Find him? Take a break? Is he going somewhere? What is he taking a break from? Aedor was relieved that his master did not ask him to follow, but he was unsure what it meant.

He wanted to ask his master if he could win, if they would see each other again, if his master would finally teach him the Rules of Greater Ruin when it was over, but Aedor could barely manage a single sentence, for he feared his voice would betray the cowardice he felt in his heart.

So Aedor kept his response short and formal, which he hoped would be fitting for the occasion.

"It will be done, Master Stormblood."

(Volume End)

A Note from the Author – The Past & Future of the Series

Dearest Reader,

Thanks so much for reading the new edition of the *Tipsy Pelican Tavern* series, which includes a new cover, new interior art, and all the final edits of the novel after having rewritten it several times over. My great hope is that the rerelease will allow the series to have a shot at finding a wider audience.

For the newcomers to the tavern, welcome! You might not know this, but the original version of this series was illustrated by me. But gone are the days when my amateur squiggles could suffice for a book cover. As you're probably aware, we now live in the age of AI and algorithms, and self-publishing just isn't what it used to be. My covers simply don't compete as well as the shiny AI-made ones, no matter what anyone says about supporting human artists. Data and book rankings don't lie.

But that put me in quite the pickle because I really didn't want to join the AI authors and use AI art in my books. I'm not here to get into an AI debate, nor do I want to judge other authors, so all I'll say is that I couldn't bring myself to use it. AI just doesn't fit my series, which is heavily influenced by Japanese light novels, an illustrated medium that partners with artists.

So I did just that.

I brought in Elfe Carter and Kantuk Creative to bring the books to life. This took months of work, finding my partners, scheduling, planning, creating base sketches, and teaching the artists about my characters and series. Literally months and months!

But in the end, I think it was truly worth it because they've done a stunning job, don'tcha think?

In fact, I'd say they've done a better job than what AI could have produced. Take that, Altman! Ha!

Alright, realistically, I know this victory is short-lived. As a technologist myself, I'm quite certain AI will come for my bread and butter soon enough. But in the meantime, I intend to keep doing what I'm doing with the *Tipsy Pelican Tavern* series by keeping it human.

If you'd like to help support my endeavors, you know what to do: tell your friends, recommend the series on Reddit and social media. Despite the direction we're headed, word of mouth is still a far stronger force than the Amazon algorithm.

Also, the audiobook is out! If you haven't already, I highly encourage you to check out the audiobook version of this novel. It took over 400 auditions (sadly, some of these were AI-generated) to find my narrators, Joshua Story and Laurie Catherine Winkel, and they did an absolutely phenomenal job. If you ever wondered what Charm sounds like or wanted to hear Arch deliver a joke with the appropriate amount of snarky irreverence, then be sure to listen to the audiobook. (Find it on Audible and my author store at shop.a ugust.art!)

The plan going forward is to complete the rerelease of Vol. 2, Vol. 3, and Vol. 4, which will follow shortly after this one, and then I will launch Volume 5, which I am currently working on. Each will feature Elfe's covers and Kantuk Creative's interior art. If all goes well, the series relaunch will be a success and will allow me to dedicate more time to the *Tipsy Pelican Tavern* series. I originally had ten volumes planned, and I deeply hope that I will get to write them all.

Alright, I know this is getting long, so let me end with a heartfelt thank-you for supporting me thus far. Your readership is what keeps me going despite the odds and setbacks. I also want to thank my Patreon supporters, who have been there this whole way despite my modest offerings: MGeo, Bullet Philia, John W., Josh, Jemention, Will, Dale, Vic X, Jennie C., Chad A., Stephen M., Martin M., TC128, Dan A., and Pipes M.

Okay, that's it for this time! See you back at the tavern soon!

All the best,

August Hei

Newsletter: www.august.art

Store: shop.august.art

Twitter: @augustdotart

TIPSY PELICAN TAVERN SUGGESTED READING ORDER

VOL 1: Even a Hero Needs a Vacation Every Now and Then

Prequel #1 - Elsa's Story: Sweat, Scoundrels, and Taverns

VOL 2: Everyone Knows You Shouldn't Rescue Maidens in Alleyways

Prequel #2 - Cassia's Story: The Final Test

Prequel #3 - Roddard's Story: A Road to Meritas

VOL 3: Rare Swords Are Only Good Until You Lose Them

VOL 4: You Can't Be an Assassin if You Have a Leather Allergy

Read at any time:

Tipsy Pelican Tavern : Origins

Read the prequel short stories for free at:

www.august.art

www.ingramcontent.com/pod-product-compliance
Lightning Source LLC
Chambersburg PA
CBHW071231300726
48975CB00002B/376